LOVE in the CITY

The Complete Collection Boxed Set

By Liv Morris

Love in the City

Copyright © 2013 Liv Morris

Createspace Edition: November 2013

Cover artwork by: Jada D'Lee Designs

Editing by: Dee Ward and Marla Esposito

This is a work of fiction. Names, characters, places, and incidents either are products of the author's imagination or are used fictitiously. Any resemblance to actual events, locales, or persons, living or dead, is entirely coincidental.

All rights reserved. No part of this publication can be reproduced or transmitted in any form or by any means without permission in writing from Author.

Liv Morris

TABLE OF CONTENTS

**Magic at Macy's
The Perfect Stranger
the panty dropper
The Love Handles Club
Drunk and Disorderly**

Magic at Macy's

by Liv Morris

Liv Morris

Ally's Love at First Sight

It was Thanksgiving Day and the first time I'd spent the holiday apart from my father, Joe. He had raised me single-handedly after my mother, Mary, left us when I was twelve years old. We had shared something in common since the day we found her farewell note sitting on the kitchen table—broken hearts, which never fully mended from the rejection she left behind. He was a betrayed husband and I was an abandoned child.

    Our collective pain could have pulled us apart, but miraculously it seemed to bring us together and solidify us as a family. We had each other to lean on, and we leaned on one another hard, especially during the holidays. So I worried about him being alone today. However, my father reassured me that he was fine this morning when I called, but I knew better as I heard the flat tone and sadness in his voice. He missed me and I missed him terribly too. Over the last couple of months, I had tried to convince myself that attending Yale was worth our separation, but today it just didn't work.

    I had thought about flying back home to be with him, but a ticket to Nowhere City, Arkansas, was outrageously expensive and my funds were tight. I barely had enough money saved up to fly home for the fast approaching winter break, so I settled on a lovely, but rather stuffy, holiday meal with some gracious Yale faculty members who lived close to campus. I hoped it would be better than hanging out all alone in my dorm room.

Though my dinner hosts were kind enough to invite me to join their family celebration, I quickly learned that I had nothing in common with my kind benefactors as we chatted and dipped our turkey into the smooth gravy.

They appeared to be from families who ate their breakfast cereal from silver spoons. My dad and I had about ten spoons to our name. All of them had different patterns on the handle and were bought at the local thrift store. We may not have possessed a lot, but it always felt like we had what we needed. Somehow, my hardworking father made that a possibility.

Not too long after our meal was finished and all the dishes were cleared, I thanked my hosts for a lovely dinner and quickly scooted toward the door. They sent a couple pieces of pumpkin pie home with me, but I could feel a sense of relief from them when I left. I guess my fake smiles were not that convincing after all. That's probably why drama was my toughest class in high school. I'd never been able to be anything but myself. Whoever made up that lame motto, *Fake it till you make it,* was a complete idiot, at least where I'm concerned.

When I made it back to my dorm, I quickly waved my hand to acknowledge the lone security guard sitting behind the glass entrance and walked through the deserted halls. All the soundless air was unnerving. Even though we studied nonstop, the word "quiet" was something only found in the five-inch dictionary on my desk.

Closing and locking the door to my room, I let out a long, slow breath, feeling safe within my little haven. But now I had nothing to do but stare at the stark white walls, so I decided to go to bed early. I wasn't sure how I'd fall asleep without the usual bustle of activity, or the slamming of doors echoing down the hallway, but finally I nodded off... most likely due to having just finished off both pieces of my host's delicious pie.

The next morning I awoke around eight o'clock. I tried to go back to sleep, but after thirty minutes of hiding away under my warm down comforter, I finally put my feet on the cold dorm floor. I walked to the window and saw that the sun was shining brightly in a cloudless sky. It was so bright I had to squint my eyes as I looked around. It appeared deceivingly warm out until I glanced down at the sidewalk and saw people passing by all bundled up in warm jackets and wrapped up in wool scarves.

Making my way to the shower, I wondered how I should spend my day. Many of the kids on my floor would return tomorrow, so this was my last free day all to myself. Since there was nothing much to do in New Haven and I'd visited all the important sites around the campus, I thought I might try to do something more adventurous.

A few weeks ago, my roommate, Sarah, had persuaded me to take the Metro North train with her into New York City and see a Saturday matinee show on Broadway. It was my first trip into the city and I fell in love with the energy there. People scurried about the sidewalks with determined looks on their faces. The street was lined with vendors selling everything from scarves to hotdogs. I remember Sarah telling me how spectacular the city was around Thanksgiving when all the stores unveiled their holiday-decorated windows.

"Ally, it's magical here during the holidays. I've got to bring you back to see it. Somehow we'll make it happen," she'd said.

She mentioned how the whole city seemed to adorn itself for Christmas. I'd always been a sucker for anything that had to do with the holidays, and who hasn't dreamed of gazing into the Macy's Christmas windows, so I decided to escape the deserted halls around me and head to New York City for the day.

    I quickly googled "holiday windows in New York" and the Metro North train schedule into Grand Central. There was a walking tour that started at Bloomingdale's, so I would just buck up a few extra dollars and take a cab there from Grand Central and walk the rest of the way with my trek ending at Macy's. The website said that the stroll by the six store windows would take under two hours. I knew that I would be stopping to shop and sightsee along the way, so it would take me most of the afternoon and into the early evening. But since the last train back to New Haven left at nearly one a.m., I had plenty of time to see all the sights.

    Looking at my alarm clock, I realized that I had little under an hour to get to the train, and once I was on board I would be in the heart of Manhattan in ninety minutes, so in a little over two hours I'd be walking the tunnels of Grand Central Station.

    Starting the day with frozen hair was not a good idea, so I hurriedly dried my locks and formed them into loose curls around my shoulders. I found my new down jacket and suede winter boots that were hiding under my bunk. I pulled them over my wool socks and hoped they'd work together to keep my toes warm. I wrapped my favorite scarf around my neck and dug my gloves out of my pockets.

    Now all bundled for the day, I made my way to New Haven's Union Station via the free shuttle from the Green by Yale's campus. I grabbed a donut and a latte at the station's coffee shop. Now that I was getting caffeinated and feeling more awake, the excitement of my little adventure was starting to set in.

After purchasing my roundtrip ticket, I headed toward the platform. Keeping my head down, I walked out the glass doors and braved the cold wind. The train would pull up at the stop any minute. I could feel the anticipation building and for some reason, I didn't even mind going by myself. I was a little surprised that I wasn't anxious about heading into the city alone. It wasn't like I was a seasoned New Yorker, but I'd be able to linger and shop as I pleased. If I wanted to drool on the glass cases at Tiffany's for a couple of hours who was going to care? Other than the poor salespeople. Also, I'd be able to indulge in one of my favorite past times... people watching.

Hearing the buzz of the train as it headed toward the platform, I turned my head and something, or I should say someone, caught my eye. A tall man was leaning against the soda machine across from me and dressed in a black wool topcoat that hit him about mid-thigh. The jeans he wore appeared to be lined in flannel because I could see the plaid material making up his cuff. His legs looked like they were jammed into his pants as they stretched tightly over his strong thighs.

The *New York Times* he was holding in front of him hid most of his upper body, but I knew exactly who it was. I'd stared at and dreamed about him for weeks.

The hot guy standing just a few feet away from me was none other than, Jack Prescott, Editor-in-Chief of the *Yale Daily News*, man about campus, and my new best friend, Chelsea's, brother. Oh, and most importantly he was majorly out of my league, even if he did just break up with his goddess of a girlfriend, Marissa.

He'd barely said a word to me since Chelsea introduced us. I was pretty sure he thought I was mute or just had a permanently paralyzed shocked face, because being in his presence left me completely speechless. I'd never been so attracted to anyone in my life and at the same time felt like I wanted to run and hide when I was around him. My behavior basically added up to crazy.

Strangely, though, I'd noticed him gazing at me during the weekly board meetings we lowly freshman attended with the editors. Last week his stares were rather unnerving and a complete turn-on, leaving me squirming in my chair and at a loss of what was being said during the meeting. But I didn't flatter myself in dreaming that his heated looks my way really meant anything. After all, he was perfect and I was far from it.

My mind wandered back to the day I'd first met Jack. It was a couple of months ago during my first week at Yale.

"Hey, Ally," Chelsea had called to me as I entered the first-floor reporter's room.

I stopped dead in my tracks because the most beautiful boy, or more like man, was examining me from where he was leaning against my desk with his long, muscular legs stretched out in front of him. My sex-starved mind imagined pushing him back against my desk blotter and remedying my sorry, deprived state.

"Ally, are you okay?" Chelsea had laughed as she tried to break me out of my trance. Just thinking back on that day was mortifying.

"Uh, yeah. I'm fine. Just coming down from my morning caffeine fix. That's all." I hoped that I made sense, but I remember how he just stared at me.

"This is my brother, Jack Prescott." She smiled, as she turned to her hot as hell brother. "I've told her all about you, Jack."

Well, it was rather obvious that she'd forgotten a few things… like his chiseled jaw line, his sexed-up hair, and those dangerous baby blue eyes. I recall breaking my stare and looking over at Chelsea, pleading for her help. But I still couldn't speak. Somehow, I'd earned a perfect score on the SAT, but place a devastatingly handsome piece of hot testosterone in front of me and my brain turns to complete mush.

"Hi, Ally," the gorgeous, blue-eyed god had said to me. "I hear from Chelsea that you're going to be working as a general assignment's reporter. Nice to meet you."

I remained dumbstruck after hearing him speak my name, but saw that he had extended his hand out to me. Somehow, I moved and placed a rather shaky hand in his, and as I did, I felt an odd warmth as we touched. My body moved forward seemingly without my help, as if on instinct. I think he felt it, too, because he looked down, puzzled, at our collective hands before he pulled away and ran his fingers through his glorious, bronze hair.

And it was that same bronze hair that gave him away today. It peeked out from the top of the newspaper. I barely saw his eyebrows as they scrunched together in concentration. Panic set in as I realized that I was about to be discovered ogling Mr. Blue Eyes. I wanted to run and hide or throw myself in front of the train. My choices were few and I needed to make a decision quick.

Thankfully, I saw a copy of the local newspaper lying discarded on the bench next to me. I reached for it and brought it up to cover my face. The train finally stopped and opened its doors. No one got off the train, but about twenty people entered as the platform lights blinked. I was careful to stay hidden from Jack as he moved to the back of the second car and faced away from the front of the train.

Discreetly, I chose a seat several rows in back of him with my newspaper disguise still placed a few inches in front of my face. I wondered where he was going and why he hadn't flown back home with Chelsea for the holidays. Perhaps his position at the *News* had kept him in town even though the staff had pre-planned editions. I guess there could always be breaking news to cover.

Well, there was no denying that he was here with me right now on this train bound for the city. And what should have been a relaxing ride ended up being one that was rattling my nerves. I found myself constantly shifting around in my seat hoping to steal a glimpse of him without exposing myself. What if he *did* see me? Would I just stand there tongue-tied as usual? Most likely.

Every time I saw him at the News building, I would turn the other way or duck into an empty office. He'd probably written me off as a complete lunatic and I seemed to transform into one when it came to him anyway. And now I'd become totally crazy about him. It was really rather sad as I couldn't seem to get him off my mind and to see him on the train… well, I started feeling sick from all the butterflies in my stomach.

Finally, the train pulled in and stopped at Grand Central Station. I decided to hide down in the seat with my paper as a mask and wait for him to exit first. After that, all bets were off. I had no idea what I would do next. But I knew that I couldn't let him out of my sight. With all the people crowding the station, I was fairly certain that I could keep a reasonable distance from him and go unnoticed.

Walking stealthily behind him, I realized that Jack had somehow turned me into a class-A stalker. Yes, it was totally his fault. I giggled quietly as I thought about visiting the mental health clinic on Monday, but until then I'd just use my time wisely and keep his beautiful backside in my view. I had absolutely no idea where he was going. He took several turns and walked through the tunnels down in the station.

Finally, he made his way up a long ramp. There weren't many people on the ramp and I worried that he might turn around and spot me behind him, but he just kept moving forward. I pulled my hair in front of my face to shield myself from his view in case he turned to look. If he saw me now, I'm pretty sure that he'd figure out that I was following him. Looking at it logically, just how did two people from New Haven end up being this close together in New York City without it being intentional?

I briefly reconsidered what I was doing. Honestly, I knew that I should turn the other way, but who was I kidding? I couldn't deny this pull I had to him, so my stalking continued unabated.

As Jack entered the main terminal lobby, he stopped abruptly and tilted his head up toward the ceiling. I followed his actions and saw the twinkling display overhead. It was beautiful how all the lights moved together so perfectly, but I was afraid to stare too long and have him walk away. The crowds were starting to get thick around us, so I decided to move a little closer to him.

He entered the 42nd Street-level access tunnel. I was relieved that we weren't going to take the subway somewhere else. It would be so much harder to hide from him. They were way too open and full of windows. Now I just prayed that he wouldn't be getting into a cab. That would bring my stalker capabilities to a definite halt. I held my breath as we moved to street level, but he put his head down and walked with a purpose toward Fifth Avenue. The sidewalks started to get crowded as we made our way to Fifth and turned left. The Thanksgiving parade tourists were still lingering throughout the city, so we were literally packed in shoulder to shoulder.

Block after block passed by as we hustled south. He slowed down for a bit as we approached Lord & Taylor's department store. I thought he might cross the street and stop to peer into their windows, but instead he pulled his collar up and continued on, picking up his speed.

Love in the City

My toes were starting to feel numb as we walked across 34th Street and turned right onto it. I suddenly realized where we might be heading.

34th Street. Where Christmas miracles happen.
Macy's!

We strolled down a long block, but as we approached the next street, I could see the trees lit up in Herald Square. I took a moment to look around and saw the tree designed of Christmas lights on the front of Macy's stone facade. The whole area looked just as I'd imagined it would—cheery, bright and filled with people.

I brought my eyes back down to street level and scanned around for Jack but didn't see him. There wasn't a head of bronze anywhere in sight. Picking up the pace I started looking around frantically for him as I worked my way to the Christmas windows. The crowds were packed tightly around them. I decided to get in line and view them then I'd head into Macy's and warm up for a bit. The day wouldn't be a total bust. It had been exciting and more than an adventure being close to Jack, sneaking peeks and playing like a spy. The last few hours sure beat hanging out in the quiet halls back in New Haven that was for sure.

As I inched my way closer to the windows, I glanced around just in case Mr. Blue Eyes walked by. But, alas, nothing... Not a damn thing.

I continued walking with the line toward the display windows. Finally, the first window was right in front of me. I stopped as I read the theme for this year's window.

They were showcasing the story of eight-year-old, Virginia O'Hanlon who wanted to know if there really was a Santa Claus. Displayed inside the window in front of me was little Virginia herself, questioning her father about the existence of Santa Claus.

I had the strangest feeling at that moment. It was almost like I was standing there by myself and the throngs of people just disappeared. Staring at the writing on the window, I felt someone brush up behind me and none too gently. But before I could turn around, I saw my reflection in the window along with the person who bumped into me.

It was HIM! Jack! He was standing right behind me and looking into the window, too, all smiles, and smirks.

Unbelievably, right in front of me mixed in the window's reflection was Virginia, me, and the gorgeous Jack Prescott. Immediately, I stiffened and was paralyzed until I felt his breath at my ear. My knees started to buckle. I think he must have foreseen my reaction, because he stepped in closer behind me and placed his glove-covered hands tightly on my upper arms. My eyes were glued to his in our mirrored reflection and I saw his lips start to move.

"Ally, turn around," he whispered into my ear.

Who could disobey a seductive whisper like that? I knew I couldn't, so I quickly spun around in his arms, my face just inches away from his wool-covered chest. I'd dreamed and hoped that he'd notice me, and, holy shit; here he was looking down at me with those eyes of his. Right then I knew I was putty in his hands.

"I thought I'd sneak up on *you* this time. You're a hard stalker to lose, Ally."

Oh, my God. He knew that I'd been following him. I wanted to die. Now. Once again, all I could do was stand there and look shocked.

"You look surprised that I knew that you were following me. Take some friendly advice—drop any thoughts you have about working for the CIA."

"That bad?" Hey, I finally spoke! Two whole words. Yeah.

"Yes, that bad. But I did enjoy the panicked look on your face when I deliberately hid from you. Are you feeling better now, Ms. Stalker?" Jack laughed as he drew me in closer to him. Our bodies were almost touching and my head was spinning. What the hell was he doing holding me like this? It didn't make any sense. He didn't even seem disturbed by my crazy behavior. He appeared to find it amusing.

"Feeling better?" I asked confused then realized what he was asking. "Oh, I get it. No, I'm no longer panicked. Well, that's not totally true."

"I have an idea and it looks like you could use some warming up." He winked at me. Oh, my God, I think he must have had me confused with someone else. This couldn't be happening to me. He took my hand into his and walked me to the edge of the sidewalk. I stood slightly behind him and watched him hail a cab.

When a cab pulled up and stopped, he opened the door for me and I slid across the seat as he followed me in. He looked over at me all smiles with a sexy gleam in his beautiful eyes. Without taking his eyes from mine, he told the cabbie where to take us. "The Roosevelt Hotel. Madison and Forty-fifth."

"Yes, sir," the cabbie responded.

"I have reservations there for the night. Is it okay if I check in early and warm up?"

I nodded my head as words failed me. Holy shit. He was taking me to a hotel. To a room with a bed. My head was spinning once again.

He took off his gloves and reached for my right hand. Slowly, he removed my glove, finger by finger. I was practically panting by the time he'd finished and laid my lone glove on the seat.

"I want to try something, okay?" he said.

I nodded my agreement.

"There's something I've been curious about since the day we met."

I sat there lost in his words and blue eyes, not daring to move a muscle.

Very carefully, he moved his fingers toward mine and placed them lightly against my opened palm. And there it was again. That strange, warm feeling moved up my arm just like it did during our handshake back in September. But this time he didn't pull his hand away. Instead, he wrapped his long fingers around mine and pulled my hand up to his lips.

He began to gently kiss each knuckle as he gazed at me with rather hooded eyes. I tried to suppress the moan that was working to escape my lips, but I just couldn't hold it back. I had my fantasy man sitting next to me in the flesh and he was pressing his sweet lips against my shaky hand. It was almost too much to believe or bear.

"You felt that too, didn't you?" He lowered my hand to the seat, but didn't release it.

"Yes, I felt it. But it wasn't the first time. I remember feeling it when we met." My words made him smile even more if that was possible.

"I felt it too, Ally. At first, I thought it was just a fluke, but there was just something about you. I can't really explain it."

What? Maybe he *was* attracted to me?

I remembered Chelsea telling me that he broke up with the goddess, Marissa, after he found himself having feelings for someone else. She'd told me that he didn't want to be unfaithful to Marissa, and he needed to see if this other person felt the same way he did. Chelsea mentioned that the other girl often avoided him, so he didn't really think he stood a chance with her. But he wanted to reach out to her anyway, give it a try.

Could it possibly be me that Chelsea was speaking about?

"So there's something about *me*?" I had to ask him this question. I just couldn't wrap my mind around his words and declaration. I needed to hear it one more time.

He tightened his grip around my fingers and shifted right next to me in the backseat. He pressed his body into mine and looked directly into my eyes.

"I can't quit thinking about you, Ally. I know that you've noticed me staring at you during our weekly meetings. Every time you looked my way, I'd get lost in your big, brown eyes. Don't even get me started with your innocent blush."

True to form, I blushed heavily as if on cue.

He laughed and traced his fingers over my cheeks. He looked at my lips then gazed up into my eyes asking for permission. I closed my eyes and parted my lips in answer.

His lips found mine, and the spark from earlier turned hot with passion. No longer were we suppressing anything. Breathing hard, he moved my scarf away from my neck and starting gently kissing me below my ear. I was aching in the most delicious way.

I leaned back into the seat and closed my eyes as Jack pulled me even closer into him.

The only thing I thought of while his warm lips kissed mine was Virginia and her Christmas wish. Like her, my wish had come true, and he was sitting beside me holding me tightly in his arms.

Jack's Love at First Touch

Moving toward the full wall of windows in my Manhattan office, I peered at the skyline and surveyed the neighboring buildings. Granite and glass were surrounding me, but I didn't feel the sterile coldness as my mind drifted. I thought back to a Thanksgiving week five years ago. I smiled remembering how my sweet wife had become mine.

It'd been the Monday afternoon before Thanksgiving break, and we were five minutes past the scheduled start of our weekly "all hands on deck" editorial meeting. I scanned the boardroom looking for Ally, rubbing my hands nervously against my thighs. She was usually one of the first reporters to arrive and always seemed prepared. I needed to see her today. Strike that; I had to see her today.

I stalled and shuffled through the upcoming assignments for the week in an attempt to look calm and in control. Where the hell was she? There was only one chair left unoccupied in the room. It was directly across from me at the other end of the long, shiny mahogany table.

Staring at the empty seat, I thought back over the last few days. It had been one hell of a weekend. Breaking up with Marissa had been a complete disaster. She knew that something was afoot before I even uttered a word. I'd lost count of how many times she'd asked me if everything was okay. What could I tell her about Ally, when nothing made sense to me?

"Sorry, Marissa. I've met someone who shows no interest in me, and I have to pursue her."

Damn, Ally'd been the main attraction in my nightly dreams over the last couple of months. The night before, I'd dreamed that I was making love to her as she lay across the very desk in front of me. Her hair had been spread in a wavy halo around her head. God, what a dream.

I couldn't deny it any longer. My attraction to her was intense and somehow growing stronger. The only problem was, my ethereal beauty avoided me like I was the Black Death.

As I started the board meeting, a flustered Ally stumbled into the room. Her face was flushed and those big, brown eyes of hers were hitting me head on. I was completely lost as a sense of relief flooded me. She was here finally.

A goofy grin spread across my face as Ally took the seat opposite me at the large boardroom table. She mumbled her apologies, but looked at me confused. It must have been my funky smile because everyone else around me shared in her puzzled look.

"Well, Ally. Glad you're here. We're just getting started. I'm going to let our managing editors take our weekly meeting from here. Patrick and Marcy, floor's yours."

Now that I'd handed over the meeting to my editors, I could get back to more important things. Like staring, gazing, and mentally undressing Ally. Watching that beautiful flush on her cheeks, I was beginning to think that she was feeling a bit uncomfortable with my constant eye contact. But I'd be damned if I couldn't look away from her.

As the meeting adjourned, I tried to catch her. However, she was closer to the door and the only way to get her attention would've required me to walk across the damn table.

Fate was working against me! I'd missed another chance of talking to her.

Over the next couple of days, I tried to run into her somehow. Really run into her. I longed to touch her again. That simple touch on the first day we met still had me craving for more. My connection to her was undeniable, but what were her feelings for me? Part of me was afraid to find out.

After spending a gluttonous Thanksgiving Day with family friends in Woodbridge, Connecticut, I returned to Yale early in the evening. I sent the next day's edition of the Yale Daily News to press, and then decided to escape the confines of my campus apartment on Friday by planning a night's stay in New York City at The Roosevelt Hotel.

I thought of inviting someone else to tag along; however, I needed some time away by myself to try to regroup. Since Ally had successfully eluded my charms, I knew I had to devise a plan to woo her.

Friday morning I rolled out of bed, showered, dressed for the cold and headed to New Haven Station. I grabbed a Red Bull and a bagel, tucked a copy of today's New York Times under my arm and met the cold day head-on. I'd thrown a few things into a backpack for the overnight stay. I didn't need much and it felt good to get away. And since someone else was manning the News' publishing tomorrow, I was free now for over twenty-four hours.

After purchasing my roundtrip ticket, I leaned against the buzzing Coke machine on the station platform.

Glancing at the ticker board time display, I saw that there was ten minutes before the next train to Grand Central arrived. As I opened the newspaper, I briefly glanced into the terminal doors and noticed the line at the coffee shop was long.

Finally, the train pulled up to the station, I folded up my paper under my arm and entered the closest car. For some reason I preferred to sit with my back toward the front of the train. I took out a pen from my pocket and started to write a list of ways I could break the ice with Ally. Twenty minutes later and no ideas, my eyes became fixed on the paper in front of me. I was drawing a complete blank.

It was baffling to me, but I felt like an insecure fourteen-year-old boy trying to feel his way up his girlfriend's shirt, hoping that his wandering hands would make it to second base without their being pushed away. Perhaps I feared that she'd reject me and I'd never get to hold her tight or smell her hair as I shared a pillow with her after making love. With that thought still fresh in my mind, I closed my eyes and drifted into a semi-conscious sleep still trying to stay aware of the train's stops and starts.

Upon reaching Grand Central Station, I stretched out my stiff limbs and made my way to the car's exit. I briefly glanced at a young woman seated a few rows from me. She was wearing one of those puffy down jackets, which hid her curves and made me curse the cold. A newspaper was gripped tightly in her small hands. Strangely, she was holding it super close to her face.

"Poor girl," I muttered wondering if she had extremely poor eyesight.

After winding through the underbelly of Grand Central, I finally made it to the main terminal. It was one of my favorite places in New York City and always a hub of activity. Stopping in the center of the expansive open terminal, I looked up to see the twinkling lights overhead. As I turned my head slightly, I caught a glimpse of Puffy-coat Girl. As I looked closer at her, I realized that she was Ally, my Ally.

It's my lucky day! Quickly turning, I tried to figure out what to do next.

Should I go and talk to her? Walk up and say "hi"?

Wait! A funny thought crossed my mind. Could she be following me? What could she be doing here standing a mere three feet away from me? She was on the same car of the train with me and had that silly newspaper practically plastered to her face. I had to know if my suspicions where correct or if it was just wishful thinking.

I proceeded to the street-level exit. Out of the corner of my eye, I could see her wrapped in that monstrous, silver coat walking closely behind me with her head angled toward the ground. Damn, she was following me. My palms started to perspire and I tried to think of a quick plan. It had to include an element of surprise. I wanted to catch her off guard and needed to play it just right.

Originally, I'd planned on taking a cab to Herald Square to do a little shopping at Macy's. However, taking a cab would've separated me from my hot little shadow. I laughed thinking that maybe, just maybe, I had read all those "stay away from me, you're not my type" signals incorrectly. Perhaps she felt the same as I did—a strange and compelling attraction, a need to be near, desperate to touch. I hoped she felt a portion of what I'd experienced in regard to her since we'd met.

I kept walking toward the glass revolving doors that led to Fifth Avenue. As I reached them, I slowed my gait to a snail's pace. Leisurely, I pushed the glass forward and the suction from the movement made a whistling sound. Once again, I spotted my sweet stalker just paces away.

She was hot on my trail and we proceeded south at a fast clip toward 34th Street. The Lord & Taylor building appeared on the right after we crossed over a couple of streets. Turning my head to watch for oncoming cars as I crossed, I kept close tabs on Ally's position behind me. At the last crosswalk, she barely made it to the other side before a reckless cab driver nearly plowed her down. Idiot cabbie. I nearly blew my cover as I fought the urge to run to her aid. Instead, I discreetly watched her dash to safety.

   I steeled myself and trekked on, taking a deep breath trying to relax, as I'd become pretty geared up. I thought about stopping at Lord & Taylor's to work my magic and turn the tables on Ally, but the crowds were too thin for my liking. My covert operation required wall-to-wall gawkers. Only a large, stagnant cluster of people would guarantee my plan's success.

   My toes started to tingle as I carefully scooted across 5th Avenue and walked down 34th to the Holy Grail of Christmas crowds, Herald Square. Just before we were in front of Macy's, I pulled my black stocking cap out of my coat pocket with one hand, tilted my head to the side and glanced at Ally. Just as I'd thought, she was catching flies with her mouth agape while her face tipped upward looking seven stories up to the top of the store's roof. She was completely overpowered by the lavish display of commercialism. Macy's has a way of putting unsuspecting window shoppers into a holiday trance of some kind.

   Having my stocking cap safely in hand, I put it on. While she was lost in the red and green haze, I darted and squatted down next to a magazine kiosk near the kick-off window. It was where Macy's preferred its herd of onlookers to begin their "ooh and ahh" finger-pointing parade.

   With my crazy hair tucked away, I crouched down out of Ally's sight. The attendant at the kiosk was beginning to wonder what the hell I was up to. He probably thought I was preparing to steal the December copy of Cosmo that my hand was pressed against. Smiling until my frozen face smarted, I looked up at the attendant from my peculiar position.

"Hey, man. I'm trying to hide from that beautiful brunette over there. She's the one in the silver puffy coat." I nodded my head in Ally's direction. The man acknowledged Ally with a wiggle from his eyebrows and grinned in a knowing way.

"Yes, man, she's hot as hell. And I'm trying to surprise her. Early holiday present and all," I lied, partially. The man brushed his hand across the thin air signaling that my plan had passed muster.

Ally moved closer to the windows, still scanning through the crowd for me. She must've realized that she'd lost my "scent" because I observed a forlorn expression upon her beautiful face. It pained me and thrilled me at the same time. She wanted me. Her exasperated appearance gave her away. It was more than a game, as she appeared to be on the verge of desperation.

After walking and circling the area on her tiptoes, she stopped dead in her tracks and dropped her head toward the ground in a sign of defeat. But I'll be damned if those windows didn't draw her like a magnet. It's nearly impossible to stand in Herald Square and ignore them.

Cautiously, I rose from my squatted position. I held my head low and moved toward her, as she stood frozen in front of a window.

Relief set in. My plan had worked. Gingerly, I walked up behind her excusing myself as I gently sliced my way through the horde.

Almost there. Her brown hair was shining in the sun like a beacon. My heart raced.

Ten feet away.

I mumbled a few, "Excuse and pardon me's."

Bull's eye.

Adrenaline was running through my body. The anticipation had revved me up.

She was completely absorbed while reading the words displayed on the window. A Cheshire Cat smile slid across my face as I secretly watched her. God, she was adorable, almost childlike as she stared in awe at the magical montage. My eyes were fixed on her face as I waited and hoped that our eyes would lock together in the window's reflection.

I quickly discarded my stocking hat, shoving it into my pocket. I tried to smooth down my stubborn mop as I gazed at Ally's petite frame. Out of nowhere, a man holding a large 90's style camcorder bumped into me, which made me more than bump into Ally. Her eyes traveled toward mine in the reflection of the window. She probably wondered who the ass was that had just collided with her so rudely.

"Hi there, baby," I thought.

I knew the second she saw me, because a wave of recognition appeared on her face, followed by a look of disbelief.

Quickly, I grabbed her upper arms. I needed contact and a simple reassurance that all was well. Leaning toward her right ear, I whispered softly, "Ally, turn around."

As she turned toward me, I wanted to kiss the shock right off her face. Kiss her neck. And really any place that she'd let me. Craving her was maddening, so I grabbed her hand and led her to the sidewalk's edge.

I hated the gloves that were separating us. My fingers were hungering for her touch, yearning to see if that energy I'd felt between us when we first made contact was genuine and real.

Luckily, a cabbie stopped for me after my first wave for attention. Opening the door, I followed her into the warmth of the taxi, smiling at her with everything I had. I wanted to reassure her and erase that frozen look of disbelief on her face. With my eyes never once leaving hers, I rambled off our destination to the driver, The Roosevelt Hotel.

Could I be asking too much from her too soon? I searched her face, but there was no resistance from her as she agreed to stop at the hotel with me.

Relief hit me and I looked down to see her hand still lying in the space between us. Her fingers were hidden by her knitted gloves. I had to remove them, touch her, and caress her. Satisfying this ache for her was almost overwhelming to me.

I reached out and gently placed her tiny hand in mine, asking her for permission, needing her to grant me my wish to let me touch her skin-to-skin.

She nodded and I proceeded to slowly and torturously remove her glove then placed my hand in her open palm with the force of our connection once again hitting me like it did during our first encounter.

Shit, it was real, she was real, and we were real. Unable to hold back any longer, I found my body sliding next to hers in the backseat. I brought my hand to her shoulder, still focused on her beautiful, flushed face.

Looking deep into her eyes, I could see it. Desire. Longing. The shock and hesitancy was replaced with surrender as she closed her eyes and parted her lips.

Damn right. I looked at her open lips and closed eyes. There was my invitation. It was my green light to kiss her delectable lips. My first kiss was tentative and slow, but as I pressed myself against her, I felt the need for so much more. Her soft almost inaudible moans were heavenly and fueled me on. But her silly coat was not meant for passionate touches, so I moved the one item, her scarf, which let me kiss more of her creamy skin. I trailed my lips across her skin while she hummed with the pleasure she felt.

I reluctantly ceased from scattering my lips across her neck. As much as I wanted to keep our passion stoked, we needed to communicate beyond what we were feeling on a physical level. I searched her face, but saw that her eyes were closed with a sweet smile gracing her lips. There was no resistance from her as I held her tightly in my arms, but it was time to talk.

"Ally, I can't get you off my mind." I paused to let my words sink in. "I can't begin to explain it. But that touch when we first met… It seemed like there was something there between us."

Now time to confess.

"I tried to deny it. Write it off as a weird fluke, but then I'd see you again either in the hallway or at our board meetings. Let's just say I was completely caught up in every move you made or word you said. Any question I had about my attraction to you was gone."

She was still and silent as her eyes looked straight into my mine. But I had no idea what she was thinking and was starting to get nervous. I wanted to know her thoughts. Perhaps I was frightening her. Damn, that would kill me.

"Ally, do you understand what I'm saying?" My fingers tightened around hers in assurance. "I want to get to know you, be with you. But am I scaring you?"

Finally, her lips moved. I froze in place waiting for her to tell me what our fate would be.

"Jack, my head's spinning. I'm shocked that you'd want me. I'm plain next to you. You… you're the most beautiful man I've ever met." Her eyes looked away shyly. "To be honest, I feel like I'm in a dream and if I am, please don't wake me up."

We both started laughing and I caressed her cheek with my thumb and cupped her face.

"You're the one that's beautiful, Ally."

I couldn't wait any longer. I needed more of her sweet lips. There was no better way to convince her of my attraction for her. Drawing her lips into mine, I passionately kissed her and pushed her coat up above her waist. Placing my hands underneath her sweater, I felt the warmth of her soft skin.

We reached the Roosevelt as my greedy hands started to wander. I settled up with the cabbie and followed her out of the cab.

Walking together hand in hand through the revolving glass door at the hotel's entrance, we grinned at each other ridiculously. I'm sure we raised a few eyebrows, but we didn't pay any attention to onlookers. We only had eyes for one another.

We made our way up the marble steps, which led to the lobby. The front desk was a few feet away on our left, and as we waited in line to register, we were still smiling like two crazy fools. Unlocking our eyes, I bent down to whisper into her ear.

"Let me check in and then we can go upstairs and order some room service. How does a bottle of champagne sound to you?"

"I'm not twenty-one yet," she said with a cute little pout. "Kind of stinks."

"Don't worry about it. The room's in my name anyway." I pulled her tighter burying my nose in her hair. She smelled so sweet.

"Thanks." She pulled back a bit and looked around hesitantly.

"Are you sure that you're okay with this? You know—us together, upstairs, alone? I promise not to push or ask you to do anything that you're not ready for. But I will warn you of this. Once we're behind the doors of our room, I'm going to kiss the ever-living hell out of you. What happens after that will be your call. I promise. You have my word."

"It'll be my call, huh?" Ally looked at me in question.

"Yes, Ally. Your call."

"There's no way I can refuse that proposition." She squeezed my hand and smirked at me.

Oh, no. What the hell was behind that smirk? I would've given anything to know. A guy could only hope, right?

After checking in, we proceeded up to the fifth floor, heading to room 506. In went the key and out went the breath that I'd been holding since we walked through the hotel's front door.

Ally padded slowly to the side of the bed. I saw the trademark monogrammed "R" square pillow on the linen white bedspread.

"It's lovely, Jack. I've never been in a hotel room this beautiful."

Needing to be closer, I moved to stand in front of her. That jacket of hers had to go, now. My eyes never left hers as I slowly unwrapped the scarf from around her neck. As it dropped to the floor, my fingers found the zipper of her coat.

"Don't worry, baby. I'll keep you warm." Slowly, inch by grueling inch I moved the zipper. I couldn't help but notice that we were both breathing raggedly. Our desire increased as the zipper traveled downward. Finally, I freed her of her coat and saw her standing there in an ice blue crewneck sweater. It hugged tightly around her full breasts.

Looking away from her heaving chest, I met her eyes and couldn't contain myself any longer. "Are you ready to be kissed to within an inch of your life?" I winked and removed any space between us.

But I'll be damned if she didn't hold out her hand to stop me in my approach.

"No, actually, I'm not ready."

My disappointment was evident. I knew that this was too good to be true. Damn, I felt crushed, but thankfully, she saved me from my misery.

"Hey, I said I'm not ready, but I didn't say 'no.'" She winked at me this time. "I need you to close your eyes and no peeking. Okay?"

I nodded as I closed my eyes as tightly as I could. This woman owned me. I'd do anything for her right now.

I felt her hands unbutton my coat and gently remove it from my body. As my eyes started to flutter, she reminded me to keep them shut.

"Keep 'em closed, got it?" Her tone was sassy and by the sound of her voice, she'd moved away from me.

What the hell was she up to? I loved this playful side of her. God, we had so much to learn about each other.

"Alright, you've been a good boy. You can open them now."

My eyes popped open and I couldn't believe the sight I saw in front of me. Ally was lying down on the bed propped up on her elbows as she bit her sweet lips. She had removed her jeans and sweater.

I closed my eyes to calm myself. Damn, this was my lucky day.

She was wearing white cotton boy shorts and a simple white bra. Her underwear matched the color of the bed's coverings.

As I moved forward, her head fell back upon the bed and her hair surrounded her like it had in my dreams… into a beautiful halo. But this wasn't some crazy dream of having her on a mahogany desk. This was real.

She was the perfect mix of a woman. Innocent yet sexy as hell. A devilishly sweet angel.

I removed my sweater and roughly tugged off my boots. My jeans were added to the pile. I stood there in my black boxer briefs fully ready to give her whatever she wanted.

"Okay, now I'm ready," she spoke seductively to me and my hands were on her legs before she finished her sentence.

My hands slid up her outer thighs to her hips. I placed my knees on the bed and leaned over.

"I think you promised to kiss me within an inch of my life. I'm waiting," she said.

God knew I wasn't one to keep a beautiful woman waiting…

Waiting! That word shook me out of my daydream. Crap! If I didn't hurry I'd leave her waiting out in the cold for me. It was almost noon. When I'd left our apartment that morning, I'd given Ally specific instructions about my surprise for her.

She was to meet me in front of Macy's kickoff window at noon. Straight up. I asked her to be facing the window, focusing on the display in front of her. A big smile lit up her face as she caught on to what I might have up my sleeve.

Racing out of my office, I hit the street and hailed a cab.

"34th and Broadway!" I practically shouted at the poor cabbie. "Get me there fast and I'll double the fare's cost!"

"Yes, sir!" the driver replied.

I reached into my pocket and checked to see if my surprise was still there. Yes, still there. Now, game on.

We reached Herald Square in lightening speed and I gladly handed the smiling cabbie a twenty.

"Merry Christmas, buddy," I said as he greedily swiped the bill from my hands.

Checking my watch, I realized that it was high noon. I ran to the front of Macy's and there she was standing in the black cashmere coat that I'd bought her for her birthday. My darling wife deserved nothing but the best.

Catching my breath, I slowed down as I approached her. The crowds were thick and she was looking intently at Macy's magical display.

Finally, I was behind her, quiet and just staring into the window's reflective glass. I nudged her gently. Our eyes met in the window. We stood there gazing with our love reflecting back to each other.

God, I adored this woman.

"Ally, turn around."

Slowly, she turned around and we laughed as I tried to draw her near to me. However, her round eight-month pregnant belly kept my arms stretched out. I reached down and kissed her knowing that she'd never been more beautiful. And that I would be eternally grateful for her giving me the best gift of all—our soon to be born child, Virginia.

"Hi, love. Thanks for meeting me. This is our last Thanksgiving together before the baby is born. I wanted to do something special for you. Reach into my coat pocket. There's something in there for you."

She placed her little hand, slightly swollen from the last stages of pregnancy, into my pocket. Then she found the gift.

A key to room 506 at the Roosevelt Hotel...

Perfect Strangers

by Liv Morris

Liv Morris

The Working Girl

My eyes are looking down as I type away furiously on my keyboard. Just a few more numbers to enter and I'm finally going to shut this computer down.

Ping, ping. Click, click.

After pressing "send" and emailing my year end report, I'm finished… Finally! Twirling around in my office chair, the walls of my little cubicle blur before my eyes.

When the spinning stops, my chair faces the partitioned offices of my neighbors. But something's missing as I scan around me. There doesn't appear to be a single head peeking over the top of the other cubicles. It looks like I'm the last holdout tonight. Which makes sense; it's New Year's Eve, after all. Only crazy workaholics stay this late on a night made for the fun type of alcoholic endeavors.

A door slams loudly in the distance. I jump out of my chair turning quickly toward the noise once my feet land on the ground. Wobbling on the heels of my boots for balance, my heart pounds away, startled. Someone in the shadowy hallway moves in my direction. Thankfully, I recognize the person is my stumpy, firecracker of a boss. He's notorious for being quite the tyrant, but I've found he's really a softhearted man, at least where I'm concerned. He walks toward me with a scowl on his face. His countenance is nothing new and a welcome sight as I realize I'm not alone in this deserted building after all.

"Katrina Williams, what the hell are you still doing here?" Mr. Stephens never yells but I know from his gruff tone and the use of my full name that he means business. "Everyone was supposed to leave a couple of hours ago. Gather up your coat and hightail it out of here."

"Okay, I'm leaving now," I respond back to him. "I needed to finish the year end reports for Bentley. I'm gone all next week, remember? And he wants the numbers by January 4th or else." I cringe at the thought.

"Kat, it's New Year's Eve for Christ's sake. And haven't you heard the news?"

I shake my head. I've been too busy with my report to even care about what's going on beyond my three partitioned walls.

"What's up, Mr. Stephens?" I ask genuinely concerned when I see the worried look on his face.

"For starters, Chicago is under a winter storm warning."

"You're kidding me? I thought we were supposed to get just an inch or two." I look out the glass walls of the building, but only see the evening's darkness reflected back at me.

"We're way past a couple of inches already. The last report I heard said the wind is really starting to pick up too." Okay. He's worrying me a bit now. "So scoot and get started on that overdue vacation of yours."

"Alright sir, I'm out of here." I stand at attention after pulling on my coat and give a little half-hearted salute. "Happy New Year, Mr. Stephens."

"Same to you, Kat. And please drive safely."

I nod and grab my purse out of my desk drawer but decide to leave the laptop here. Out of sight means out of mind. At least that's my plan for the next few days.

I shout one last goodbye over my shoulder as I wind through the labyrinth of office desks toward the elevator. I hear some cursing coming from somewhere behind me. I laugh at Mr. Stephen's silly mutterings. How his sweet wife puts up with him and his sour moods is beyond me.

Standing in front of the elevator, my foot taps impatiently. What's taking so long? I push the down button a few more times for good measure. Finally, the doors slide open and I practically jump in. As the cage starts to descend, I do a little happy dance. My vacation has officially begun. Yay, me!

I'm free for a whole seven days and plan on being a lazy sloth. Days filled with wearing yoga pants and watching old Audrey Hepburn movies are awaiting me. Oh, and ice cream. Lots and lots of chocolate ice cream.

Unfortunately, the lazy times won't start until tomorrow because tonight I'm meeting my parents for a late dinner. It might be a bit of a snoringly good time for New Year's Eve, but it's better than the alternative. The usual New Year's Eve party at which I'd make an appearance would likely be attended by my ex-fiancé. He's a super big jerk and I'm avoiding him at all costs. Unless I have a GQ looking date by my side, that is. This would counteract his Victoria's Secret looking replacement for me.

Unfortunately, I wasn't able to arrange even a semi-hot date for tonight. Since breaking up with the ex, my dating life has amounted to a couple blind dates that were orchestrated by my so-called friends. All of the dates, utter disasters.

So, I'm off to meet my sweet parents, hoping they'll have mercy on me and not ask if I'm seeing anyone new.

They know how hard the last few months have been on me. It's rather mind-blowing to come home early from work and find your fiancé in bed with the hot neighbor down the hall…

Well, it definitely took the wind out of my sails. Now if I could just find someone to re-inflate them. Hmmm… Maybe there will be a hot waiter or bartender at the restaurant tonight. I could go for a little harmless flirting. Of course, I'll need at least two strong drinks to play that game. Maybe even more with my parents supervising me.

God, I'm hanging out with my parents on New Year's Eve. Could I be any more lame? Probably not. At least I have my job to keep me busy. I've thrown myself into advancing my career since my breakup, and my latest promotion puts me way ahead of the ex-fiancé in the income department. Gloating isn't my normal style but right now, I can't help it.

The elevator doors open to the garage parking in the lower levels of the building. There are only two cars in view, Mr. Stephens's and mine. My sporty little SUV is all shiny and new. It was a little post-breakup present to myself. It should be a big help with tonight's weather, too.

Pulling out of the parking garage, I'm hit with a wall of snow. The weatherman said flurries were likely this afternoon, but this is close to being a complete whiteout. My palms are starting to sweat now.

I grip the steering wheel tightly and curse the white stuff blowing around me. Dammit. I hate driving in the snow. One would think being raised in Chicago would give me mad snow driving skills, but I have no love for the snow. I'm always a ball of tension behind the wheel when it starts sticking to the ground.

Since the roads are completely snow-covered and getting treacherous I inch my way toward Lake Shore Drive. There's a red light up ahead and thankfully I ease into a skid-free stop and exhale. Removing my white knuckled fingers from the steering wheel, I pull my phone out of my purse. I need to make a quick call to my mother, let her know that I'm going be late. Real late.

"Kat!" My mother's voice is strained and anxious. "I've been worried sick. Have you left work yet?"

"Yes, I'm just about to get onto Lake Shore. But I wanted to give you a heads-up. The snow is crazy right now. Traffic is horrible, so I'll probably be late."

"Oh, sweetie. I know how you hate driving in snow. Maybe you should wait until the roads are better?"

"I'll be okay. This is Chicago, Mom. If there is one thing they can do, it's clean up some snow. I'll be fine."

"Promise you'll be careful and turn around if it gets worse," she begs.

"I promise. Please don't worry. I'll be okay." I try to comfort her and I think it works because she changes the subject.

"I baked one of your favorites today. Apple pie. As a matter of fact, I'm going to thaw some steaks. We'll just eat at home tonight."

"Sounds good. I have no idea when I'll get to the house." I see cars starting to move in front of me. "Oh, Mom, the light turned green, better go."

"Bye, Kat. Drive safe, dear."

I say goodbye and end the call, as both of my hands are needed on the steering wheel. My neck and shoulder muscles tense up as the car moves forward. Hopefully, I can talk Mom into giving me a little shoulder rub when I get home.

As my car inches along, my usual radio station breaks to broadcast a Special Report. Chicago's mayor is asking, or more like pleading, that all motorists clear the roads because the street plowing crews are making little headway against the heavy snowfall. Add rush hour and

New Year's Eve travelers to the mix, and the roads were totally jam-packed leaving a complete gridlock across the city.

I just need to get home. *Home.* That's my focus now. Mom's cooking and maybe some hot chocolate will be waiting for me. I imagine Dad sitting in his comfy chair by a roaring fire. I can almost hear the wood popping and feel the warmth from the flames.

Now I really do hear popping sounds as car horns blare all around me. A bus has begun to swerve erratically in front of me and my foot presses hard onto the brakes. I clutch the steering wheel for dear life as my car skids toward the side of the still moving bus. It's now sideways across all the lanes of traffic on Lake Shore Drive.

Danger Ahead

As the bus fishtails in front of me, I get a sick feeling in my stomach. The car next to me swerves out of the bus's way and ends up in the ditch facing the opposite direction. I continue to slam on my brakes, but realize a chain reaction wreck is about to take place and I'm going to be a part of it.

The next few seconds transpire in slow motion. I pump my car's brakes, turn the steering wheel as I've been taught, but still my car spins out of control. It becomes clear that my fate is in someone else's hands, so I close my eyes preparing for the inevitable crunch of metal. But it never comes. Instead, I feel a thud against the passenger side door. My head keeps moving and hits the window at my side, hard. Now my car has come to a halt, so I open my eyes to see where I've had landed. My vision is a little blurry but eventually focuses.

Somehow, I've ended up parallel to the bus with my car's right side pressed against the back wheel well. I'm sure I have a large dent, but the most important thing is I've thankfully survived to live another day. Putting my car in park, I rest my forehead against the steering wheel and say a silent prayer. Though my head hurts a little, my life was somehow spared.

Taps at my window draw me out of my reverent moment. I look out to see a young man staring at me through the glass. He's mouthing something and motioning for me to roll down my window. I reach for the button and roll it down.

"Are you alright?" the stranger asks.

"I think so," I reply, rubbing the small knot forming by my left temple. He smiles down at me with a beautiful display of white teeth. I want to restate my condition, as the snowflakes blow around him. He makes me feel anything but okay. I must've hit my head harder than I realized.

"You look a little pale. Why don't you come and sit in my car?" His eyes have a look of concern, but I think I see a smile lurking behind them. "I have a feeling we're gonna be here for quite awhile."

He points to the bus that's hugging my car and blocking all the lanes in front of us. "Someone will have to come and tow away the bus before we can even think about moving our cars."

I watch snowflakes land on the young man's black cashmere coat and can see a signature Burberry scarf peeking out from around his neck, which leads me back up to his face. It's hard to look away from him. I've heard people call hot guys beautiful, but this guy really fits the description. He has a strong jaw line, high cheekbones, and intense, dark brown eyes that continue to study me. He is, without a doubt, one hundred percent delicious.

I need to pull myself out of this beautiful boy daze and answer him. He wants me in his car, with him. Um, that sounds like a plan as I throw caution to the wind.

I've seen the movie *American Psycho*, but right now I'm freezing and stranded in the damn snow on New Year's Eve with a head that's hurting. I decide to take my chances and smile up at him, feeling warm already. *I did mention that he was gorgeous, right?*

"Sure, why not?" I finally answer back.

After grabbing my purse and rolling up the window, I turn as he opens the door for me. Next thing I know he's holding my hand and sheltering me from the wind and snow with his body as he walks me to his car. Jeez, I thought beautiful guys like him were all jerks.

Oh please, oh please, Mr. Tall, Dark and Handsome, prove all those urban rumors wrong. I want to believe in miracles today.

Once I'm inside his car, I look around me. Quite impressive. I have no idea what kind of sports car this is, but it's one sweet ride and expensive too. I can just tell.

I run my hands over the smooth, leather seats as I melt into their soft luxury. I'm thinking he's an attorney at this point, probably for one of the big firms downtown. But he does seem pretty young to have such a sweet ride. Family money, perhaps?

The driver's side door opens. His long suit-covered legs stretch into the floorboard as he moves into his seat. I find myself straightening up and feeling a little nervous. It isn't everyday that a guy like him invites me into a car like this. Actually, it's never happened to me. Maybe that little bump on my head is making me dream because this whole scenario seems a little surreal to me.

Cashmere Knight

I look up into his eyes. They're shining at me. His hair has snow scattered throughout the brown waves. He runs his fingers through them and smoothes away the white specks. My eyes move to his mouth. His lips move and I simply can't look anywhere else.

"I guess I should introduce myself. I'm Drew Michaels." A glove-covered hand reaches across the middle console toward me. My hand stretches out to meet his.

"Hi, Drew. I'm Katrina Williams. Kat, for short."

"Hi, Kat." He pronounces my name slowly and just above a whisper. Like he's tasting it. I'm pretty sure my body heat has melted any snow left on me. Somehow, I need to pull myself together and respond back.

"Thanks for letting me sit in your car. It's awesome, by the way." I smile up at him. His head almost grazes the car's interior roof.

"My pleasure. I really mean *that*, by the way."

Did he just wink at me? I'm sure he did.

"I'm glad you're okay. Your car may be a different story, though." He looks me over concerned. "You're all right?"

"Just a little head bump from hitting the window. Nothing big, really." I neglect to tell him there's a small knot on the side of my head and that I'm feeling a bit dizzy. The dizzy part may be his fault, after all. It's the "hot guy talking to me" syndrome. I've had it a few times over the years. Makes me a bundle of nerves among other things.

"Head injuries are nothing to scoff at. Here, show me where you hit your head." He moves closer to me. I get a whiff of his cologne. It's spicy and very, very nice. I point to the small bump and breathe in deep. He does smell so good. I sigh as he touches me, very, very gently.

"There's a good size bump." His face is scrunched together in concentration. He has my head in both of his hands. He rubs the matching spot on the other side to compare the two. "You really need to get checked out. I've had my share of head injures. Football."

"Oh, I feel all right. Maybe a little dizzy and a dull headache. Had worse skipping coffee." I chuckle.

"Well, as soon as the police get here, I think you should go to the hospital. Have someone take a look at you." He's so serious. I nod in agreement and wish his hands were still touching me.

Reluctantly, I move back into my seat away from him. It's feeling colder now that I'm closer to the glass window. A slight shiver moves through me as I rub my hands over my tights-covered legs.

"Here, let me turn on the seat warmers."

"That would be great. Thanks." He really is a sweet and perceptive guy. Best snowstorm ever.

"So you work downtown?" he inquires.

"Yeah, I work for Fifth Third Bank at the State Street Building. I mostly focus on demographic studies. Target marketing and the like. Boring stuff."

"I don't work too far from there." He seems really interested in me. I feel slightly giddy as he continues. "I'm in the M&A department at Sloan and Farthing Partners."

"Oh, an accountant?" I raise my brow. "I had you pegged as an attorney."

"I'm afraid not. Just a corporate accountant. Nothing sexy, sorry." And there's that wink of his again. He's beyond adorable and the sexiest accountant I've ever met.

"You must make a lot of money to afford the monthly payment on this car." After speaking the words, I immediately want to retract them. What a nosy thing to say but Drew seems rather amused by my verbal diarrhea.

"Would it help if I told you I got quite the deal on it?" He laughs while looking amused.

"I'm sorry. It's really none of my business."

"It's okay. I've always had a thing for expensive sports cars. When a merger I was working on closed last summer, I used every penny of my bonus for a big down payment. Probably an impulsive decision, but I've enjoyed every single mile in this seat."

"I'm enjoying this seat too." And I am enjoying it, immensely. The view of him decked out in wool and cashmere, the smell of his cologne, and the feel of fine leather are a dangerous mix to me. I'm not sure yet, but I have a feeling that I'm going to be in trouble if we stay huddled in this car too long. My mind is starting to wander and wonder.

What would his lips feel like against mine? Would his kiss be gentle or passionate? If he started something, would I even want to stop him?

Probably not.

But I've lived "no boys allowed" since The Cheater got caught, well, cheating. And I've often hoped some plague would descend on him or his most prized part. But this guy, Drew Michaels, was the complete package.

Handsome, sweet as honey, and obviously successful. I pray he's straight because guys like him are an endangered species in my experience.

A comfortable quiet falls between us and we silently listen to the traffic reports on the radio. All over Chicago, roads were closing due to the snow. When a reporter announces that Lake Shore Drive is being shut down because of a jackknifed bus, we look at each other knowing that we're in for a long wait.

"Looks like we're going to be holed-up in here for awhile," he says, sounding frustrated.

"Probably so. I hope someone can make it through and move the bus. Otherwise, we're screwing, I mean, screwed. Screwed, yeah, that's what I meant to say." I want to bury my face in my hands or in his actually.

"Kat, you're funny." He smiles at me and I melt a little more into the seat. "I'm beginning to think you'd keep a guy like me on my toes. I like that."

"I'd like that too." I feel my face heating up and probably turning a bright red. "Jeez, I could really use a drink or a whole bottle right now." My laugh is a nervous giggle.

"Hey, I bought some brandy for my parents. It's in the backseat."

"Do you think it's alright for me to have a drink? You know with my head and all."

"Probably a little bit to warm you up would be okay." Once again I'm treated to his sexy little wink. Who needs brandy to warm them up when he's doing that?

He starts leaning my way and reaching behind me. Yes, I am definitely screwed.

Warming Up

He's looking straight into my eyes, only inches away from my face, as he pulls a bag from the back of the car. Sadly, he sits back up and places it on his lap.

"I bought this for my father." He points to the bag. "It's his favorite brandy and came in a set with two matching glasses so we're covered."

I watch as he pulls the bag's contents out. The bottle contains a rich amber-colored liquid. Brandy, I assume.

"Martel XO Cognac 80 proof. It doesn't get any better. Here, hold this glass while I pour you three fingers," he instructs.

I focus on two things in his last words he spoke—80 proof and three fingers. I'm pretty sure that I need to be careful, because the brandy he's pouring into my glass smells stronger than any liquor I've ever smelled.

"Maybe we should work up to three fingers. Start slowly." I giggle, inappropriately. "I think this stuff could put some hairs on my chest and I'm not sure how I'll explain that to my waxing girl."

Holy crap. My waxing habits seem a little too personal for a "we just met an hour ago" conversation. However, he appears amused by my words and keeps pouring the amber liquid into my glass while he chuckles, most likely at my expense.

"I wouldn't let you drink something that puts hairs on your, um, chest," he says, and the dirty rascal continues to snicker. "So you're safe for now with your waxing girl."

"Funny." I scoff and bring the glass up to my nose for a quick sniff. "I have to confess that I've never tried brandy. Should I sip it?"

"Never tried brandy, huh?" His eyes twinkle with amusement. "Place the bottom of the snifter glass in the palm of your hand. Your body temperature will warm up the brandy."

"Like this?" I ask him after removing my gloves and tentatively placing the brandy glass in my palm.

"Yes. Now take slow sips and let the brandy flow down your throat. You should feel a warmth as you swallow."

I follow his instructions, sipping and slowly swallowing. I watch as he focuses on my lips and then my throat. I'm pretty sure he swallowed too, though he hadn't drunk anything yet.

After that gulp by Mr. Michaels, I decide to up the ante a bit. Getting stuck in a snowstorm with a hot guy doesn't come along every day, or any day for that matter, so it's time to seize the moment. Carpe Diem.

With my eyes focusing on his, I take another sip, and run my brandy-coated tongue over my lips and wink. It's my turn to pull out the charm. At least that's my hope.

He stares at me for a bit and then shakes his head with a smirk on his lips. I laugh as he removes his scarf, unbuttons the top of his cashmere coat and loosens his tie. I swear there's some steam rising from his collar too.

"What's the matter, Drew? Getting a little hot?" I purposely purr my questions. He shrugs his shoulders and I decide to keep pressing him. "Perhaps you need a little help with that tie."

I turn toward him and lean in closer as he nods like an obedient little boy. Perhaps, my tongue and wink combination were a little too much for him, as he appears slightly stunned.

My fingers work quickly to release the knot in his red, silk tie. Slowly, I pull on one end while I gaze up at him coyly through my lashes. Inch by inch, the tie gradually falls away from beneath his collar. He lets out a soft moan as I collect the fallen end from his lap. Gathering the tie in my hand, I decide the rearview mirror would be its best resting place.

"Let's leave your tie on the rearview mirror. Who knows, we might need it later." I pause and realize I might have been to forward. "Just kidding."

"You're really something else, Kat." His sexy smile is mixed with a sweet shyness.

"So I've been told." My sarcasm isn't hidden.

"What did you think of the brandy? Too strong?"

"It's different. Maybe an acquired taste?" I swirl the amber liquor in my glass after taking another sip.

I'm beginning to feel warm now too, so I sit up in my seat, purposely unbuttoning my coat and wiggle my arms free one at a time. It now hangs empty at my sides.

"Getting a little hot, too?" he questions, slyly.

"Yes, between the brandy and you, I am." I arch my brow at him and look around for the other brandy sniffer that he took out of the gift bag. "But where's your glass? I think you need a drink too, Mister."

"Is that so?" I watch him reach for something on the floor in front of him. Sitting back up, he now has the other brandy glass resting in his hand.

"You've three fingered me; now it's your turn." We both look at each other, jointly shocked by my words.

Hung By Her Tongue

"God, I can't believe I just said that out loud." My face is heating up and I want to bury it in my hands. "We hardly know each other and I'm talking about fingering, my waxing girl, and using your tie for God knows what."

"You have nothing to worry about. I can't remember the last time I've had this much fun with someone. You're quite entertaining."

"Really?" I ask, totally surprised. "My mother thinks I need to learn how to, and I quote, 'control my tongue.' But every time I meet someone I'm attracted to, I start saying things that are totally inappropriate."

"And this lack of filter issue only happens when you're attracted to someone?" He quizzes me, while cocking a brow my way. He's one sexy gentleman. Lucky old me.

Crap, he caught the "attracted" remark I made. I'd better explain a few things to him.

"Yeah, I tend to speak like a crazy person when I'm around a hot guy. I have a chronic condition of hormone-induced Tourette's."

Looking into his eyes, I continue. "You are my worst case yet."

"Why's that?" he asks with a devilish smirk, seeming to enjoy my discomfort.

"Jeez, I think that's fairly obvious," I declare. "You've looked into the mirror, right?"

"Yes, daily, when I brush my teeth, comb my hair, boring, necessary stuff like that," he dutifully outlines his morning mirror routine. *Whatever...*

"Well, then I'll just have to quote my favorite line from the movie, *Zoolander.*" I stop and pause before reciting the punch line in my best Derek Zoolander accent. "You, Mr. Michaels, are really, really ridiculously good-looking."

He starts to laugh in this unbelievably cute way. I can't resist it and join in too.

"You've got to be kidding me," he chokes out between laughs. I find it difficult to believe that I am really *this* funny. Maybe he hangs around dull, stiff-lipped people. Who knows? But either way he needs to know that I'm as serious as the boring people he likely socializes with.

"No, you really, really are. You're one of the most handsome men I've ever seen. I'd call you beautiful, but you'd probably not like that tag. Most men think it's weird or something."

His eyes stay locked on mine as the glow of the dashboard lights reflect off his face. His gaze becomes serious. All previous humor is missing.

"Thanks for the compliment, Kat." His voice is soft, gentle. I want to reach over and take his hand, but I can't break this moment just yet.

"It's hard to believe you have no idea what a catch you are." My words make him bashfully bow his head. Could he be any more adorable?

"Okay, here's the list I've compiled in the hour we've been together." He looks wary, but I continue on. "You're sweet, handsome and successful. I didn't think guys like you really existed."

There's a moment of quietness once I quit speaking and the atmosphere between us changes. It makes me want to reach out and touch him perhaps caress his hand with my fingers. I've never, ever desired someone like this. This "thing" I'm feeling toward him is pretty strong.

Throwing care to the wind, I decide to reach across the console and boldly take his hand in mine. His next breath comes out in an audible gasp as our fingers touch. His eyes look down and watch as our hands entwine together.

Holding his hand up slightly I ask, "Is this okay?" He nods and I smile, glad to know I'm not being too forward.

As we continue to hold hands, I feel something intense in our connection and touch. I can't help but hope he's feeling something for me too. Next thing I know he brings my hand up to his perfect lips.

As he gently kisses my knuckles, it's clear we're both feeling something now. I close my eyes and hum quietly while his lips caress my skin. It feels heavenly. My entire body moves toward him and our shoulders touch, coming together over the center console.

After his gentle kisses cease, he continues to rub my hand with his fingers and whispers, "You feel so soft, so warm."

"Thanks. This is the best wreck ever." I sigh contentedly and he laughs.

"You've been in quite a few wrecks then?"

"No, just this one. Best and only." I smile up at him. Our hands are still clasped together.

"I'm beginning to wonder if we'll be rescued before midnight," he speculates.

"God, I hope so. It's not New Year's Eve unless I see a ball drop." I turn red and he laughs. I'm beginning to see a pattern here. I speak in my unique form of Tourette's and he seems to think it's as funny as hell.

"You have a knack for saying things that seem innocent but could also be dirty. Quite the talent." He smirks and I die a little or maybe a lot.

"Yes, my mother has trophies all over the house from my exploits." I turn away from him rather embarrassed but my movement makes him hold my hand a little tighter. He's not letting me go and I'm happy about that.

"Sorry, Kat. I'm kidding. Truth is I find your 'condition' pretty damn cute." He smiles and it makes me smile back. "I have an idea. Let's play a little game. Get to know one another. Whatta ya say?"

"Maybe a little strip poker followed by a quick game of Twister?" I let out a quick snort because that was bad even for me.

"That's rather progressive for a first date, don't you think?" And he's back to rubbing my fingers and I feel myself melting back into his lovely leather seats.

"A first date?" I don't think he's joking.

"We could call it that. Stranded in a snowstorm. It's a pretty unique way for two perfect strangers to meet."

"Yes, it is," I have to agree with him. "I've had a second, third or maybe even a twentieth date that wasn't this memorable."

Unhappily Rescued

Lights come shining through the back window of the car. They're flashing red, illuminating our little space. I know what they mean. Our time together is up, finished, and I feel sad.

I need to get my disabled car towed and Drew will probably drive off after wishing me well. Maybe he was headed to a friend's party where a girl is happily waiting for him. By tomorrow, he'll forget me and I'll be trying to forget him. But I know that's impossible. It may take some time to get this guy out of my head… and heart.

"Looks like we have company," he says curtly. He doesn't seem thrilled to see the lights either. A little flicker of hope lights up within me. Maybe just maybe…

A knock on the window startles me, and I watch as Drew lowers the window to see who's there. Snow whirls into the car as the outside air is exposed. It's blowing hard, even harder than it was when my car hit the side of the bus.

"Good evening," a gruff male voice says to us. His face is partially covered by a thick scarf. "I'm Officer Kowalski. You'll need to evacuate your car and follow me to the rescue vehicle."

"You want me to just leave my car here?" Drew questions. He sounds freaked at the thought of leaving his beloved car here.

"There's no other choice. The bus can't be moved tonight and the snow trucks won't be clearing this area until tomorrow. So this car isn't going anywhere tonight."

"Okay. Give us a second to get our coats and gloves on," Drew replies back, frustrated, I can tell, and rolls up his window.

"Wow, this is crazy," I say, hoping to lighten his mood. I pull on my coat and grab my purse. It's time to brave the snow. "I'm ready to go."

"Why don't you climb over the middle and exit out my side? I want to help you in case you're dizzy when you stand up. Remember, the bump on your head?" I'm touched that he cares.

"Okay, let's do this." I watch as he opens the door.

Heating Up

Drew grabs my hand and helps me maneuver over to the driver's side. I dread facing the snow and wind. My body starts to brace for the shock. Once I'm by the door, his hands take mine and help pull me out the door.

"Oh my God," I yell, completely startled by the cold wind's fierceness. It whips through my wool coat and hits my legs. The black tights and red boots I'm wearing might as well be made of thin gauze. Nothing will stop me from freezing now.

"Come on, Kat." I hear Drew somewhere in the whirlwind. My eyes are watering as I try to open them. I've lived in Chicago all my life. The lake-effect winds are nothing new to me, but this blizzard is beyond anything I've ever experienced.

Drew pulls me tightly to his side. I cling to him as if he's my last breath. It feels like he's dragging me. My feet are having trouble moving in the deep snow. The next thing I know he's picking me up and cradling me in his arms. Like a small child, I curl into him and wrap my arms around his neck. Holding on tight, my face burrows into his chest and I'm comforted by his spicy cologne. He smells all man. Masculine and strong.

"We're almost there," he shouts. His body vibrates against my cheek.

After a few more steps, Drew stops and lowers me. He places a hand on my head and tucks me even further into him. The wind has stopped beating against me and something meets my backside. I think it's a seat.

Thank God, we're in the rescue vehicle. I open my eyes and scoot over on the bench seat so Drew can join me. A blast of warm air coming from the heater's vent draws me forward. I can't get enough of its warmth as even my covered fingers are tingling.

"We made it." My words are slurring together due to my nearly frostbitten lips.

Even before I'm finished speaking, he has me in his arms. Again, I melt into him. He could be rather habit forming and I could get used to being his addict. I giggle at my thoughts.

"What's so funny?" he asks while looking down into my eyes.

"Oh, I think I'm becoming addicted to you."

"What are you talking about, Kat?" There's a look of amusement on his face. He's just so darn handsome.

"I have these crazy symptoms. Butterflies in my stomach, heart beating a little too fast, and the worst one of all… I keep looking at your lips."

"Funny thing… I have the same symptoms too." He gazes down at my lips, and moves his mouth closer to mine. We touch. It's a short, sweet kiss as the officer who helped us is now trying to get our attention.

"Pardon me, lovebirds. But you all need to buckle up before I take off," he scolds us from the front seat.

I find myself smiling and feeling giddy. Drew likes me. I can see it. Feel it.

"Officer, my name is Drew Michaels. My friend here is Kat Williams."

"Your friend, you say?" the officer questions.

"Well, we weren't together before the storm," I state and glance over at Drew.

"Actually, she was driving the car in front of me. She hit the bus and I had her join me in my car." He's staring back at me now. It's really unbelievable, this pull I think we're both feeling for each other.

"My car's a little banged up," I explain.

"Don't forget that bump on your head." Drew's face turns toward the officer. "I think she should have a doctor look at it."

"Great." I laugh. "We just met and he's already telling me I need to have my head examined."

"You kids," the officer shakes his head and mutters. "As a precaution, I'm taking you to the hospital, Miss."

I sit back in my seat, dejected. Off to the hospital we go. Not a very fun way to spend a New Year's Eve. Maybe Drew will ask for my phone number when we get to the emergency room. If he doesn't, I'll ask for his because there's no way I'm letting this one get away. This chance meeting needs to be explored, along with other things…

True Confessions

My purse lays across my legs and I feel some vibrations on my knee. It dawns on me that it's my phone. It's still by the time I dig it of my purse's side pocket. I don't really even need to view the screen to know who was just calling me. After a quick glance, my screen shows over ten missed calls. Pretty sure I'm in deep trouble with my mother. Better give her a quick call.

"My mother." I hold up my phone and show Drew the list of calls and texts labeled "Mama Bear." I cringe at her nickname, hoping he won't ask for details.

"That's a lot of missed calls. Maybe Mama Bear thinks you're heading out to a party in the snow."

Oh no! I have to confess what my true plans were for the night. New Year's Eve with my parents. I should lie, make up some story, but I can't. Instead, I decide to tell him the truth then watch whatever cool factor I might've possessed disappear.

"Actually, I was heading up to their house on the North Shore for the evening." I prepare for the pitiful look and distance he'll want to put between us now.

"No kidding?" he asks.

"Yes, me, my parents and Times Square on the television. All kinds of excitement." I just can't bear looking up into his eyes. Instead, I scan the scene out the vehicle's window, hoping we're getting close to the hospital.

"We're quite the pair." His fingers gently touch the side of my cheek. With a little pressure he turns my head toward him. "I was going to do the same thing tonight. Though there were about forty other people joining my parents and me."

"Really? I haven't hung out with my parents on New Year's since I was in middle school. I just didn't want to go out this year." I don't say any more because the only thing left to discuss is why, and my ex-fiancé isn't about to make any appearances tonight.

"My parents go all out and entertain their entire circle of friends each year," Drew says. "When I was younger I'd try to sneak a drink or two left unattended. Then in high school, my mom decided that she'd rather have me at home drinking than out with my friends. Been a permanent fixture at their party for years."

"I feel better now. I thought you'd think I was a complete loser." I watch his facial expressions become serious.

"Never." The way he stresses this word convinces me that he's telling the truth. My whole body relaxes. My mind is at ease now.

"Alright," interrupts the officer. "We're at Northwestern folks."

We peek out the windshield for the emergency room signs. The vehicle pulls up to a sliding glass door entrance. I face Drew and try to suppress the knot in my stomach. I'm not ready to say goodbye. Not now and maybe never. It's odd. I've known him for a mere hour or two and it seems like so much longer. We've really hit it off in our time together.

"Well, Drew, I can't thank you enough for all you've done for me tonight." My face has to be showing my sadness in leaving him. I scold myself for feeling like this. What a stupid girl to have let him get under my skin so quickly.

"Are you trying to say goodbye?" His brow scrunches together in confusion and then he smiles blindingly at me. "You're not getting rid of me that easily. If it's okay, I'd like to come in with you. Moral support and all."

"Really?" I ask.

"Yes, really." His finger traces over my face. "Why the sad face, Kat?"

"I... I didn't want to leave you."

"Good, because I'm not going anywhere," he reassures me and faces the officer. "Thanks for helping us tonight. Who do we need to call about our cars?"

"Here's the card for the towing company we use in cases like this. You should call them around ten tomorrow morning. My guess is that nothing will be moving off of Lake Shore until sunrise."

Drew pockets the card. I don't even bother asking the officer for one because Drew said, "who do *we* call." I really like the way that sounded.

"Thanks again and Happy New Year." Drew opens the door while reaching for my hand. We're leaving the vehicle and heading toward the emergency room's entrance.

Watch Over Me

Once inside, I'm surprised to see an empty waiting room. Usually, this place is packed. I've been here for minor issues and waited for hours. Hopefully, tonight will be a quick in-and-out visit.

Drew takes charge and guides me to the registration desk. After all the paperwork and insurance information is exchanged, we take a seat and wait for my name to be called. I'm very thankful to have him by my side, but I'm also not sure if he wants or should be with me when I see the doctor. I bite my lip, worrying about where to go from here.

"What's the matter?" He's watching my teeth push into my lip. For being practically strangers, he has an uncanny way of reading me.

"God, this is so awkward, but when they call my name, I'll just head back on my own?"

"How about I go back with you and stand outside the door. So if you need me for anything, I'll be there."

"Where did you come from Drew? You're a little too perfect," I tease.

He takes my hand in his and I haven't forgot how good he feels, so comforting. I sigh and lean in closer to him.

"Perfect would be a better description of you." He's so good at turning the tables back on me.

"See. That's what I'm talking about." If I wasn't holding his warm hand right now, I might believe I was dreaming up this guy.

"Katrina Williams." I hear my name being called out by someone. We rise out of our chairs and head toward the nurse across the room. She holds a chart in her hand and has a door propped open with her leg.

"I'm Katrina," I tell her when we're a couple feet away. "That was quick. I just signed in."

"It's the snowstorm. No one is out in this weather." She appraises us quickly, likely wondering what the heck we're doing here. Her eyes then read over what appears to be my chart.

"It says here possible head trauma?" She speaks to us as we walk to a nearby curtained area. It's a little room with a small hospital bed and some medical equipment.

"I hit my head when I swerved into a jackknifed bus on Lake Shore. Nothing big, really. I don't even have a headache anymore."

"Lake Shore," the nurse repeats slowly. "Were you two stranded out there?"

"Yes, after the bus blocked the lane, the snow started to pile up and no one could move their cars."

"It's all over the radio. They're saying about one hundred cars are stuck out there." It's impossible to miss the concern in her voice. She motions for me to sit on the bed. I obey and notice that Drew is still standing near me. So much for waiting outside my room and I'm glad.

The nurse takes my vital signs and records them on a page inside my chart. She presses a few keys on a small laptop sitting on a tall table toward the end of the bed.

"Rest here." She lightly touches my shoulder. "The doctor should be in in a few minutes."

As soon as she moves beyond the curtain, I remember something super important. My mother.

"Crap. I still haven't called my mother. She's gonna kill me for sure now." I cringe as I imagine her reaction to what I'll tell her. I'm definitely in a heap of trouble.

Somehow, Drew has been carrying my purse for me since I registered with the front desk. Truthfully, I can't even remember handing it to him. It's like we're a couple already. I hold out my hand and eye my purse, which he hands over to me.

I pull the phone out and call my mother. Predictably, she answers before the first ring even finishes.

"Kat! Please tell me you're okay?" I've never heard her so worried before.

"Well, yes and no." I prepare for her freak out.

"What do you mean?" she sounds panicked.

"There was this bus on Lake Shore Drive. It fishtailed and I sideswiped it, but the hit didn't even set off my airbags."

I hear her yelling to my father. He must be in the adjoining room. The only words I can make out are "Kat," "Wreck," and "Lake Shore."

"That accident is all over the news. Where are you now? Are you still in your car?"

Now I'm getting ready to tell her the good part. "I was rescued by a tall, sweet and handsome stranger. His name is Drew. He's with me here at Northwestern's ER. There was a little bump on the side of head."

"How bad is your head?" she asks me. I can hear her repeating everything I say to my father.

"Mom, why don't you just have Dad pick up the other house phone?" I hear a little click.

"Kat, are you okay?" My dear father is worried too.

"Dad, I'm fine," I reply.

"She has some man there helping her." The way Mom says this leads me to believe that she's not buying the knight in shining armor story.

"He was in the car behind me, Mother. After seeing me hit the bus, he had me sit in his car."

"Oh, I see." She's softening up. I hear footsteps approaching and see a man in a white coat moving the curtain.

"Mom, the doctor is here. I need to go. I'll call later. Love you."

"Love you too, Kat." Both my parent's speak in unison. I glance over at Drew and he's smiling and laughing. Great, just great.

The doctor walks toward me with my chart in his hands. "Good evening, Ms. Williams. I'm Doctor Leonard."

"Hi," I reply and see Drew moving toward the doctor.

"I'm Drew Michaels." I watch the two men shake hands. It looks like Drew is here to stay. Yay, me.

"Evening," responds the doctor. "So you have a head injury from a car accident this evening. Show me where you hit your head."

I point to the side of my head and pull my hair away from my bump. The doctor gently rubs his fingers over my skin and starts running through some neurological tests. He says this will determine whether I need to go get X-rays or an MRI.

Dr. Leonard seems pleased with my answers and results and decides that I don't need any further treatment or tests. To say I'm relieved is an understatement. Next, he's facing Drew and I'm getting a little nervous now.

"I don't believe she has a concussion, but you need to wake her up every two to three hours tonight. Ask her a few questions each time you do. Like, what her name is, who the President is? Just a precaution."

Drew's grinning from ear to ear and I'm doing the same. This doctor has no idea who we are but he obviously believes that we're a couple. I can't wait to see how Drew handles this one. I decide to leave my mouth shut and enjoy the show.

"Well, I'm pretty sure I can handle that." Drew's answer makes me laugh.

"Good. Here's a sheet detailing what I'd like to have you do tonight. I know it's New Year's Eve, but no hanky panky tonight." I burst out laughing now. Hanky panky? Did he really just say that?

Now the doctor's looking in my direction and I stifle my giggles, though it's hard. "That's disappointing. I'm rather fond of hanky panky."

The doctor appears shocked and Drew silently laughs. Good to see that my verbal gaffes still amuse him.

"Well, happy New Year, you two." The doctor continues, once again looking toward Drew, "Keep an eye on this one."

I swear I see the doctor winking and Drew responds to him with a knowing look. Some kind of unspoken guy communication has just taken place and I think it's also pretty darn cool because I'm the center of it.

"Will do. Thanks, Doc." Drew shakes the doctor's hand one more time and then the doctor leaves us.

"Well that last little bit about waking me up every two hours was... interesting," I say. Drew has this sexy, amused look in his eyes. Hmmmm.

"Yes, *very* interesting." He pauses. "So, your place or mine?"

the panty dropper

by Liv Morris

Prologue

It's close to two in the afternoon on Saturday, February 14th. My heart pounds away due to a crazy mix of joy and nervousness. I check my lipstick and hair one more time in the mirror before my father comes to escort me. Without him, it's unlikely I'd be sitting in this dressing room surrounded by yards of ivory satin.

    I'm here because a year ago today my life changed 180 degrees on a holiday I had cursed for years. Who could have guessed that it would become my most treasured day of year? One can never underestimate fate.

Fate

Today is Friday, February 14th. Yes, it's that day...

As a single, unattached woman, I've loathed this holiday for years. The fact that two serious boyfriends had conveniently broken up with me the week before Valentine's Day is likely the main reason. And adding to the rejection, I had to return my already-purchased gifts for them, though I did keep all the chocolates for myself. A friend told me under the circumstances, the chocolates were calorie free. A slight consolation.

When the calendar turns to February, I dread the upcoming parade of roses and candy. And stupid red hearts start appearing everywhere, seeming to mock me and my singleness.

I'm okay with being single for the most part. It isn't my first choice, and truthfully, I would love to settle down with a sweet and decent guy. But so far, Mr. Right hasn't shown up at my door. His appearance remains elusive in my life, but I have faith that he's out there, somewhere... I'm only twenty-six years old and refuse to feel desperate or panicked yet. Instead, I'll let my mother do all the worrying and hand wringing concerning my love life. God knows she's become a pro at it.

My career as a flight attendant appears to be a stumbling block for many guys. In fairness, I'm away from home more than I am actually here in San Francisco. One guy I dated said he was tired of spending lonely nights by himself on his couch eating takeout for dinner. He even asked if I might consider quitting my job.

I couldn't quit my job in this economy or any for that matter. I love what I do. When I told him that he was asking too much from me, I watched him get up and walk out the door. Deep down inside I know that I'm better off without him, but it still stings, especially today, the day anointed for lovers.

I might adjust who I am for someone, but I'm not willing to completely change myself just to please them. Looking into the mirror and seeing my frizzy hair is hard enough. I need to also see a reflection of someone that doesn't make my stomach turn.

As Shakespeare said, "To thine own self be true." Words to live by I suppose.

My flight segments wore me out today. They bordered on tortuous. Friday happens to be the worst day of the week for Valentine's Day to fall on. It adds up to planes full of couples canoodling in their seats as they jet off for a romantic weekend somewhere to enjoy strawberries and champagne. I tried not to scowl at them but my aggravation was likely obvious. My behavior was nothing to be proud of. Envy never really is.

During my last segment back to San Francisco, I'd had enough of all the couples for the day and was teetering on doing something that might make the nightly news. Nothing too violent, of course, but the thought of pouring a few drinks over a pair of steamy lovers to cool them off did cross my mind. Especially when one of them looked like an ex of mine.

It took some restraint, but I'm proud to report that I left the airport sans handcuffs. I decided that harboring ill will against something I really want in my own life creates bad Karma. And I'm not stupid enough to mess with her.

So now back at my apartment, I'm safe from a world, which has gone painfully red for the day. My best friend, Monica, lives a couple of floors below me. We spoke yesterday and decided to spend tonight watching a movie, painting our nails, and crying into our wine glasses about how we need a man. Sounds kind of pathetic, really, but we need something cathartic to purge this day from our system. Wine and bitching mixed with a few tears usually does the trick.

After changing into an oversized t-shirt and black yoga pants, I go deep-sea diving in my large tote and find my phone swimming somewhere on the bottom. Monica is expecting my call, so I locate her number and press on the phone's screen.

"Hey, Em. You're back home?" Monica answers quickly. She's likely ready to forget this day too.

"Yep. Got back about thirty minutes ago. Both of my flights were filled with starry-eyed lovers. I could only take so much after a while."

"My day wasn't much better. By noon, I wished I'd called in sick. Everyone around me in the office received flowers. Even that witch, Melody. When the delivery man sat pink roses on her desk, I almost screamed, 'What about me?'"

"God, that sucks, Monica. Maybe she sent them to herself," I say with a laugh. "We need to wash away this day with a bottle or three of wine."

"Sounds good. Maybe we can watch a comedy tonight. I need something funny or I'm gonna need to hide all my knives." Now we were both laughing.

"How about that Kate Hudson movie? The ten days to do something one." I couldn't remember the exact title, but I enjoyed watching Matthew McConaughey squirm in it.

"Perfect. I'll bring some..."

As Monica was speaking a loud knock came from my apartment's front door. It wasn't angry pounding but it was loud.

"What was that noise?" Monica asked after the knocking stopped.

"Someone's at my door. I didn't buzz anyone up so it's probably my neighbor," I say approaching the door.

I peek through the peephole and nearly faint dead away when I see who's standing on the other side.

"Oh my God. You're not going to believe who's at the door. It's The Panty Dropper."

"The what?" Monica questions.

"You know. The hot guy in our building I call The Panty Dropper. The one I'd willingly be a sex slave for."

"No way. What the hell is he doing there? Wait don't answer that. For God's sake, Em, answer the damn door."

I look out the peephole one more time and am startled as he knocks forcefully once again. He's probably ready to give up on anyone being home.

"Hold on," I whisper to her.

I place the phone down on the entryway table and laugh when I see myself in the mirror above it. Not exactly the look I would go for if I had a choice, but he's at the door and I can't let him get away.

Quickly, I smooth down my frizzy hair and bite my lips for a little color. And with a shaky hand I turn the knob and pull. But I'm simply not prepared for the sight and close proximity of the most beautiful man in the whole universe, or my building at least.

So instead of saying hello, I find my mouth gaping open, guppy-fish style, as I stare up into his ocean blue eyes. I've never had an opportunity to see him this close up before and it's completely overwhelming and paralyzing.

"Hi, are you Emily?" He finally speaks and hearing my name roll across his tongue warms me up in a place somewhere between my head and toes.

"Yes," I purr back at him trying to channel a sex kitten of some kind. It probably isn't working considering my hobo attire.

He smiles at me sweetly and I just know he witnesses silly girl behavior like mine daily.

"I'm Ethan Murphy. I live upstairs in apartment 814 and these roses were left at my door. I'm pretty sure there was a mistake."

Roses? I shake my head a bit to bring myself out of a fixed stare. As I do, I notice a pretty bouquet of red roses in his hand. I look back up at him confused.

"I'm not sure I understand what you're saying." And before I know it, I'm throwing the door wide open and asking him to enter my apartment. "Come in."

Right now, I don't care if he's like the crazy from *American Psycho*. Watching his suit-covered body walk across my threshold makes any thought of danger slip from my mind. His suit is navy blue, add a tie to match his eyes, and he looks like he just walked off a photo shoot for Brooks Brothers.

He moves closer to me and steps to my side, shoulder to shoulder, and holds up a small envelope, the kind given with flowers. Before I can really focus on what's in his hand, I take a calming breath and get a whiff of his cologne. It's woodsy and crisp. Nice, dreamy nice.

"I think the doorman misread the envelope," he says. "It clearly says 614 not 814 on the front."

My eyes glance over the envelope and it's clear that the flowers were supposed to be delivered to my apartment, 614, not his.

Staring at the lone apartment numbers on the front, I realize my name wasn't written on it... just the numbers, which is odd, as he knew my first name. Since we've never met, he must have opened the envelope to look at the card inside.

"Do you mind?" I ask while reaching for the envelope. Once in my hands, I turn it around to the back, and sure enough it's been opened. I pull the card out, dreading to see what I already suspect is on the little piece of cardstock. The words jump out at me, making my face turn a deep red, not quite the color of the roses, but pretty damn close. They're from my father. He's given me flowers on Valentine's Day since I was a young girl.

I cringe even more as I read over the card.
Dear Emily,
Will you be my Valentine?
I love and miss you,
Dad.
Holy crap!

After a few more moments of silence, I look up to see Ethan's eyes focused on my face. Relief rushes over me as I see him smiling all sweet and sexy.

"My dad," I say shyly while raising the card. "He does this for me every year."

"That's really cool," he responds sincerely. "Sounds like a great guy."

"He is, but it's rather embarrassing."

We're now leaning against my entry wall facing one another. He's looking at me and I'm looking at him, both of us smiling. It feels nice, different. I've almost forgotten that I'm decked out like a slob. In this moment, it doesn't seem to matter.

"I guess it gives your boyfriend a little competition." His words end almost like a question. "He has to top dear old Dad."

"Boyfriend? I wish." Wait, did I just say that? My eyes immediately fall to the ground, but his slight laugh brings them up again.

"So, no boyfriend?" This time he asks a definite question like he cares whether I'm dating someone. Oh good God. Would someone please pinch me?

"Nope." I say with a stupid pop to the "p." But that makes him smile even more and I see this little dimple on his left cheek. I stare at it and bite my lip to hold myself back because he's beyond gorgeous.

"Well, here are your flowers." He moves the roses toward me. I want to touch his fingers when we make the exchange. Just a little touch. Who knows if I'll ever have this chance with him again?

I place my forefinger over his pinky and glide my finger against his as I grasp the flowers. His composure stiffens, but more out of surprise than retreat. Hmmm... I think we have cause and effect here.

"Thanks," I reply after the flowers are safely in my hand. "I appreciate you bringing them down to me."

"No problem," he says as he moves away from the wall and toward the door. "Guess I better head back upstairs."

I want to scream, DON'T GO! Instead, I start to follow his movements as he approaches the door.

"Thanks again." I throw out a couple of words to keep the conversation going, hoping that maybe he'll stay a few seconds longer. His fingers cover the doorknob and he starts to turn it.

Damn, he's leaving. I feel my face turning into a full blown pout. Attractive, no doubt.

He pulls the door open in a super slow manner. So slow it has to be deliberate. My heart nearly skips a beat as it hopes...

Then his movement stops and he turns around to face me. There's a slight smirk on his lips.

Oh please, oh please, I silently plead. Ask me anything.

"I'm not sure what you have planned tonight." He pauses as his eyes scan over my clothes likely assessing what I'm wearing or not wearing. Definitely not "going out" threads.

"Well," he continues. "I bought some food to cook on the way home. Nothing fancy. Just pasta. Would you like to come up for dinner in about an hour? I need to get the place presentable."

And there it is. Plain as the nose on my face. I'm sporting an earsplitting grin and have to lock my knees to keep from jumping up and down. There's no way I can answer him and look cool at this point, so I just go with it. Here comes the real me...

"Oh yes, I'd love to join you." *Love* and *you* in the same sentence don't seem to scare him. In fact he appears relieved. Guess even Panty Droppers have insecurities. Good to know.

"Great." His enthusiasm can't be missed and we now have matching grins. Just too damn cute. "I'll head up and start on the presentable part."

"I'll do the same." At his questioning look, I explain, "The presentable part." I laugh as I tug at my five sizes too big t-shirt.

"You're fine and look comfortable." He has to be kidding, but I don't think he is.

"I'll upgrade my comfortable though," I say.

"Okay. See you in a few." And he winks at me. Winks and smirks, then closes the door. I fall against it and slide down to the floor. I think my move is called a supported swoon.

But I can't rest on my laurels for long, I have one hour to turn from sweatpants girl into a snappy, casual hottie.

I get up, still a bit shaky, possibly from adrenaline and hormones. Both seem to be on overdrive. Reaching for my phone on the entry table, I pick it up and touch the black screen. I need to see the time. I have to pace myself. But instead of the time, I see my call with Monica never ended... Holy shit, she heard the entire exchange I had with The Panty Dropper.

"Oh my God, Monica. I'm so..." She doesn't let me continue.

"Don't say another word, Em. I'll be right up." And the call goes dead.

Ready, Set, Go

While I'm waiting for Monica to arrive, my vocabulary has consisted of three words. Oh. My. God. Spoken repeatedly as I walk around in circles by the door and occasionally glance at myself in the mirror. Which doesn't help at all.

Finally, she knocks and I swing the door open to see her arms loaded down with clothes, shoes and a couple of makeup bags. She walks right past me, not even stopping to say hello.

"Em, follow me," she says over her shoulder. I'm stunned but shut the door and follow.

"Yes, mistress." I giggle.

"Oh, you have no idea. You will do everything I say, *capiche*?" she laughs but I can sense she's not to be trifled with right now.

"Can you believe it?" I ask as we enter my bedroom. "He invited me up to his apartment."

"He invited you," she stops and assesses my attire, "looking like that?"

"Do I look that bad?"

"Yes, but all the more reason to think he really likes you for you." She speaks while placing everything in her arms on my bed. The spread takes over the entire thing.

After she's finished and her arms are empty, she turns to me and points to my master bath. "Into the shower. Exfoliate and shave... everything."

"Everything?" I think I know what she means, but, really, I've never had sex on a first date. No matter how much I've had to drink. Surely, she doesn't think I might drop my panties for him in spite of his nickname.

"You heard me. Use the razor everywhere!" She's looking at me and seems annoyed.

I back into the bathroom, afraid to say anymore. She returns to the bed and searches through the items on it.

"I don't think this will work." I watch her toss a couple pairs of jeans onto the floor as she talks to herself. "These skinny jeans are perfect, though."

She moves to the other side of the bed and sees me standing by the bath's door. Her disapproving glare makes me scurry toward the shower.

"I'm going," I yell, grabbing a towel and new razor.

~~~~~

Freshly showered and shaved, I'm standing beside Monica in my bathrobe. She displays the outfit that I'm wearing tonight. There isn't room to question her. The thought of even doing so scares me, to be honest.

She's chosen a pair of dark jeans with a little subtle acid wash over the front. I pull them off the bed and see that they've never been worn.

"Monica, I can't wear these. The tag is still attached." I hand them back to her and watch her gently pull the tag from the jeans.

"There. Put them on. I want to see how they fit."

I obey and drop the robe to the floor and jump as she lets out a gasp.

"What the hell are you wearing? A tank and black cotton briefs?" She holds up some sexy panties. "I found these in the back of your drawer."

"I can't and won't wear them, because he's not going to see them. I've never slept with anyone on my first date." I look her dead in the eyes. "Never."

"Is this a hard and fast rule of yours?" she asks. "Because I overheard your exchange together. Remember? I could feel the chemistry between you through the line."

I giggle and tilt my head. "I know. There definitely was something..."

"Well, your old yoga pants didn't scare him away so keep what you have on, but don't forget to bring a condom just in case."

She thrusts the jeans at me again and I take them for good this time. I squeeze myself into the legs and with a few little jumps the jeans make it over my hips. I hope they give a little after wearing them. They seem too tight, but after sucking in my stomach I get them buttoned.

"Tell me they stretch," I say. "Because I can only hold my stomach in so long."

"Quit whining. You look great." She takes me by the arm. "Now, hair and makeup before the shirt goes on."

I'm being lead into the bathroom. "Sit on the toilet, lid down." I start to laugh and she joins me.

"Thanks so much for helping me tonight. I feel bad that I'm ditching you." I place my hand on her forearm. "You're a great friend. You know that, right?"

"Same to you, Em. We've been through a lot together these last couple of years." She stops for a second and smiles. "Here's how you can make up for tonight. Have something naughty to tell me tomorrow."

She just doesn't give up. We laugh and she gets busy with the blow dryer, tugging my head in every which direction. It'll be a miracle if there's any hair left when she's finished.

After finishing my makeover, she finally allows me to look into the mirror. It's amazing. She's made my frizzy hair look shiny and bouncy. Those two words have never been used to describe my hair.

"Wow. How did you get my hair to do this?"

"It's the serum I used. My stylist swears by it and I have to agree. I've never seen your hair so tamed." She smiles big, proud of her creation: me.

"I'm going to buy a vat of this stuff," I remark while touching my hair. "And my eyes look smoky but not porno. Perfect."

"You look great if I do say so myself. But we aren't through. Next is the top and shoes."

"Okay, Personal Shopper. Finish me."

We walk back to the bed and I see the shirt set out for the evening. It's a black chiffon blouse with sleeves gathered at the wrist. The hem is longer in the back giving it a flowing look. It's feminine and not over-the-top sexy or dressy. "I love this top," I murmur as she helps me get the blouse on so my hair stays in place.

"Now the shoes." She has a pair of red pumps dangling from her fingers. I know these shoes, but I've not seen them in ages. They're her "one-night stand" pumps.

"Not happening. I know what you're up to." I back a few feet away. "I can hear my panties dropping on the ground just by looking at those evil things."

"What are you talking about? It's Valentine's Day. Red works." She's approaching me with the shoes and I curse the fact that we wear the same size.

"True, but those shoes are dangerous. Every time you've worn them out they end up on the floor of an unknown man's apartment."

I hear her muttering but can't make out what she's saying. She kneels to the ground and has me lift my leg. I acquiesce and put the shoes on. Damn if they don't fit great.

"Alright, I'll wear them, but I'm breaking their bad reputation tonight," I state.

"Whatever." She hands me a tube of lipstick. "Wear this one tonight. It's the perfect red for you."

"I don't wear red."

"How many Panty Droppers have asked you out in your life?" I look at her defeated. "Exactly, so pucker up and go with it."

"I don't think I've ever seen you this bossy before." I'm standing in front of the mirror over my dresser applying the lipstick. She's right, the color looks great.

"I'm your biggest cheerleader tonight and don't mean to come across bossy. But an opportunity like this doesn't come knocking at your door every day." We both catch the irony and burst out laughing.

"So true." I stand up and face her, placing my hands out to the side. "What do you think?"

"You look great," she approves. "There's something about you tonight. I bet he can't keep his hands off you."

"It's strange. I feel different too." I'm nervous in an excited way, not the usual *I wonder if he likes me* mood. It's pretty clear he does. The connection was there earlier.

"One more thing." Monica reaches into her bag of tricks and pulls out a bottle of whiskey. "Show me to your shot glasses."

"I don't think this is a good idea," I warn.

"Just one. It'll loosen you up. Besides you never get sick when you mix alcohol. You old rock gut."

I place two shot glasses on the counter and watch the amber liquid pour from the bottle. We pick them up and tap them against each other.

"Here's to Valentine's Day. Who knows? It may become the best day of your life."

"Yeah, who knows? Cheers." I place the glass to my lips and slam the whiskey back. "Wow. I forgot how wicked that stuff is. I'll need a breath mint for sure now."

Monica digs around in her purse and hands me some mints. "We can't have you reeking of booze."

"Oh, I almost forgot. I need to spray on some perfume." Before the whole word perfume is out of my mouth, I see Monica holding her cherished Chanel No. 5. "Jeez, you're quick."

She has me hold out my arms like she's spraying me with bug repellent. I'm afraid that she's overdoing it, but her movements are quick and few. It's like I've been spritzed not doused, so hopefully, I won't overwhelm him.

Him. Ethan, The Panty Dropper. I can't believe my luck.

Glancing at the clock on the microwave I see that I need to leave now or I'll be late.

"Well, this is it," I tell Monica bending down to grab my tote. "Wish me luck."

"I hope you both get lucky." Monica can't quit the push for us to have sex and I give her the stink eye. "Hey, I'm living vicariously through you tonight."

"I know." After giving her a hug, I head to the door. "Thanks for everything. I mean it. And if I'm never heard from again, his name is Ethan Murphy, apartment 814."

"Got it," she says with a smile. "I'll stay and clean off your bed, though I hope you don't sleep in it tonight."

Funny, but something inside of me just might be fine with that too.

Dinner is served

I take the elevator up to his floor. It's just two flights via the stairs, but I can't risk twisting my ankle in these heels. As the elevator carries me up, I get almost giddy. The door opens and I walk out into the hall taking a few deep breaths to calm myself down.

There are fewer apartments on his floor than on mine. Since it's the top of the building, I'm imagining they're more spacious, penthouse style. The thought makes me wonder what he does to afford such a place. He seems fairly young, around thirty or so.

Well, I'm going to find out a lot about him. I raise my hand and form a fist.

Here it goes.

My knuckles tap on the door. Hopefully, the knock was loud enough for him to hear.

Literally, two seconds pass and the door swings open. He's in dark jeans with a black fitted shirt. His sleeves are rolled up to the elbows. But the killer for me is that he has on a burgundy apron. Nothing says sexy like a man cooking me dinner while donning an apron.

I sense trouble and think I just heard a nail in the coffin of "I don't sleep with someone on the first date" get pounded into the wood. He's smiling and I smile back.

"Hey. Come on in." He shuffles to the side to make room for my entrance while his eyes move over me. Stopping at the shoes. "Wow, you look great."

Monica was right. Damn her and these wicked pumps.

"Thanks. So do you. I love the apron." I lightly brush my fingers across the part of the apron covering his chest as I pass by. He stiffens like the last time when I touched his finger. Seems like he's sensitive to my touch. In a good way too. I pause after walking past him, waiting for him to lead me into his apartment.

Something about his smile has taken away the butterflies in my stomach. I've never felt this at ease on a first date. Amazing since he's The Panty Dropper. I think it's the fact that I feel welcome here. Being invited into his home is different than meeting at a busy, noisy restaurant or club. There isn't anything formal about tonight at all. Just two people having dinner, getting to know one another. How well is to be determined.

"Dinner is close to being finished," he says turning toward me after shutting the door. "I have to confess that I've never cooked for anyone before."

"Really?" I respond. "Should I be scared?"

"Probably, but if the sauce stinks then we can blame Ragu." He laughs and I really like the sound when he does.

"Ragu has never let me down," I confess.

As he comes to stand next to me, I feel his hand on the small of my back and it's my turn to stiffen at a touch. He gently pushes against me as he walks out of the entry area. I purposely follow him slowly, this way his hand stays pressed against me. It feels heavenly. I believe I'm in all kinds of sweet trouble tonight.

We arrive in his open kitchen and living room area. The space is big and bright. There's crown molding, high-end granite and shiny, stainless steel appliances. His place looks nothing like my rental just two floors below. Everything seems customized. I look at him confused.

"Your place is unreal. I don't feel like I'm in my own building. How did you talk them into letting you do all of this?" I wave my hand across the whole room because everywhere I turn there's something that seems out of the ordinary.

"Well, actually I own this apartment," he answers me sheepishly.

"I didn't realize that you could own an apartment here. I figured they were all rentals. How did you pull that off?"

"When I said I own this apartment, I really should say I own the building too." Now he's appearing even more embarrassed.

"So you're my landlord then?" I say teasingly.

"I'm afraid so. And a very rude one too. I haven't gotten you a drink yet. How does some red wine sound?" Oh he's good, real good.

"You don't want to talk about being the EM Properties, LLC, that I write my rental check to, do you?" I want to know more about him now, as I'm totally intrigued.

"Have a seat at the bar. I'll get you some wine and explain."

"It's just unexpected." I follow orders and take a seat on the bar stool, hoping the jeans have stretched a little to make bending at the middle easier. And they have, thank God.

He sits a half-full wine glass in front of me. "You're the only person in this building that knows my secret. Are you good at keeping them?"

"I've been told I'm like a vault, so I think you're safe."

"A vault? Meaning impenetrable?" I snort and he blushes. God, he's getting more and more irresistible.

"Well, I wouldn't say that." I wink for fun. Turnaround is fair play after all. He smiles back so I know we're good. "Does the onsite management know?"

"No one knows. Including the doorman and super." He's shaking his head. "With living here I prefer it that way. And as long as they receive their paychecks and are treated fairly, they seem okay. I have a manager contracted to be my go-between."

"I'm actually amazed. I would've never guessed."

"The whole ownership thing happened because of my job. I work for a real estate investment trust. I travel around the country looking for distressed properties to add to our portfolio." He's smart, successful and gorgeous. Add a genuine sweetness to the mix and I feel like the luckiest dinner guest of all time.

"I've never heard of a real estate trust." I'm way out of my league here. I'll need to concentrate to follow along.

"I won't bore you with the details. But the partners at my company didn't want to invest in this building, so I asked if I could buy it personally. They not only agreed, but helped me find financing."

"You're really young to be this successful. I bet your parents are proud of you."

"I think so. Funny how that means more as I get older. Nothing like having my father say, 'Well done, son.'"

His sweetness might just be irresistible. I glance down at Monica's red pumps and smile.

"My parents feel the same way. They've always supported my career decisions and helped me along the way. But it feels good to be totally supporting myself now."

"Yes, it does. So I told you what I do; now it's your turn." I watch him move to the stove and check on something in the oven. I sip more of my wine before I answer him.

"I fly for my job. Literally. I'm a flight attendant." I can tell I have his full attention now. He's lowered the knife he was using to cut up the vegetables back down onto the cutting board.

"Really? So you understand the travelling thing pretty well too."

"Totally. I'm gone around twenty-one days a month. Most airlines use fifteen days as a base, but I tend to pick up a few extra days here and there. Maybe someone's child is sick or has something going on at school. It's easy to find extra days."

"Time wise, that sounds a lot like me. I'm on the road every weekday. Occasionally, there will be a property here in the Bay Area, though I can't remember the last time that happened. Maybe when I did the due diligence for this building."

"So you're all over the country?"

"Pretty much. One week I might be in New York, then the next week it's Saint Louis."

"Oh, I've had a couple layovers in Saint Louis. Great place for Italian food."

"The Hill, right?" he asks.

I nod. "Best Italian food I've ever had."

"The whole Hill area is such a unique community and unexpected for that city."

Another sip of my wine and I'm done with my first glass. I've not had anything to eat since lunch, so I'm wondering if I should slow down.

"Your glass is empty. Can't have that." He grabs the glass before I can protest, and refills it to almost the top. Interesting...

"I bet we've been to a lot of the same cites." I throw caution and likely my morals to the wind and take a drink of the wine. "Do you have a favorite?"

"It's hard to pick just one. I have a few favorites, though."

"Me too."

He takes a big drink of his wine, finishing off his glass and pours himself another one. The red is flowing tonight.

"I really enjoy New Orleans. The food and people there are great. Do you fly into there often?"

"I actually went to Mardi Gras last year. Talk about wild." I notice him looking at my chest and I just know he's wondering if I showed anything for beads.

He coughs and checks the oven again. Maybe I shouldn't have said wild so enthusiastically. Damn alcohol. He probably thinks I'm easy now. A boy in every city kind of gal. Oh crap.

He pulls a casserole type dish out of the oven and sits it on the burners. It's bubbling at the top and smells divine.

"It's done," he says laying aside his oven mitts. "I've never seen that side of New Orleans. I'm usually with business colleagues, so my trips have been more subdued."

"Honestly, I only watched the crazy from the periphery. Let's just say it was interesting."

"I bet."

I'm pretty sure he's relieved after I tell him that I wasn't a wanton hussy in New Orleans as his sweet smile has returned.

He goes to the refrigerator and brings a bowl to the counter. It's a green salad with chopped up Romaine lettuce. I sip my wine as I watch him gather up the vegetables and toss them into the salad. He looks up at me and smiles so big I even see that sweet dimple appear.

There's just something unbelievably sexy about watching him cook. So I return his smile though I'd rather be kissing that dimple right now.

"I think we're ready to dish up our plates. I made my favorite. Spaghetti casserole. Like I said, nothing exciting."

"But it looks and smells great."

I watch him slowly remove his apron. Even the simple movement of him raising it over his head and straightening his shirt makes me want to stick a dollar bill as a tip in his pocket. He's just that smooth.

I steady myself as I rise out of the chair just in case my lower half has gone numb from my tight jeans. All's well as I make my way around from the counter bar to stand by Ethan. Even with my heels on he's probably a good four inches taller than me. He looks me over again like he did when he answered the door. It feels inappropriately nice.

"I mentioned earlier that you look great didn't I?" He's playing with me now.

"A girl can never hear that enough," I say while lightly touching his arm. This time I keep the connection and don't pull away.

He stares at my hand and brings his eyes up to mine. They're hooded and a darker blue than before. He's definitely turned on. We both are. And before I know it, he's gently spun me around pressing me against the counter's edge.

He releases my arms and places his hands on each side of my face. His touch is warm and I feel his thumbs gently rubbing my skin. It's sweet and enduring and my eyes remain fixed on his.

I lean into him as he leans forward. His eyes move to my lips and I know he's going to kiss me. And he does...

Turning his head to the side, his lips softly meet mine. Our bodies are only touching via lips and his hands. I want to touch him too, so my hands find his waist. It seems like the best place to land. I feel the top of jeans and gently rub his skin through the shirt. Solid, there's nothing soft about him.

His kisses become harder, more intense. The kind I can get lost in. And just when I think he's about to draw me into his arms, he pushes back instead and his hands fall from my face. His lips are gone from mine, but their touch lingers like a phantom. And I know one thing's for sure. That was the best first kiss I've ever had.

As we both catch our breath, I see his lips and I start to laugh. Not just a chuckle or snort, but a breath stealing, full-fledged laugh. I try not to but I can't help it. My red lipstick... It was everywhere. Like, Ethan the clown, everywhere.

He seems confused by my odd reaction, as he should be, and all I can do is point to his lips as I laugh. Finally, he gets the hint and rubs his fingers across them. Now the red is smeared even more than it was, on his lips, face and fingers. I quickly grab a paper towel by the sink and wet it down.

"Ethan," I spit out between laughs.

I take the wet towel and gently wipe the red off his face. He's kind of laughing with me now, which is a relief.

"I'm so sorry," I say after finally cleaning him up and calming down. "What a way to ruin a great kiss too."

"So, great kiss, huh?"

"Very much so." I make sure our eyes are connected before I continue. "Likely the best first kiss ever."

"Really?" He's all grins.

"Really," I repeat like an echo. "I usually don't wear red lipstick. It's obviously a beauty hazard."

"But it looks good on you."

He glances down at my shoes and I suddenly feel the need to divert. Maybe it's my hollow stomach. I'm not sure.

"We probably should plate up dinner." I point to the stove. "It's looking lonely."

"You're right. I got a little carried away. But when you touched me..." He stops without finishing.

"Hey. I enjoyed it a lot too," I reassure him. "Maybe we can get carried away after dinner. No lipstick, though."

"I like that idea." He gives me a little bump with his hip as he walks by me toward the plates on the counter. Stinker.

"Hey." I give him a little punch on the arm as I walk up next to him. Funny we turned off the kissing, but we can't keep our hands to ourselves. I hear Monica's voice from earlier saying he wouldn't be able to keep his hands off of me, and I wonder what else she might be right about.

We fill our plates and head to his dining table. It's set with black and gray placemats. They go perfectly with his plates. He even has cloth napkins set out for us. Very impressive and very metro. He sits at the head of the table and I sit to his left.

"This is a stylish table setting for a man who never cooks for company." I take my first bite of pasta and it's pretty damn good.

"Everything on the table is a gift from my mother."

"Well, then cheers to your mother. She has good taste." I raise my wine glass and take a sip. It appears to be full again. He's pretty sneaky. I don't remember him refilling it.

"Yes, she's an interior designer by trade."

"Nice."

"She helped me redesign the apartment and decide on what to purchase for furniture. I eventually just gave her carte blanche to do whatever. With my traveling schedule I couldn't keep up with the approvals."

"Good decision. The place looks like it belongs in a magazine."

"She wants to get it in a local publication here in the Bay. But I'm concerned about being exposed as the building owner."

"That makes sense. It's hard to believe that you've kept it a secret so far."

"I guess it wouldn't be the end of the world. But I don't want people knocking at my door with problems. It could get ugly."

"Ugly, like a knock on the door at midnight from someone who's locked out of their apartment. Or even worse, has a stopped up toilet." We both laugh.

"Exactly. That's the reason I have a reliable super on site. When I'm home, I really want to be home, not dreading a knock at the door. Travel has a way of wearing me out."

"I hear you there."

We continue eating and sipping on our wine. As we finish, he opens bottle number two or is it three? Either way, I'm feeling slightly tipsy. I wonder if it's part of an evil plan. I'm pretty sure I've drunk more than him too. He was busy cooking and I was busy staring…

"I need to slow down on the wine. I think I'm holding my fourth glass now."

He says nothing out loud but I can tell from his face that he finds it amusing.

"I need to pace myself." He picks up our plates and carries them to the sink. Totally mum. "I'm not kidding." He's smirking at me now. "Aren't you going to say something?"

"You want the truth?" he asks.

"I think so." My answer is a plea to be gentle. He sits down at the now cleared table. Cleared of everything but the wine.

"Tonight has been great." He briefly glances down to the table like he's gathering courage to continue. "I can't remember when I've had such a good time getting to know someone."

"I feel the same too." My words are a confirmation that there's something between us. "But what's with all this wine, mister?"

"I like the way it makes your face blush." His hand covers mine as it lays flat on the table. I feel his fingers slide under my palm. "With each glass, your skin lights up. It's so beautiful."

"Wow." I'm shocked. Oh boy. What do I say to this one? I'm flushed even more now. I feel it. My eyes stare at our intertwined hands as I search for what I want to say or do.

"I've embarrassed you?"

My hair is a covering around my face as I shake my head to let him know that he hasn't. Actually, the words he spoke make me want to jump up and kiss his beautiful face. But even with my wined-up brain, I know things are moving fast. Getting too real. The kiss in the kitchen, my hand that he's holding now a little tighter. I just don't trust myself. And I'm afraid to look up; he's just too tempting. But I have to…

"You haven't embarrassed me at all." Our hands are magnetic. Pulling away from him is difficult, but I finally manage it. I need to break our connection for a minute.

"I'm making you feel uncomfortable." He scoots his chair away from me and I want to grab it and bring it back closer. I'm completely conflicted with myself when it comes to him.

"Please don't think that." I hope my eyes speak more than my words. "I've enjoyed everything about tonight. That's the problem."

"Problem?" he asks. "Enlighten me."

"Well, I've been attracted to you for some time." I can't believe I'm confessing this. Monica would kill me. I might even kill myself.

"This *is* enlightening." He glides the chair closer again and I'm relieved. "So, before we met today?"

"I've seen you working out in the building's gym. It's great by the way."

"Thanks, but I would have remembered seeing you. I'm sure." He appears to be concentrating, probably trying to remember me from before today.

"I doubt it." I think he's given up on searching his memory as his face relaxes. "I lurked in the back when I saw you at the gym. I was sweaty and gross. You on the other hand…"

"I'm sweaty and gross at the gym too."

"You're the sexy version of sweaty. Believe me." I really emphasize those last couple of words with a little attitude. I think one day after a "gym experience" he earned the nickname, The Panty Dropper. It was the day I hid behind some weight machines and watched his backside while he ran on the treadmill. This train of thought isn't helping me at all.

"It's crazy how we met today." He stops and the mood between us shifts to serious. "I feel like I've known you for years. It's odd, a good odd, though."

"Reincarnation maybe?" The mood is lighter again as he laughs at my question.

"Would you like to see what's on TV?" he asks cautiously. "We could rent something off cable."

"Sure."

He pushes back his chair and stands and I follow his lead into the living area.

It's open to the kitchen with a wall adorned with the largest big screen television I've ever seen. Beautiful built-in cabinets filled with books and modern decorations encase the television as it fits perfectly into the center. The surroundings form an altar to the god of the room.

"That's some TV you have there."

We've moved toward the couch and he motions for me to take a seat. Do I choose to sit in the middle or at one of the ends? Or maybe somewhere between the middle and the end? I decide on between the middle and end. So confusing. He mirrors my decision by doing the same. We have a little space and can easily reach out and hold hands. Not that we should or will.

"I'm not a big TV person." His words make me giggle. He raises his brow probably wondering what brought on my response.

"For someone who isn't a 'TV person' you have a gigantic TV." I use those annoying finger quotes in a teasing way when I repeat his words.

"Remember, I gave carte blanche to my mother. I guess she thinks that every bachelor builds the room around the TV." We laugh and he starts scrolling through the cable channels.

"I was going to ask what your favorite TV shows were but since you don't watch much..." I stop speaking, hoping he'll continue.

"I watch a few shows when I'm out of town in the hotel room at night. Helps me unwind."

I angle myself toward him on the cushion and bring my legs up where they're now folded under me. My arm stretches across the back. He turns and mimics me with the exception of his legs. One bends, the other stays on the floor. He's almost crossing his leg at the knee. Our bodies form an open circle as he places his arm over mine.

I lean against the back of his couch settling into the soft cushions. It's more comfortable than I thought it would be.

"This couch is great."

"My mom," he states. "She knows I wanted comfort. Looks were second."

"Lucky for you. This has both." My fingers rub the upholstery.

"Her true masterpiece is my bathroom."

"Really? I hate my bathroom." My hand covers my mouth as I realize he owns my bathroom. "Oh crap. I'm sorry. It's just that..."

He interrupts as I try to recover from insulting him. "It's okay. Why do you think I redid mine?" He smiles and reaches for my hand. "Let me show you."

He's standing in front of me clasping my hand and helps lift me from the couch. Seeing the bath means we venture into his bedroom. A little warning bell is going off somewhere in my head, drowned out by the wine, literally. But I'm too curious to pay attention and willingly follow him. Our hands are magnets once again. Sure enough we've crossed into his bedroom and it's ultra-modern and male.

"I was out of town for two weeks when she finished the work. Was a great surprise."

"Your bedroom." I glance around the room. "I love it. It really fits you too."

"You think?" He seems hesitant. "Maybe too modern?"

"No, it says, 'I'm a serious grown-up.'"

"Never thought about it that way. Definitely moved away from the college look from before."

We take a few more steps and stop at a door. He cracks it a bit and then shuts it quickly.

"Had to check and see if I picked up all the towels." He gently tugs me toward him. "Close your eyes."

I do as I'm told. He pulls my hand and I move with him and quietly hear the door open. As we progress forward I can feel the floor go from hardwood to something smoother, like tile. A couple more steps and we stop. He lowers my hand and tells me to open my eyes. I slowly peek at the room and then turn to scan it. It matches the blacks and grays in his bedroom. Black, gray, and white. Amazing.

A large mirror dresses the wall above the double sinks. My reflection stares back at me. Ethan's right, I'm flushed. Glowing. Wine and him. Has to be both. I run my hands through my hair and face him.

"It's unbelievable." My hands glide along the sink. "Really."

The walls are straight lines of horizontal glass tiles. Grays meet black and mix with white. My eyes end at the shower. The same tile on the walls extends there too. The shower is an invisible space as it's encased in glass from floor to ceiling.

"You like it?" he asks curiously.

"Love is more like it." I open the heavy glass door to the shower. It has to be seven feet tall from the step-in ledge to where it's flush with the ceiling. The glass connection is tight as a drum, sealed.

"Look up at the ceiling," he instructs. I see a rainfall shower head. A personal favorite. I've stayed in a couple of hotels that have them. I never want to leave once I'm under the water's stream. So relaxing.

"God, I love taking showers under these." I throw my head back as if the water's cascading down on me. I can almost imagine its touch and feel its warmth.

"Emily." I hear Ethan's strained voice and find his eyes on me. He's looking at me with an "I want to devour you" fire in his eyes. Something inside me silently hopes he does.

It's clear to me. Right now, one of life's crossroads stands a couple feet away from me. Either I answer the desire in this man's eyes with a kiss and maybe more, or diffuse it with a rejection by walking past him coldly. I see no other route out of these walls of glass as he stands at the opening. Slowly, I approach him, still trying to decide. But the second I hear him whisper my name again the battle's over. He's won.

"Good damn, you win, Ethan." His arms are spread and flexed high on the glass door's edge. My hands meet behind the back of his neck and settle in the soft waves of his hair.

"Good damn?" He smiles all sexy. "Don't you mean God?"

"No," I explain while twirling locks of his hair in my fingers and trying not to get distracted from his scent. "It's more, 'damn, I'm giving into you' and I'm pretty sure it's going to be 'good.' See I can't resist you anymore. Not gonna even try."

Ethan pulls me to him in an embrace. His hands are drifting to the edge of my shirt and I feel warm fingers skim across my lower back. Desperate. Now that I've given in, that's how I feel. Our lips remember and continue where we left off in the kitchen. Nothing is tentative now. We've broken through the awkward and now we're heading to the bed.

When he scoops me up in his arms, my hands clasp behind him holding on to his collar. My eyes find Monica's red heels and I push one shoe off with the toe of the other. I kick my foot and the red shoe goes flying off.

"I shouldn't have worn these," I mutter between breaths and kisses.

"God, I love them." His voice is raspy. His breathing's short. I maneuver the other shoe off and it goes sailing. He lays me down on the white comforter. My hands fan out and it feels crisp and cool under my touch.

"But they're one-night stand pumps." He's standing over me, silent. I watch him tugging his own shoes off. "And I don't do one-night stands. Ever."

"Oh, Emily, this *isn't* a one-night stand."
"Well, good damn."

Warm and blissful, I lay across his chest. We've given all we can to each other tonight. His arm and comforter drape over and anchor me. I snuggle into him further and my eyes start to close while I smile in contentment. What a night. What a guy. I say a little prayer of thanks that sixes can look like eights. Otherwise the doorman might have never made the wrong delivery.

~~~~~

As I slowly wake up from a sleep-induced fog, I remember where I am. In bed. With Ethan. The touch of the sheets and the smell of him are familiar to me now. His warm body spoons mine and we fit together perfectly. I want to stay here cocooned in his bed all day. I'm afraid of losing our connection and hope the light of day doesn't melt away what we had together. Either way I won't regret it. Last night was worth it.

I gingerly open my eyes, roll over and see Ethan, all disheveled hair and scruffy face. He's in full-blown panty dropper mode. And from the look on his face, I have a sneaking suspicion that fate and red heels worked some magic. He's sporting the biggest grin. It smoothes away any worries of where we might stand now. His dimpled grin sweetly calms me. I end up laughing while telling him good morning. He pulls me into his arms and makes sure it's great.

Epilogue

It's 2 p.m. on Saturday, February 14th, exactly a year since I met Ethan. My dear father leads me to the closed doors leading to the church's sanctuary. Our arms are intertwined. Slowly, we make our way to the entrance. We stop and wait until the ushers open the doors. I hear my chosen processional song and know that we're about to be revealed.

My father whispers softly as the doors open, "Be happy, Emily."

Holding back tears, I answer back, "I am. Very much so."

He escorts me toward the altar and my love where very soon I'll become Mrs. Panty Dropper.

The Love Handles Club

by Liv Morris

Dedication

This short story is dedicated to the original Love Handles Club. A unique group of men who meet on Thursday nights somewhere near our nation's capital. These men and their life-long friendships inspired me to write this fictitious story.
Bradley, Bob, Dave, and Matthew, many thanks!

Chapter 1: Bradley's Turn

"Okay, there's one more signature left and we should be done here."

I watched Stephen Jensen, my attorney, place the last remaining document in front of me and signed where he directed. A sick feeling gripped my stomach as ten years of my life was erased with a simple stroke of the pen.

"Well, that should do it," he said while gathering up the papers spread across the conference table. "I know this finalization has been a long time in coming, Bradley. But I think in the end it was fair."

"Fair or not, at least Natalie and her father's company are out of my life. For good." I stood and reached out to shake his hand. "Thanks, Jensen, for getting this settled. I just hope that I never need your services again."

"Me too, Bradley." Jensen returned my handshake with a sad smile. "You take care of yourself and try to put this behind you."

"Will do."

While exiting the glass-covered office building, I felt a deep, cleansing breath escape my lungs. I looked up into the cloudless Dallas sky as the warm afternoon breeze blew through my hair and it felt good. I felt good and... free. Finally free.

As I walked toward my car, the reality that I no longer had any tie to my wife of ten years hit me. The thought of calling Natalie my "ex-wife" made me laugh. It was bittersweet, but finding humor in the clustered mess of our marriage's end gave me a bit of relief.

No one around would've noticed, but there was a definite weight off my shoulders. I felt it down to my bones. Removing the heavy load hadn't come easy. But I had no regrets. That part of my life was over and now it was time to finally move on.

It had been a long and lonely year since I'd filed for divorce from Natalie. I'd played it safe after the official filing, even though I'd caught her having an affair with another senior executive at our company. I didn't want to give her any ammunition against me. I had so much more to lose, so I'd remained faithful to her until I signed the divorce papers today.

It had been over a year since I'd been with anyone. I missed being around a woman and not just for the sex. Though that would be nice too. Real damn nice.

Hell, I was sick of being alone. I wanted someone to be with, share a dinner out instead of the usual take-out at home. I guess after all the crap I'd been through in the last year, I still believed in love. I had to. It was the only thing that kept me from becoming a bitter man.

My cell phone rang once I was inside my parked car. Looking at the screen, I saw that it was Dave, my best friend since elementary school, likely calling to check up on me and see how I'm doing. Dave had stood by me throughout the yearlong divorce battle. He was my rock.

"Hey, Dave."

"Hey, man." He always sounded upbeat. It was his happy go lucky way. "How did things go? You met with the lawyers today, right?"

"Yep. I'm officially divorced. Just left their offices."

"Wow. Thank God it's finally over. You can move on now." He had no idea how much I wanted to do just that.

"My thoughts exactly." I turned on the car to get the a/c circulating. The sun had heated up the interior and I felt like I was sitting in a sauna.

"You can begin tonight. Love Handles at seven." Dave had a convincing way of telling people what to do. I think he missed his calling as a diplomat for the State Department.

"I'll be there, but I plan on getting a car service tonight. I have a little celebrating to do and don't want to worry about how much I drink."

"I'll swing by and pick you up around 6:30. It's no problem."

"That'd be great. Never one to turn down a free ride." We both laughed.

"The girls are joining us tonight. Hope that's alright."

Usually, just the guys hung out together on the weekly Love Handles Club night. But occasionally some of the wives and women we knew from our high school days joined us. Looked like tonight was one of those nights.

"Sure, I haven't seen them in a while. It'll be good to catch up. Who knows, one of them may have a lead on a job for me? I'm gainfully unemployed now."

"You may be unemployed, but you should be set for life with the divorce settlement. Unless Natalie and her father didn't buyout your shares of the company as planned."

"I'm good. Everything got worked out with them buying me out of the company. My attorney says it was a fair deal. I say it's done." I really didn't want to talk about the specifics. "So where are we meeting tonight? The usual?"

"Yes, The Londoner. I feel like playing a game or two of pool."

"Bob humiliated you last week, if I'm not mistaken."

"Yes, it was ugly. I need to save face tonight," he continued. "Oh, I almost forgot. We have someone special coming. Someone that I think you'll want to see."

"Whoa, Dave. I just signed the papers a few minutes ago. Please tell me you're not trying to hook me up already."

Dave had been carrying around a list of women he thought would be perfect for me. I, on the other hand, wanted a little time to breathe. I wasn't quite ready to jump into the dating game tonight.

"Oh, it's nothing like that. It's Kelly. She's joining us tonight." He paused and so did I.

After a few seconds I finally replied in almost a whisper, "My Kelly?"

"Yes, your Kelly. Is that alright?" His question had a hesitancy to it.

"I guess so." But truthfully, I wasn't sure how I felt about seeing her after all these years. "It's been a long time. I saw her at the reunion a few years ago, but I didn't even get to say hello. Right after we made eye contact, her jerk of a husband ushered her out of the banquet hall."

"Yeah, I remember you telling me about that. Well, I have some good news for you then." Dave paused increasing my anticipation. "She's coming alone. Tina's bringing only her and I don't know the whole story but she moved back here from Atlanta…"

"So she's back in Dallas?" I interrupted. "Permanently?" I should've been happy with the news that she was here in our hometown. But having my first love around with her possessive husband wouldn't be an easy pill for me to swallow. The thought of running into them somewhere filled me with dread.

"Tina said she's moving back to Dallas and the husband isn't. I think they split up. But don't quote me on that."

Thoughts began to jumble in my head at the possibility that Kelly was single now too. I needed to find out for sure before I let my mind even toy with the idea.

"Well, it'll be good to see her. And thanks for giving me the heads up, Dave."

"What are friends for? Maybe you two can celebrate tonight. Your freedom and her homecoming."

"Let's avoid divorce talk, if you don't mind. Deal?"

"Deal," Dave answered with gusto. "Listen, I have a conference call in a few that I need to prepare for. I'll see you at 6:30."

"Okay. See you later."

I tossed the phone aside and pulled out of my parking space to head back home. I needed some time to mull over what Dave had said. Hell, I was going to see Kelly Parker tonight. I really couldn't begin to wrap my mind around that fact.

My hands started to sweat and it had nothing to do with the day's heat either. I knew the cause. Regret tinged with a sprinkling of fear. Pretty much what every heartbreaking jerk like me should feel after coming to his senses too late.

Yeah, I'd broken her heart. Likely shattered it to pieces. I have no excuse for my nineteen-year-old self. I was a dumb knucklehead back then. If I had those teen years to do over again, I never would've done the idiotic things that led to our break-up.

Kelly and I had met our freshman year in high school. She had attended a private, religious school before she switched to Highland Park High. I remembered seeing her in my second period class the first day of school.

She was nervous. It was easy to see. And who wouldn't be? We were a snobby bunch of rich kids and didn't embrace newcomers easily. I moved to her side in hopes of rescuing her. I also wanted to be the first one to introduce myself to the pretty girl standing alone. There was just something about Kelly. I could still see her looking up at me with those pretty brown eyes, big as saucers. She seemed so fragile, vulnerable.

Standing next to her, I'd looked down and said "hi." She'd smiled back at me and from that moment on, I'd been wrapped around her little finger. We'd just clicked. During our four years of high school, we'd shared everything two crazy, lovesick kids could possibly experience together. However, everything had changed when we'd gone off to different colleges after graduation.

Kelly had selected Baylor University in Waco. Or I should say her parents had chosen the school for her. They were deeply religious and thought it best to have their impressionable daughter attend a nice Baptist college.

I'd gone off to the University of Texas in Austin and joined a rambunctious fraternity. Not a very smart idea if you wanted to keep a long-distance relationship going. I'd convinced myself that I was immune to the temptations of booze and willing women. Sadly, I'd been wrong and ended up living like there wasn't a beautiful girl two hours away expecting me to be faithful.

After being apart for two months, Kelly had come to visit me over UT's homecoming weekend in October. She hadn't suspected that I was cheating on her, as everything between us had seemed fine. When we'd talked on the phone, I had kept up the ruse of being a devoted boyfriend. What a complete jerk.

However, my secrets hadn't stayed hidden for long. During her short stay on campus, she'd found out I was seeing other girls at school. Just the thought of how that weekend had gone down made me dread seeing her tonight.

Kelly had arrived at my fraternity house on Saturday morning before the big football game. I'd brought her up to my room where several of my frat brothers were enjoying some pre-tailgate partying.

The drinks had been strong and one of the guys was wasted and forgot Kelly was coming down to visit me. I'd warned everyone to keep a lid on my skirt chasing. I sure as hell didn't want her finding out what a dick I was or where else my dick had been, for that matter.

However, my drunken friend had spilled my secrets as soon as Kelly'd walked into the room, shouting that I'd found another hot girl for this week's football game. I'd tried shutting him up, keeping him from saying more, but he hadn't stopped. Each word had been like a punch in my gut and likely a dagger to Kelly's heart.

Her beautiful eyes had filled with tears as she searched my face for an answer. I couldn't say a word to confirm or deny what she'd heard. She knew the truth because she knew my heart and it'd told her that I was a lying cheat. There'd been no defense for what I'd done.

After a few seconds, everyone around us had gone back to partying acting like nothing earth shattering had happened right in front of them. They continued drinking and talking about the game later. But Kelly and I had stood a few feet inside the room facing each other. Neither one of us moved a muscle or said a word. We'd looked into each other's eyes for a long, long time. Then she'd whispered the last words I thought I'd ever hear from her...

"Goodbye, Bradley." I remember them like it was yesterday.

She'd turned away from me, tucked her overnight bag into her side, and walked out of the room. I had no idea where she was going or what I should've done. My legs felt frozen to the floor beneath me. So I did nothing. I let her go. Biggest damn regret of my life.

I still can't figure out why I didn't chase after her. Maybe I felt she deserved better than me and it was probably true. Who knows what goes on inside a stupid nineteen year old's brain?

When I finally came to my senses a few hours later and tried to find her, I was too late. Tina, her best friend from high school who also was at UT, told me that Kelly had gone back to Baylor brokenhearted.

No matter how hard I'd tried to reach out to her, she refused to see me again. I'd lost her for good.

Funny what stood out in my mind after all those years. I'd given her a little kiss before we entered through the front doors of the frat house. It'd ended up being our last one.

Chapter 2: Kelly's Turn

Tina, my lifelong best friend, found out that I was back in Dallas. I wanted to lay low for a while, but our mothers belonged to the same bridge group and saw each other every week. So my mother shared my arrival with Tina's mother, Bitsy, because she worried I was isolating myself from the world and, truthfully, she was right. I'd avoided everyone since I'd left Joe and Atlanta behind. I needed some time to process the failure of my marriage, but I felt ready to get back to my life here once again. Even if I had no idea what that might be.

So when Tina called a few days ago to invite me to the weekly Love Handles Club get-together, I decided it was time to get out of the house. She explained that the club was formed by the guys we'd hung out with in high school. They planned weekly nights out together at local watering holes in North Dallas.

It sounded like they wanted to keep the fun of their youth alive. And from what I remembered, they knew how to have a good time. Hanging out with them had positively been the most fun time of my life. I missed them. And being honest with myself, I really missed one particular Love Handles' guy the most. Bradley. I'd be a millionaire many times over now if I had a dime for every time I'd thought about him over the last fourteen years. He was the reason my stomach had butterflies. My nerves had almost made me cancel, but in the end I knew I had to see him. At least one more time.

So now, I found myself sitting outside The Londoner in my car on a Thursday night. The others wouldn't be coming until around seven, which was in about thirty minutes. I wanted to get there early and be the first to arrive. I hated the thought of a grand entrance and would rather be in place waiting for everyone as they arrived.

Exiting the car, I walked to the entrance and pulled the heavy wooden doors open. The place had the feel of a genuine London pub. The walls and ceilings were decorated with UK sports paraphernalia. The smell of fish and chips even hung in the air. Truly authentic.

The pool tables were in the back of the pub and I saw a few tables to the left of where they were situated. They seemed like the perfect place for a large group to sit. I just needed to make a pit stop before I claimed them because I wanted to stay seated as long as I could tonight. Delay all the shocked faces for as long as possible. I still couldn't believe that I was braving seeing everyone especially since Tina said Bradley was going to be here too.

First things first though. I'd worry about seeing him later. I scanned the pub's walls and found the illuminated sign for the restrooms and headed toward them. Avoiding the mirror when I walked in, I quickly did my business and washed my hands. As I let the water rinse the soap away, I looked into the mirror checking to make sure my hair and makeup were okay.

I definitely looked different from the last time they'd seen me at the ten-year reunion a few years ago. I had to beg Joe to let me go and he'd relented as long as he was able to be there too. I agreed to his terms, but I think he knew how disappointed I was that he demanded on attending with me. He didn't want me being alone in a room with Bradley. I think he knew that seeing Bradley again was the main reason I wanted to go. And he was right.

Once we were at the reunion and my eyes had found Bradley, Joe made me leave. I think it was the beginning of the end for me. It just took about five years too long for me to come to my senses.

There was so much unfinished business between Bradley and me. I've always regretted how I'd completely shunned him after I found out he was lying to me and likely sleeping around with other girls. He called, wrote and begged relentlessly to see me after I'd left him. But I'd been a heartbroken mess. Joe, my now soon-to-be ex-husband, had taken advantage of my weakened state.

Joe had known exactly what he'd been doing when I'd arrived back at Baylor crying and inconsolable after fleeing from Bradley. He'd pounced on my vulnerability and I'd had no clue. I'd thought he was the greatest guy in the world. He'd listened to every detail between sobs. Helped me forget all the pain and appeared to be someone who would never do the kind of things Bradley had done to me.

What a silly young woman I'd been. The true reason behind Joe's compassion hadn't shown itself until after we were married. I'd been too caught up in the persona that he'd put together for me. My knight in shining armor.

He'd known my weaknesses and had played me well. He'd wanted someone to control or reside over really. Being my husband wasn't what he'd wanted. He'd wanted to be king, a ruler over every detail of my life.

Thankfully, I was in Dallas now, far away from Joe and his controlling ways. When I'd left him a few weeks ago with only the clothes on my back and what little I could fit into a suitcase, I'd decided to never look back and question what I was doing. It was for the best. My future was no longer in Atlanta by Joe's side.

"Excuse me, ma'am." A voice pulled me out of my memories and I looked up to see a young woman standing next to the table. "Will there be other people joining you tonight?"

"I think there will be around ten of us maybe even twelve. I thought this long table would work."

"It's the largest one we have in the restaurant." Her smile was big and bright. "Would you care for anything to drink or eat until the rest of your party arrives?"

Good question. What could I drink tonight? I needed something that would look like a mixed drink. Keep the appearance that I was indulging with the rest of the gang.

"I'll take a seltzer water with a lime. And I'll continue to have those the rest of the evening if that's okay?"

"No problem." She looked at me curiously. "Can I get you anything to eat?"

"No thanks. I'll just wait until everyone is here."

"Okay, I'll be right back with your drink."

I had a cover now and it would come in handy. I didn't want to stick out for not drinking. I could blend in with the rest of them for a little while at least. Sticking out would come soon enough. Literally.

My server sat my seltzer drink down in front of me and I sipped through the stirring straw. It was refreshing and cool. I'd been so thirsty lately. I'd forgotten how dry it was in Dallas this time of year.

There was some movement toward the front of the pub. I turned my head to see what was going on, and my body froze instantly when I saw the handsome and older version of my high school sweetheart standing by the front door.

Seeing him tonight was more intense than I thought it would be. No one, which really meant Joe, was standing by me gauging my reaction, so I completely reacted. The heat I felt when he scanned the restaurant and our eyes met, nearly made me slide from my chair and walk across the floor to him. But I needed to stay seated, planted in my spot. The magnetic pull I felt so many years ago when I was anywhere near him still extended between us today. Well, at least it did for me.

Dave was standing next to him with a funny little smile on his face as he looked from me to Bradley. He appeared pretty pleased with what he saw and I was too. I watched Bradley's shocked face break into a grin then he lowered and shook his head.

Hopefully, that was a good sign, but my nerves were totally frayed as I watched them start to walk my way. It seemed that my heart rate increased with each step they took. My stomach was tied up in knots. I couldn't remember the last time I'd felt this close to having a panic attack.

Once a lanky, tall young man, Bradley had filled out very nicely. Indeed. His shirt stretched tight across his broad shoulders and abs. I didn't understand how the two men got away with calling themselves Love Handles as neither of them had an ounce of flab that I could see. They looked toned and fit. Especially Bradley...

Their walk across the pub seemed to take forever. Finally, they were standing right in front of me. I was sitting at the end, next to the head of the table. Dave came around and gave me a big hug. I hugged him back but stayed attached to the seat of my chair. If he was expecting me to stand up, he didn't show it. Instead, he quickly took the head spot next to me. One hurdle down, next up was Bradley.

The logical chair for him to take was the one opposite me. But would he? That would mean we'd have to make a lot of eye contact tonight. Who knew? Maybe even our feet or legs would touch on occasion under the table?

Bradley didn't disappoint. He pulled out the chair right across from me and folded his tall frame down onto it. I sipped at my drink again. It definitely was hotter in here now with him across from me; staring at me with those deep, blue eyes, the color of bluebonnets. And those long lashes. God, I'd loved looking into his eyes as we'd made love.

I had to stop myself. This train of thought signaled danger, so I began to silently chant, *I can do this, I can do this*. But I was a goner when he started to speak to me. All my resolve melted away.

"Hi, Kelly." Hearing him say my name brought back so many old feelings. Good ones.

"Hi, Bradley." I had said his name so many times in my mind. It was hard to believe that I was saying it to him in person.

Chapter 3: Bradley's Turn

The second I saw Kelly after entering the bar, my whole body stilled. I had the feeling of being transported back in time. She didn't look much different than when she was nineteen and I ached to get closer to her. But Dave was doing the meet and greet as we arrived and we hadn't moved past the entrance. The drawback of knowing everyone at this place.

Finally, we started heading her way. Her face shone with the sweetest smile as we approached. I caught her eyes glancing over my body and chuckled. Sweet little Kelly was checking me out. I'd put on a lot of muscle over the years and was no longer the lanky young boy she had once known. Hopefully, she liked what she saw.

When we arrived at Kelly's table, my heart was pounding hard against my chest. I wasn't sure what to do. Speak first? Shake her hand? Concerned and a bit panicked, I breathed a sigh of relief when Dave moved toward her first and wrapped his big arms around her little frame. I remained where I was standing, just past arms' length. I didn't want to freak her out by hugging her too. Though the thought of having her in my arms sounded pretty damn tempting. She stayed in her chair, which was a good thing. Otherwise, it made the fact that we didn't hug even more obvious. This way we avoided awkward.

Dave sat down after releasing Kelly from his hug, and I joined him at the table. My eyes never left Kelly's and hers never left mine. She practically glowed as she smiled at me.

Boy, the years had been good to her as she didn't look a day over twenty-five. The nineteen-year-old girl whose heart I'd broken now hid behind a more mature and beautiful face, but her smile appeared just the same to me. Bright and contagious.

Her hair was like the young Kelly I knew. She'd always worn it long, so I was surprised when I spotted her at our ten-year reunion with her hair above the shoulders. The familiar long strands were back now and sexy. My fingers itched to run through them.

We said hi to each other and the distance we'd had between us started to fade. Dave began carrying on about how great she looked. My mind wandered off because it was my turn to check her out now. My view ended at her chest as the rest of her was tucked under the table.

After we'd broken up, no one had compared to her. Firm, round and a little too big to fit into the palm of my large hands described her boobs. So soft to the touch and sweet tasting on my tongue. And those pink-colored nipples of hers...

Memories of me taking them into my hands and feeling them against my lips crossed my mind. My flashbacks of being with Kelly were vivid and powerful. Like it'd been yesterday. I now felt myself starting to get hard. Damn, the things we did. We were pretty adventurous for being so young, especially the last year of high school.

I wondered if she could tell what I was thinking. If the lust-filled memories pumping through me right now showed in my eyes. She had known me so well and had been the recipient of my horny teenage behavior. There was no need trying to hide my feelings from her now. I was done with playing games.

All afternoon, I'd told myself I would do what I could to get to know her again, prayed she'd let me back into her world. My first steps should've been engaging in some conversation with her instead of gazing at her eyes and chest, but I continued to gawk like a pervert.

Not having had sex in a year wasn't helping me either. I needed to reign myself in right the hell now. So I tried to concentrate on what Dave was saying instead of Kelly laughing and biting her lips.

"So you've been back in Dallas for a couple of weeks now?" Dave's words might get her to open up about her future here.

"I've been here almost a month now." Her eyes were on Dave and occasionally switched to look at me.

"If you plan on moving back here for good, there are some awesome real estate deals right now." I threw my thoughts into the ring.

"Thanks." Her one word answer sure didn't give anything away. I still had no clue if she was back permanently.

"Excuse me, you two." Dave rose out of his seat and I was tempted to move right into it. Closer to Kelly. "I'm going to get a tab set up for the group. I'll be right back."

"Sounds good," I replied.

"Did a server come to the table already?" Dave asked. "I see you have a drink Kelly."

"Yes, the blond girl over there." Kelly motioned to the bar. "She took my drink order so I'm assuming she's our server."

"Alright you two try and behave yourselves." Dave started to walk off but stopped. "What do you want Bradley?"

"I'll take a Heineken. Thanks."

"I'll be right back." Dave winked at Kelly. He knew exactly what he was doing. Leaving us alone. By ourselves. And I was very thankful too. It gave Kelly and me a few minutes to talk before the Love Handles' crowd arrived.

"So," I commented and paused. Great one-word conversation starter.

"So," she replied. We both started laughing which seemed to ease the tension between us. It was only natural we felt a bit uncomfortable, since our last contact, face to face, had been so many years ago.

"It's so good to see you, Kelly." I laid it out there. Decided I might as well go for broke.

"It's good to see you, too." Her eyes pierced through me as she spoke those words. Like they were trying to convey a deeper meaning.

"You look wonderful by the way." I took a quick breath before continuing. "More beautiful now than when we were in college."

A blush spread across her cheeks upon hearing my compliment. They weren't just idle words. It was true. She was beautiful. It only reinforced how much of an idiot I'd been all those years ago.

How could I have turned my back on such a beautiful woman? She was the whole package. One any man would love to have as his.

"You're making me blush," she shyly replied. "I've changed a lot lately, but thanks for the sweet words."

"They aren't just words, Kelly." My face became serious to match the tone of my words. "I've missed you. Wondered so many times how you were. If you were happy."

Maybe I was getting too heavy. Coming on too strong. She'd just left Atlanta so I assumed things with her husband were on the fritz. But dammit, I couldn't pull back if I tried. I'd done that years ago and a royal jerk had filled the void I'd left behind. It ended up being the biggest regret of my life. So I felt like it was an all or nothing chance to reach out to her tonight.

"I've had the same thoughts about you over the years too." Her voice was quiet. Just above a whisper. "I hope you've been good."

Holy shit. She'd had the same thoughts too? Did that mean she missed me? Wondered what I was up to like I'd wondered about her? My heart soared hoping we were on the same page when we looked back at our past together. Could we possibly have another chance together? One with a different ending? What did I have to lose at this point? I had to hope, but there were so many questions lingering between us.

And how should I answer her last comment? How do you tell someone the last few years of your life sucked? You'd married the wrong person and wished they were the one you married instead. Honesty was the best thing with her now. Nothing hidden or secret. She needed to hear the truth from me. No matter how girlie it sounded, I needed to speak from my heart.

"My life has been crazy over the last ten years. I made a big mistake getting married right after graduating college. I've finally put it all behind me now. I'm looking for a clean slate." I didn't want to bring up my divorce. Not yet anyway. So I decided to speak of my years with Natalie vaguely, not giving the full story away.

"I understand that all too well." A sorrowful look spilled from her eyes as they gazed at me. They reflected a life laced with sadness.

"Maybe we should think of new beginnings. Whatta you say?" I tried to cheer her up. Hell, I needed to do the same thing too.

"Sounds nice." A forced smile spread across her face. "Actually, it sounds perfect."

I watched as her head tilted down toward her drink. Her smile faded and something deep within me ached to know what caused this beautiful woman so much heartache.

"I have to say I was surprised when Dave told me you were going to be here tonight." Her face turned up to me and her eyes were once again looking into mine. "Are you here on a long visit or something more permanent?"

"I've moved back for now." She wasn't divulging much and I didn't want to push. Though I wanted to know it all, the why's and what's, it was really none of my business. What we had together was a lifetime ago. We were kids back then. Right now I was really a stranger to her.

"Well, welcome back to Dallas," I said with the biggest grin my face could muster.

"Thanks. I appreciate that." She mirrored my smile and this time it didn't seem as forced. "It feels good to be back here."

As we sat grinning back and forth at each other, Dave arrived with my beer. Thank God, because damn I needed a drink.

"Here you go, Bradley." I reached for the beer he offered and had to stop myself from downing it in one big pull.

"Thanks. I hope our server can keep up with me tonight." Dave laughed but Kelly looked concerned. "I'm teasing, Kelly. It's just been an intense day. Having you here has made it better, though."

"Yeah, Bradley has had a day." Dave, now once again seated next to me, hit me on the back. I prayed he'd keep his big mouth shut about my divorce finalizing.

"Sorry to hear you've had a bad day, Bradley." Kelly spoke so sweetly. Her words wrapped around me like a hug.

"Thanks. My day's definitely improved since I walked in here." I lifted the bottle of Heineken in front of me toward the middle of the table. "Here's to old friends and unexpected reunions."

We clinked our drinks together and sipped, but my eyes never left Kelly's face. I couldn't put my finger on it but something was troubling her. Maybe it was being with our old group of friends, including me, her long ago ex. Or having curious eyes upon her followed by questions she wasn't ready to answer. Knowing Dave those questions were likely about to begin.

"Have you seen any of the old gang since you arrived back here?" Dave started in with the questions as I predicted.

"No one," she answered. "I've been laying low. But when Tina called and invited me tonight, I figured it was time to reconnect with my roots here. And the people who helped me love Dallas so much."

I watched Kelly closely as she spoke. She hit something deep down inside me when she uttered that last sentence. Maybe it was how her eyes sought mine and fixed on them intently. I really needed to contain what I was feeling for her. Hell, we hadn't talked to one another since we were kids. It's not like we could just pick up where we had left off. The thought of it seemed too impossible.

"You missed us didn't you?" Dave teased. "I know we've all missed you. Some more than others."

Damn him. Dave had to go there. But what he said was true. We'd all missed her and a few of the gals, mainly Tina, had blamed me for Kelly's distancing herself from everyone. But after the years passed, they realized that it'd been her husband who was keeping Kelly under lock and key. Other than a few phone calls with Tina, no one had any luck connecting with her.

But here she was... in front of me... no asshat husband in sight... a sight for sore eyes and my sore heart to be honest.

"I have missed you all. Some more than others too." She glanced toward me as she finished speaking but looked quickly back to Dave.

"I'm pretty sure you missed me the most, right?" Dave's words made us all laugh.

"It's true. You always made me laugh. Something that I'd almost forgotten how to do." Her mood shifted suddenly. The sadness resurfaced.

"Well, having you laugh tonight will be our main goal." Dave placed his hand across the top of her shoulder, a comforting gesture. "This gang of misfits knows how to have a good time. Right, Bradley?"

"We do," I agreed. "I think that's why we're still hanging out together on Thursday nights. It's like our church. Keeps us all going no matter what life throws our way."

"I can see that." Kelly's smile was back. "I'm glad I came. When will everyone else get here? Tina said she might be running a bit late."

"Tina's late is relative," I explained, looking at Dave for back up. "Usually, everyone is here by 7:30 Tina by eight."

"The guys get here on time for the most part. When the gals join us, the evening starts a little later," Dave said. I saw him looking up toward the door and waving his hand. "Looks like we have company."

I turned around to see Matthew and Bob heading our way. Their eyes lit up in surprise when they saw Kelly seated at the table with us. I was the only guy Dave had told about her coming tonight and I loved seeing their faces. Shocked didn't quite describe their reaction. They appeared almost as stunned as I had been. Matthew took quicker strides almost jogging toward the table after seeing her, so naturally he was the first to arrive.

Chapter 4: Kelly's Turn

"Holy shit. Who do we have here?" Matthew asked. "I swear she looks like our Kelly. A prettier version but still... Someone's been holding out on us. Dave?"

"Hi, Matthew. It's been a long, long time," I replied quickly. I hated being the center of attention but it was unavoidable tonight.

"Long? Try forever." He walked around to me. My palms started to perspire. I hoped I didn't have to stand up.

"Fourteen years," I heard Bradley say. Matthew scooted around the back of my chair and took the seat next to me. I breathed a sigh of relief. No standing after all.

"Hey, what about me?" Bob protested as he stood next to Bradley across the table. "Don't I get a hello?"

"Hi, Bob." I smiled up at him and realized he still had that sweet baby face from his high school days, minus a little hair on top. "Who could forget you?"

"God, Kelly, you look great. Really, I can't believe it. Haven't aged a day." Bob's sincerity was always his most endearing quality. So hearing his compliment made me feel like I didn't look too bad after all.

"Thanks, Bob. I appreciate it. And you still have that same sweet baby face I loved." Bob sat down next to Bradley. I was now surrounded by the guys I had been the closest with during high school. One was my first lover, the others were like brothers. It felt good to be with them. All the familiar feelings that I'd forgotten came rushing back to me. They warmed me up. Comforted me. Filled a void that was bigger than I had realized.

"So what's the deal, Kelly?" Matthew asked. "Besides being surprised, I'm also wondering what you're doing here. The last I heard you were living in Atlanta."

"I've moved back to Dallas for now." I had a feeling I would be repeating what the heck I was doing here all night. Maybe I should've written it all down, handed out a memo.

"No way." This time Bob chimed in. "Tell me you left that douchebag of a husband."

"For Christ's sake, Bob. Give her a break." Bradley admonished. "We haven't seen her in ages."

"No, it's okay. Really." I tried to smooth things over because I knew that Bob was right. Joe was a complete bastard. He controlled everything about my life, down to how I wore my hair. But no more.

"I'm sorry, Kelly. I didn't mean to be so crude but he never set right with me. What kind of man keeps his wife away from her best friends?"

"Well, if it makes you feel better. He's staying in Atlanta." I paused. "Permanently."

After I told them where Joe was, I looked across the table right into Bradley's blue eyes. His lips curled into a grin. A slight, no teeth showing grin, but he appeared pleased. And I was pleased that he was too.

"So tell us what you've been up to since high school." Dave brought up a loaded subject, my life over the last fourteen years. I had no idea where to begin. I decided to summarize as best as I could.

"Well, after my freshman year, I transferred to Emory University in Atlanta." I paused knowing where my story led, straight to Joe. "Joe graduated from Baylor and was accepted to Emory. I followed him there and we were married the summer after his first year of law school."

While I spoke, I avoided Bradley's eyes. My head refused to turn in his direction. I felt so uncomfortable talking about all of this now.

"The rest of the story is pretty simple. I became involved with Junior League, charity committee work, and focused on being the perfect wife." I'm pretty sure my bitterness wasn't hidden. "I succeeded at a few things, but failed miserably at one. Thus, I'm here now sitting with you all."

Funny how a little reality can throw a cold blanket on a fun evening. Several of the guys shifted in their chairs uncomfortably probably wondering how to respond to me. I thought I'd rescue them, change the subject.

"Enough about me. Tell me what you all are doing. I remember you all having pretty big plans after graduating high school." I glanced around the table. All eyes were on me and the look on each of their faces showed sympathy. I cringed thinking about what their reactions would be when they saw what I was hiding under the table.

Each one of the guys shared what they'd pursued as a career. They all had applied themselves and were living out their dreams. The only one left to share what they'd been up to was Bradley. Everyone got silent waiting for him to start, but he didn't look like he was beginning anytime soon. His head remained down toward the table as he fiddled with the label on his Heineken. His eyes were hidden, as an awkward silence seemed to grow. Thankfully, a woman's voice sounded out behind him breaking the tension.

"Hey, Kelly." It was Tina, all smiles and peppy energy. "I can't believe it! Look at you! Wow!"

"Hi, Tina!" How I'd missed all her enthusiasm. We'd cheered together back in high school. It was a gift of hers, making people smile. She walked over to me and I knew the moment was about to come. I'd be standing soon. My secret no longer hidden.

"I can't tell you how I've missed you. Give me a hug."

Her arms opened up to me. Reaching out in an invitation. All I had to do was stand, but my legs felt like lead, heavy and not co-operating. Finally, they started to flex and lift my body, awkwardly heavy in the middle as it adjusted to my new weight gain. I braced myself against the table and slowly rose. I braced my heart too.

Fully standing now, I saw Tina's shocked face. Her eyes were fixed on my stomach taking in my five-month baby bump. I'm fairly certain everyone's eyes at the table were doing the same. The silence was pretty damn loud actually. Even Matthew stopped mid-sentence.

Tina's eyes flew up to meet mine, but they were glistening. I think my hesitation for coming tonight was apparent now. It all made sense to her. Tina pulled me into a big hug, one that I gladly welcomed. Silly me, I felt the fear and tension of having my secret known leave me in the form of tears. Maybe they were tears of relief. I wasn't sure, but I couldn't stop them now if I tried.

Tina pushed away from me slightly and looked into my eyes. Hers spoke to me without a word. She understood. I'd left my husband, pregnant. Who does something like that? God, my story was long and screwed up. Somehow I'd have to stick with the condensed version tonight.

"Hey guys, " Tina said. "I think Kelly and I need a minute here. Will you all excuse us?"

"Sure," I heard Bradley reply. He spoke softly. Even with one word, I heard his concern.

"Come on, Kelly." Tina placed her hand around my shoulders and started to steer me toward the restroom signs nearby. But I hated to leave the guys with so much drama. It was a fact that I'd have to face, a pretty damn obvious one. So I tried to throw out a little joke before heading off with Tina.

"Don't worry guys. It'll all be worked out in four months." A few nervous laughs followed, but Bradley looked at me. He said nothing out loud, but his compassionate gaze soothed my heart. He looked like he wanted to be the one with his arms around me. Something unspoken passed between us and I knew he'd be there for me. It was as if he said aloud, "Kelly, I'm here for you."

I turned my head and smiled up at Tina. "Nothing like a dramatic hello after being MIA for fourteen years."

"Grand and shocking. Now I understand why you wanted to be the first one here tonight." She let out a nervous giggle. "I can't believe my mother didn't know. I guess yours has kept this secret. Has to be a first for her."

"I think she's in total denial that I left Joe, I'm pregnant and I'm divorcing him." I watched Tina open the bathroom door and followed her inside. "Not a great homecoming for her, or me really."

"No it's not." Tina grabbed a few tissues by the sink and handed them to me. "Here."

"Thanks." I wiped the tears from my eyes and glanced into the mirror. I was a flushed, bleary-eyed mess. "I guess you want to know what the hell happened right?"

"Only if you want to tell me the details," she said. "I'm curious, but mostly concerned about you. Are you okay?"

"As okay as can be expected." Then I began to share. "It's over between Joe and me. He's convinced that the baby isn't his. Even wanted me to, in his words, 'get rid of it.' So much for his being pro-life."

"No way." Tina's face was a troubled mix between disgust and shocked. "I knew he was a fake from day one. I mean, it is a choice, no doubt. But he's a hypocrite to ask that of you since he's been gearing up for years to run as a pro-life candidate for governor."

"What Joe lets the world see of him, is a façade. Nothing about his public side is real." I lowered my head. This shit was harder to confess than I'd thought. "After he asked me to get rid of the baby, I had to leave him. It was the last straw."

"You're really brave, Kelly. He controlled everything in your life. I'm sure you've felt all alone in your decision."

"I have. Not a single friend in Atlanta helped me. I left our house with only a suitcase. Most of my clothes didn't fit me anyway. I mailed some keepsakes from high school to my parents' house. Gifts that Bradley had given me, actually. Joe never knew the story behind them."

"Wow. You've been through hell." Her acknowledgment of my plight comforted me. Even my own mother didn't want to hear the details. She kept telling me to give Joe another chance, but all he was getting from me was a cold chance in hell.

"It's been intense and hard. I wake up in my parent's house each morning and wish I was eighteen again. Just graduating from high school. Then I try to get out of bed with this stomach of mine, and reality hits me."

"In all of it, Kelly, I'm proud of you. Joe has never deserved you and he sure as hell doesn't now."

"It's funny. As my plane took off for Dallas, I felt so relieved and free. No Joe sitting by me watching my every move. It was the first time in years I made a big decision for myself. And one that directly shoved my fist in Joe's face."

"No kidding," Tina agreed. "Has the bastard tried to talk to you?"

"He called my parents. I left my cell phone on the kitchen counter so he knew that he couldn't reach me that way."

"Nice. You thought of everything."

"Actually, I'd wanted to leave him for a long time, but I tried to stick it out. I'd made a commitment to him. Better or worse. But his worse became more than I could stand."

"So have you talked to him?"

"After calling my parents relentlessly, I finally decided to speak to him." I lowered my head and trembled slightly as I remembered Joe's words. "He called me every name in the book. Told me that he'd been having an affair with his co-worker for years and he'd never give me a dime in a divorce. Basically that he'd make my life hell."

"He told you all of that?" I nodded my head in confirmation. "That had to hurt."

"His words didn't faze me. I felt nothing when he told me. My feelings toward him are gone." I took a short breath and leaned against the sink's countertop. "I don't even hate him anymore. I was furious at one time, before I left, but now there's nothing there."

"I'm so sorry, Kelly. I can't believe what you're going through." Tina placed her hand over mine. "I want you to know you aren't going through this alone. I'm here for you. Anything you need. Just ask. Okay?"

"You don't know how much those words mean to me. I've been a terrible friend to you and here you are giving me your support. Thanks." Now I was crying again. What a mess.

I found myself in Tina's arms once again. She held me tightly and told me everything would be okay. I hoped to hell she was right. I decided to have faith in her faith. Mine was completely spent.

"Let's freshen up your face and head back to the table. I know you haven't seen these guys in years, but they're all wonderful men now. They're like my brothers. I know they'll band together and be there for you."

"They really are a great guys. I think I probably freaked them out though. I'd been hiding in my chair since Bradley and Dave arrived."

My eyes turned to the mirror and what I saw reflecting back at me would scare them even more.

"Look at me. I'm a complete mess." I turned to Tina. "Do you have any powder? Maybe some lipstick?"

"What southern girl leaves home without her powder and lipstick?" We giggled at her remark. It was funny and true. She reached in her purse and handed me the makeup.

"I feel better now that we've talked. I've held everything in since I decided to leave Joe. No one has wanted to listen to me. My friends in Atlanta wouldn't return my calls or emails." I laid the makeup down and squeezed her hand gently to emphasize my words. "I appreciate your being here for me."

"I'm here for the long haul." She softly patted my belly. "You're going to need a few extra hands around to help you when this little one's born."

"It's overwhelming when I stop and think about raising this child on my own. I don't have a job here and no one will hire me in this condition. At least my parents are letting me stay with them."

I quickly dusted my face with her powder. It calmed down the angry red splotches left from my crying. My bloodshot eyes were another story.

"Your parents will come around," Tina said encouragingly. "They just need a little bit of time, Kelly. Our folks are set in their ways. It takes them awhile to accept the curves and bumps in life."

"I hope you're right. They've started to see what a jerk Joe really is. He's withholding money from me. Making all kinds of excuses. Remind me never to marry an attorney again."

"Speaking of attorneys," she began. I looked at her puzzled. "Dave told me this afternoon that Bradley finalized his divorce today. It's been a long, hard year for him. Actually, the last few have been. Unfortunately, you two have a lot in common. But one thing is different, he had a good attorney. Something you need a.s.a.p."

"Joe wants us to use the same attorney in Atlanta. I know he's railroading me, but I don't have access to any of our accounts. No money means I can't afford my own."

"We'll figure this all out. Trust me. Once the guys know what you're going through, they'll start pulling some strings. Before long, Joe won't know what hit him." Tina started walking to the door. "Let's get back out there and join the Love Handles, whatta you say?"

"Sounds good. Though I'm not sure what to tell them."

"Leave that to me if you'd like. I can get the subject started and rescue you if need be."

"That'd be great. Thanks."

I started to follow Tina out the door, but stopped in my tracks when I spotted Bradley leaning against the wall opposite the door's opening. His hands pushed deep into his front pockets as his eyes searched my face, looking for some direction I think. There was only one direction for me, toward him.

My feet moved to him as if they had no choice. A feeling of deja vu flashed through my mind. We had similar meetings in the halls of Highland Park High; Bradley waiting for me outside my classes after the bell rang. Everything in me wanted to pretend that we were back there one more time, innocent to all life's pains and struggles. But when Bradley glanced at my belly, I was quickly reminded that I was a thirty-three-year-old pregnant woman who'd left her husband. Nowhere close to the young girl of my youth.

"I think I'll head back to the table. Let you two talk," Tina stated. Turning my head toward her I gave a quick smile of thanks, but she was gone before I could speak a reply.

"So," I said with a shy glance to the side. My eyes returned to the floor between us.

'So," Bradley echoed. We were back to the same silly awkwardness we had when Dave left us alone earlier.

My head was still tilted down. I wasn't brave enough to face him eye to eye yet. I needed to muster up some courage quickly. There was no escaping him now. We were standing so close to one another. I could even hear him breathing.

I saw Bradley's hands reaching for mine right before they touched me. He curled his fingers around mine and gently shook them. He wanted my attention, so I looked up to find his eyes. Those beautiful blue eyes. A calm sea of blue for me.

And mine then filled with tears. A sea of a different kind. Tumultuous. I felt the tears falling down my cheeks. What was wrong with me tonight? I couldn't hold my feelings in no matter how hard I tried. I was an emotional wreck. But Bradley didn't seem to care. He brought his thumbs to my cheeks and gently wiped away the trail of my tears.

"Kelly, I'm so sorry. For everything." His voice cracked and I tried to see him clearly through the clouds in my eyes. But it looked like his eyes were swimming like mine.

I was too upset to utter a single word and he must have known, because he drew me to him. A large solid wall that cushioned me like a pillow as I sank against him. My tears now turned to sobs. I shook with the weight of my feelings. His hand rubbed my back in slow comforting circles as he quietly spoke soothing words. Telling me that everything would be all right. I melted further into him as he whispered to me.

After a few minutes in his arms, every tense muscle I had gave way and a deep sigh escaped my lips. I circled my arms around his waist relishing in him. He felt so damn good. It felt so good to have someone strong to lean on. Strong. In control.

His words, his arms, his comfort... They were the solace I needed and craved.

As I relaxed, the tears stopped flowing and I felt my body start to still. After a few deep breaths, I peered up into his eyes to find him looking warmly at me.

Chapter 5: Bradley's Turn

My arms wrapped around Kelly's tiny body. She seemed so fragile. I was afraid to hold her too tightly as she was the first pregnant woman I'd ever held this close. I'd often dreamt of having her in my arms again, though this may not have been the exact scenario. But being here to calm her trembling body as she sobbed into my chest, well, there was no other place I wanted to be. My place was right here with her.

As she cried, I wondered what had led her here. What made her leave Joe while being pregnant? Honestly, I was as mad as hell that she was hurting and alone. She didn't seem like the kind of woman who would separate from the father of her child without a good reason. I wondered what the bastard had done to her. My mind raced with possibilities.

I reined in my angry thoughts to focus on what she needed right now. I wanted to do something, anything, to make her pain go away. I wouldn't let her down this time. I just prayed she'd give me a chance to help even if only as a friend. I couldn't expect anything more.

Finally, she stirred and her face turned up to mine. I smiled down at her, trying to assure her that she was welcome in my arms. I loved having her so close, but she was wreaking havoc on me physically. I tried to ignore the softness of her breasts pressed against my chest. The sweet scent of her perfume. Her hands wrapped around my waist. God, she was killing me and I couldn't push all the lustful thoughts out of my mind. It had been well over a year since I'd had a woman in my arms. And she wasn't just any woman. She was the one I'd missed and hated myself for losing.

I wanted to kiss her tear-stained cheeks. Feel her soft lips against mine. I felt myself getting hard as my thoughts continued down a dangerous path. Damn, I shouldn't have been thinking like that. Kelly needed a friend not a man wanting in her pants. Somehow, I had to stop my body's reaction to her. She was pregnant and hurting, surely, I had enough character somewhere deep inside to stop myself from lusting after her. Though my yearlong celibacy wasn't helping one bit either.

Thankfully, she pulled slightly away from me, her body no longer making direct contact with mine. But then I realized her hands were gripping my waist tightly. Too damn close to where my body wanted her. Still, I could breathe a little, calm my shit down hopefully.

"I'm so sorry, Bradley. I don't know what's wrong with me. I'm not usually a crier," Kelly finally spoke. I was relieved she'd calmed down enough to talk. I felt her hands move from my waist then watched her fingers rub beneath her eyes.

"No apologies needed. I'm glad I can be here for you." I wanted to add, "Like I should've been years ago," but let it drop. That talk would come later hopefully.

"I'm sure I look an absolute mess." She bowed her head like she was trying to hide from me. "Great impression right?"

"Like I said, no apologies, no worries." I lifted her chin up with my fingers making eye contact. She needed to see that I was serious about what I said. "And you've never looked more beautiful to me."

"Oh, Bradley, you can't say things like that and expect me not to start crying again." Her eyes started filling with tears again. "It's been years since I've heard someone call me beautiful."

Years? You had to be kidding me... That jerk of a husband. He had no idea what he had in her. I felt the anger resurfacing that I had shoved aside. Joe was a bastard. No other word for him. This woman needed to hear that she was a beauty every single day.

"I don't know what you've been through, but it sounds like you've experienced a little bit of hell."

"You have no idea. But it's over now. Thank God." She glanced at her stomach. "Well, it's not all over really. I can deal with what's ahead now, though."

A couple of women walked by us as they headed to the restrooms. Their faces showed concern, probably wondering what was going on between Kelly and me. I smiled and tipped my head their way to give them a little reassurance that everything was okay.

"You're a brave woman to be facing..." I glanced to her stomach, "everything on your own. I have an idea. Did you drive here?"

"I did," she replied. "I borrowed my parents' car. Just like I was sixteen again." She laughed almost seeming embarrassed.

"Dave brought me tonight. I was planning on having a few drinks, but I was thinking maybe we could go back to my house. I have some steaks I could throw on the grill. How does that sound?"

"I don't know." Kelly hesitated and pulled her pouty lower lip between her teeth. Damn if it didn't turn me on.

"We could sit out on my deck. Enjoy the nice spring evening and catch up." I was pulling out all the stops and holding my breath that she'd say yes. I'd get down on my knees and beg if I had to.

"Well, I do feel a little spent and maybe not up for a big group after all. All these crazy emotions of mine…" She focused intensely on my eyes before continuing. "I do feel better talking with you, though. You always got me, Bradley. I never had to explain myself to you. And God knows I could really use a friend like that now."

"Same back to you, beautiful." Without thinking, I let my fingers push a stray strand of her hair away from her cheeks. Those soft, tear-stained cheeks. It took all I had not to pull her to me again. However, I think her use of the word "friend" made me realize that we had to cross that bridge first… becoming friends again after so many years apart, but I had a feeling we were well on our way.

"Thanks, Bradley." She smiled sweetly at me. I swore my heart skipped a beat. She was killing me and I loved it.

"Why don't we stop back by the table, speak to the gang, and then…" Kelly interrupted me before I finished my sentence.

"Head out like a baby?" She said then started to laugh, the "I can't stop" kind. And I joined in too.

"Damn," was all I could get out as we laughed together. I think it was just what she needed too.

I followed her to the table as she walked my hand pressed against the small of her back. My fingers lightly rubbed her and she didn't seem to mind. She glanced to the side and gave me a big smile. It was a smile to let me know that she was doing all right now. I hoped that my encouragement gave her a little strength.

Matthew was the first one to see us as we moved closer. His face perked up and a sense of relief was evident on it. "Hey, guys," he said as we stood by the table. Kelly didn't take a seat so I was following her lead and remained on my feet.

"Hey," Kelly said back. "Sorry about all the drama. It wasn't my finest moment. I thought I was better prepared for..."

"No need to explain, Kelly," Matthew interjected. "Tina gave us a quick rundown. And I can speak for each one of the guys here and say we're going to do everything possible to help you.

"Wow, you don't know how much I appreciate it. I can't even begin to tell you. For the first time in months, I don't feel alone in all of this."

Kelly's voice faded away at the end and I worried she was going to cry again. But she turned her head my way and smiled after she spoke. She was okay. I think she just needed her old friends around her showing her they cared and supported her. No woman should go through this alone and now she knew that she wouldn't be facing it by herself. We were there for her.

"Would you all be upset if we bugged out?" I looked at all the faces around the table and watched big smiles appear. Yeah, they were probably thinking what I was hoping... Kelly and I back together once again. Just like old times.

"Of course not," Tina replied. "We can all catch up later this weekend. Remember, I'm having you all over to my house. Pool opening."

"Oh, I forgot about that." I winced knowing the divorce finalizing had occupied my mind more than it should have. "I plan on being there."

"Kelly, I hope you can come too," Tina said. "I was going to ask you tonight. Saturday night around seven. Hamburgers on the grill by the pool. It'll still be too cold to swim."

"Thanks, Tina, I'd love to come. But I don't think I'll let myself be seen in a swimsuit anytime soon," Kelly responded.

"I'm glad you can come and don't even think about the bathing suit," Tina continued. "You look terrific. Right guys?"

Tina looked straight at me and winked. She knew exactly what she was up to. All the guys chimed in and agreed with her. All the compliments must have been good for Kelly as she beamed. I had a feeling her self-esteem was shot and I think this group of friends was just what she needed to rebuild it.

"Aw, thanks," Kelly said sheepishly. "You sure know how to make a girl feel good."

"It's true, Kelly," Tina chimed in. "I was a swollen mess at the end of my first trimester. You're only showing in your tummy."

"For now, maybe, but I have a feeling things are going to change."

I felt it was time to take our leave, so I spoke up. "Kelly, you ready?" I asked. "I've got some steaks with our names on them back at the house."

"Wow, look at you Bradley," Dave nearly shouted. I gave him a not too gentle or subtle punch on the arm to get him to shut up. After watching him flinch, I was pretty sure he got the message.

"Sorry, just kidding," he tried covering his tracks. Whatever. He teases all the time, but this was a little too much for me, and likely Kelly too.

"I'm rescuing her from all of you guys for the night." I had to laugh. Kelly laughed too. Thank God.

"I think we have a lot to talk about too." Kelly's eyes looked into mine as if she wanted to say more and I hoped she'd have a chance to later.

Finally, Tina came to our rescue and spoke up, " You all enjoy yourselves. How about we do lunch tomorrow, Kelly?"

"Sure," Kelly replied. "I'd love to."

"Let's meet at Cafe Pacific in Highland Park Village about noon."

"Sounds great. I love that place and haven't been there in years."

Kelly stopped and scanned the table, stopping at each one of the guys sitting there. I think we could all tell that she had something more to say.

"Thanks for all your support tonight. I was super nervous about everyone's reaction to seeing me, especially being in this condition." She looked down at her stomach but kept her smile intact.

"I'm so glad you came tonight, Kelly. You can count on us too. No way we'll let you go through this alone." Dave smiled reassuringly at her.

She placed her hand on Dave's shoulder and bent down to kiss his cheek, which instantly turned red. Who knew old Dave could blush? I had to laugh.

"You're so sweet," Kelly said to Dave as she teasingly ruffled her hands through his hair. I think having her here was good for everyone, not just her.

After another round of goodbyes, we were finally heading to the door. My hand stayed placed on the small of her back the entire walk to the entrance. It was hard to believe how this day had turned around for me. I woke up with divorce papers on my mind, and now I felt the body heat against my palm of the only woman I'd ever truly loved. I couldn't imagine a better ending to this day and it wasn't even over yet.

Chapter 6: Kelly's Turn

Nearly eight weeks had passed since I saw Bradley at my first Love Handles gathering. That night was nerve racking, crazy and wonderful all mixed into one. In my mind, I still can see his face as he walked through the doors of the pub. He took my breath away then and still does now.

We'd left the pub early and went back to his house, a lovely home in Highland Park, not far from where he'd grown up. I knew that he'd done well for himself; Tina had told me a few bits and pieces over the years, nothing specific, though. I'd never asked questions either, as I didn't want to hear about him being happy with someone else. But I had no idea what he'd been doing to achieve the kind of wealth that a home like his would cost. It was phenomenal. Over the top beautiful. And big, Texas-sized big.

However, in all of its beauty the house seemed lonely to me. A big mansion with only him wandering around in it. The thought of this made me sad. All this achievement on his part, but no one to share it with. Perhaps that was why he wanted to bring me back to his house. He'd been alone for too long and seemed to enjoy having me there with him. He grilled up some delicious steaks and never let my drink get even half-empty. He was so attentive and caring. The sweet young boy I'd known had become a beautiful grown man. Thankfully, the sweet in him had never left or changed, though. He was the same Bradley that I remembered and adored.

After dinner, we sat silently on his patio by the pool, gazing off at the horizon's last fading rays of light. He gradually started to open up to me about his life as the last of the sun disappeared and twilight's darkness wrapped around us. Perhaps it shielded us from seeing each other's faces, protecting us as we spoke of our hurts and disappointments. Our dark days stayed there in the dark.

His failed marriage was the first topic he brought up. How it was doomed from the start. He'd met his now ex-wife in college. Her father owned a large defense contracting company in Dallas and needed a male heir to take over his company when he retired. His father-in-law felt his daughter wouldn't have been taken seriously in the male-dominated defense industry, but he'd thought Bradley had been a perfect fit, a natural born leader and sharp as a tack.

For Bradley it was a twofer, a wife and a company. For a young man getting out of school without a job secured, he caved and grabbed the carrot dangling in front of him. He swore there was never any true love between them. It started as a partnership and ended as a failed business agreement.

His share of the business had been substantial, as he'd helped to take the company public. Once that had happened, his personal portfolio had become worth millions. But his personal life had added up to nothing. And before long he and his wife were sleeping on opposites ends of the house. This part of his story was difficult to hear. I knew all too well what it was like living inside a passionless marriage. It left a person hollow with a sadness that couldn't be lifted. Memories of that hopeless feeling still haunted me.

He and I had been through some shitty years. We'd both married the wrong person and it had taken years for us to realize or admit to our mistake. I told him how Joe had been waiting for me when I arrived back at Baylor after leaving UT so many years ago. Mentioning that fateful day was difficult, I could feel the tension between us increase, but it had to be said. There was no moving forward without speaking about our past.

I softly spoke of the day I'd left him standing in his fraternity room. I told Bradley that I'd called Joe in tears as I tried to drive back to Waco. Joe almost talked me into pulling over and waiting for him to come get me, but somehow I'd pulled myself together and made the two-hour trip. Once he'd seen my car pull into my dormitory's parking space, he'd come running toward me full speed. My tears had started falling in streams again too. I found myself engulfed in his arms. He'd comforted me, hushed my whimpering sobs.

But now looking back at that young, vulnerable girl, I knew the truth about Joe's comfort. It was a cold and calculating love meant to get him what he wanted to possess... me. I'd never quite figured out why Joe decided that I was the girl for him. The one. The only. And once he'd put on his charms, I was really no match for him. I was sad and broken. He'd been too eager to fix me, so I'd let him. It became a pattern for us. Joe, deciding what was best. Joe dictating what I would do.

I remembered Bradley trying to apologize to me. He begged me actually, but I told him that we were both young and needed to look beyond that day. I shouldn't have run off, but I had. We each had regrets and if we were going to continue to be friends, I felt the past should be buried along with our past marriages. We needed to start our friendship or whatever we had anew.

Initially, I worried that our reconnecting was on overdrive, progressing far too fast. But after a couple weeks of trying to keep things between us as friends, I decided to give in and follow my heart, throw caution to the wind.

And I was so thankful that I did as it led me back into the arms of the most beautiful man I'd ever known. Every time we talked on the phone, exchanged texts, or got together in person, our relationship grew, became stronger. He was patient and didn't push me, and under the circumstances I found myself in, I appreciated his restraint. I could tell he wanted more between us from almost day one of our being back in each other's lives. However, it took me a little time to come around. I was pregnant, newly separated from Joe and facing a wall of problems trying to divorce him.

All my troubles, not to mention the pregnancy, didn't seem to bother Bradley. He took all the insanity I was dealing with in stride. He held my hand and encouraged me every time I felt like giving up, which happened countless times a day. He kept my head above water when I felt like I was drowning. I owed him so much... especially after today.

We were on a plane heading to Atlanta to have a meeting with Joe and his attorney. My stomach felt queasy at the thought of facing Joe again. It was D-Day for me, and Bradley too.

Joe had stalled on every attempt to settle our divorce quick and painlessly. He wanted me to suffer and his threats had become outrageous as my newly hired divorce attorney fought for me. My attorney said he'd dealt with many control freaks in his days, but he'd never seen anyone like Joe. His behavior was epic, apparently.

The first thing my attorney did for me was secure some funds for my living expenses. Legally, Joe was required to give me access to the accounts we'd shared when I left him. He had no right to take the money from our joint account and reopen it under his name only. Just because he had access to the money and could transfer it, didn't make it right in our case. Pretty stupid move on his part considering he was a lawyer too.

I really didn't care about the money too much, though. Sure, I needed some for the baby and myself, but I just didn't have any fight left in me. Maybe it was the struggles I'd had over the last few years being married to a harsh man. Trying to be the perfect wife. Hoping that he would notice me for who I was and not always trying to get me to be something I wasn't. Live up to some imaginary standard he had in his mind. Joe had basically worn me out, beaten up my confidence without raising a fist.

Ironically, Bradley knew all of this without my having to give him graphic details. It was unspoken between us. I'd been treated horribly and he wanted to right any wrongs he could, so I let him help with the divorce. Maybe he shouldn't have stepped in, but he insisted and I was truly thankful for his help. I couldn't do it on my own as exhaustion ruled me most days. Maybe it was the pregnancy and moving back home under the circumstances. I'm not even sure. I needed support from someone who cared about me, wanted what was best for me, and perhaps even still loved me.

Bradley and I hadn't brought that word up yet, but we loved being together. He said he loved my hair, my lips, and the sound of my voice. The list of what he loved about me and what I loved about him was long, pages long. We hadn't admitted to being "in love" with one another again. For me there was likely never a stop to the love I'd felt back fourteen years ago. It was always lying beneath the surface sometimes dormant, other times coming alive in my heart and mind as sweet memories came back to me.

But today I was the lucky one. Not only was he in my heart and mind, he was also seated beside me on our plane to Atlanta. I felt his fingers weave through mine and I opened my eyes to find him smiling reassuringly at me. He knew I was nervous today, petrified. I knew he was anxious too, but he wouldn't show it. He would be strong for me and I would be forever grateful to him.

"We should be landing in a few minutes," he said. His thumb lightly rubbing circles on the top of my hand. His touch soothed me, gave me strength.

"I figured we were close." I tried to smile back but I just couldn't find one in me without having to force it.

"Hey, it's going to be okay. I promise." His stare became more fixed, serious, as if he wanted to scare the worry away.

"You're right. We're prepared, but nothing could be worse than having this divorce drag on for years and years."

"I don't think Joe wants this divorce to drag on. He just wants you to cave. Give into his demands. He didn't figure on your having an army to back you up."

"True. I think he thought I'd be a pushover just like I'd been in our marriage." My eyes searched his face before I continued. "You've saved me in so many ways, Bradley."

"Likewise, beautiful." He brought my hand to his lips and gently kissed my knuckles. "I'm here for you and the baby. In all ways, if you want me to be. Remember that today when we're sitting across the table from Joe. I'm the one who cares for you. The one who lo—"

He stopped mid-word. A word that began with an "L" left unspoken on his tongue. I knew that word and wanted to hear him say it too. But I wouldn't ask or beg.

"Dammit, Kelly. I wanted to tell you how I truly felt about you when we were doing something special. Like staring at the starry sky while I held you on my deck by the pool. After today's meeting and this mess was over. Not like this when you're in turmoil."

"Your being here with me is special." I squeezed his hands hoping he'd continue on with what he was telling me. Those words he didn't say were the very words I longed for, and needed to hear.

"Okay then." He turned his body to me as much as he could in our cramped seats. Taking my other hand into his, he leaned his body toward me. We were whisper close to each other. His breaths became mine too. I prepared my heart for what he was about to say to me. I felt my eyes starting to glisten with tears.

"The very first time I saw you, I knew that there was something different about you. When you looked up at me, stared back into my eyes for the first time, I felt a special connection that's still there for me today." He paused slightly, taking a breath to continue on. "It never went away. It's like I carried around a piece of us, together, in my heart. My love for you was always there inside of me. Never dying and probably keeping me from loving anyone else. It's only been you, Kelly. Only you."

Damn pregnancy hormones. My eyes were spilling buckets of tears. One after the other, after the other. He brought his hands to my face, our fingers still entwined, and wiped the streams away. More tears followed, though, after he'd cleared them, so he brought his lips to my cheeks and began kissing the salty torrents. They all belonged to him now. His lips were tender as they caressed me, comforted me.

"I love you with all my heart, Kelly Parker." He went back to kissing my cheeks, but continued whispering to me. "You are the love of my life."

I needed to respond, but I could hardly catch my breath. His words. Oh, his sweet, sweet words. I could live on them like manna. They nourished me. Made me feel whole for the first time in years.

"Bradley, you are the love of my life too." His lips were on mine now. We had kissed a few times over the last few weeks, but nothing like this. The passion was intense. I wanted to crawl onto his lap and get lost in him. I didn't even care who saw us together. After a minute or a few seconds, who knows, I had to pull away to inhale a bit of air. His kisses left me lightheaded and dizzy.

"I love you," I panted trying to catch my breath. "No one but you."

"We can make this work," he said while using a spare cocktail napkin to wipe more tears from my face. "I want to make this work. For better, for worse. No matter what we face today. Do you understand what I'm trying to say?"

Holy shit. Did he mean marriage? I'm pretty sure he did, as some of his words were taken straight from the traditional wedding vow. I wasn't even officially divorced. It should have seemed wrong to even think about us together, married. But the thought, the sweet idea of us, together forever, well, I couldn't think of anything more I wanted in the whole wide world.

"I think I do," I replied. "The thought of not having you in my life to love and be with makes me feel ill. I need you, Bradley."

"You're mine, Kelly. Mine." His eyes appeared feral. An "I want to devour you" look came from them. I felt a quick shiver run down my spine. I desired this man like no other. I wanted to be his and wanted to make him mine too.

"I'm yours." My words were quietly spoken between us. Nothing more needed to be said. He placed his hand behind my neck, weaving his fingers into my hair and drew me to him for another kiss. His lips pressed hard and passionately to mine once again. Heat flashed through me. My breasts ached for his touch. My body hummed in its desire for him. Every cell of my being was on fire. In all the years I'd been married to Joe nothing came close. Nothing.

"Yes, mine." He pulled his lips away briefly to speak. But they were back, possessing me once again. We were shamelessly making out like teenagers in our seats. Our hands wandered everywhere they could without touching too intimately. I placed my fingers on the skin of his back beneath his shirt, going for broke, letting my fingernails rake over him. This time he was the one with shivers as I ran my nails across him slowly.

He mirrored my movements as he snaked his hand up my blouse. I was protected from view by his body and the windowed wall of the plane behind me, pinned in. The hand touching me was hidden as I leaned back into my seat with him bending over me. First, he was safely rubbing my back, exploring my skin with his touch. Then I felt him inching up toward my bra line in back.

It had been so long since a man had touched me like this. His exploring fingers, still undercover, slid around to my front. I felt him cupping my breast, cradling it in his hands. He slipped his finger into my bra's cup and pulled down the lace, freeing me. Finding my hard swollen nipple, he ran his thumb across it. His forefinger joined in and they gently worked together pinching and pulling. My breathing was out of control. I wanted this man. Needed this man. I started to moan quietly. The sound of my own voice startled me back to reality. We were on a plane. In public.

God, we needed to stop. Now. If no one had been around, our clothes would've been off in seconds. Thankfully, we were seated in the back of the first class area with a partition behind us. Private and hidden. The seats beside us were empty too. Only the poor flight attendant was likely getting the full show.

That thought made me release his lips and straighten up to look around. No one was watching us, thank God, but what were we doing? I straightened my top and my eyes found his. A worried look swept across his face. He brought his fingers to my cheek.

"I want you so much Kelly." He took a few deep breaths. We both needed to calm ourselves down. "I've never wanted anyone like this. I got a bit carried away."

"I feel the same. And, yes, we were a little out of control. But to be honest, I loved it." I giggled like a young schoolgirl. Actually, that's how I felt. Young and discovering love all over again. A heady feeling.

"Tonight," Bradley paused, getting my undivided attention. "We have two adjoining rooms at the hotel. I don't want you stepping a foot into yours. You'll be sleeping with me."

My heart skipped a beat. We had purposefully chosen to stay chaste as our relationship crossed beyond friends. Just a few stolen kisses here and there. For some reason, I thought it was best to wait until I was divorced. Add the baby to the mix and things got confusing fast. I wasn't sure how to handle being pregnant with one man's baby while making love to another. It was hard to wrap my head around that to be honest. Seemed a bit warped, but my whole life was twisted right now. A big mess. The only positives were Bradley and the precious baby growing inside of me.

But his kiss. His fingers on my breast. I was done with the worry and done for him too. I wanted him in ALL ways now. No holding back. We had years to make up for and nothing was going to stop me. So I guess sleeping with him tonight was a start. A long overdue one.

"I like the sound of that," I purred back at him. "What do you have in mind?"

"My lips everywhere on that sweet body of yours. My fingers following them." I shifted in my seat as the heat of his words set me back on fire.

"You're killing me," I whispered. "I'm about to come undone."

"Oh, believe me, you will later. I promise." His voice was raspy. "I can't wait to get my hands on you."

"I don't feel too sexy right now, though." I glanced down at my stomach pointing at my belly with my finger though I was sure he knew what I meant.

"You're as sexy as hell to me. Don't forget it." I cuddled into his sides after hearing his words.

Bradley has been so supportive of the baby and me. He's even gone with me to my last two doctor's appointments and laughed when they called him the baby's father. Never once had he corrected the nurse or doctor.

There was so much to think about today, though. Joe and his reaction to our meeting stayed on the forefront of my mind overshadowing everything. Joe had become our future's biggest obstacle. I felt my mood get serious as if a dark cloud had moved over us.

"What if Joe stalls? Doesn't agree to my attorney's offer?" Fear started to rise up inside me again. I couldn't help being afraid of Joe's reaction. I knew him. I'd seen him cut his adversaries down to nothing. He used his power as Deputy District Attorney to crush people, left them a whimpering mess. Hardened criminals feared him. A wayward pregnant wife was no match against his brutality. My hands started to perspire as I pictured seeing Joe again.

"Please don't get upset." Bradley said trying to soothe me. "I can see it in your eyes. You're going there again.

Remember we have the best in Dallas, paired with the best in Atlanta."

"You're right... I think." I was so confused. "I want to believe you, Bradley. You have no idea how much I do, but I lived with that man. I know what he's capable of. My leaving him wounded his pride. Embarrassed him. Joe doesn't do embarrassed."

"We have some arrows to shoot at him, Kelly," Bradley said reassuringly to me, making me remember the plan. "Ones that would be even more embarrassing to him. Remember, it's his political future now that's his main concern."

As I was getting ready to respond, I heard the flight attendant's voice over the intercom. "The captain has just turned on the 'fasten the seat belts' sign. All electronic devices must be turned off and stowed at this time. Seats and tray tables must be returned to their upright and locked positions as we prepare for landing. We should be on the ground in Atlanta in ten minutes."

"Hey, Kelly." Bradley's hand wrapped around mine. "Trust me when I tell you that it will all be okay. We'll walk out of that office with papers signed. Okay?"

"Okay." My answer wasn't that convincing, though.

After landing uneventfully and getting off the plane, we gathered our bags at the luggage carousel. My attorney from Dallas was flying on our plane too, even staying at the same hotel so he joined us as we waited for our bags to appear.

My doctor told me I'd be okay to fly, just to drink more than my normal amount of water, which led me to the next question for my escorts.

"I need to stop at the ladies' room before we get in the car to the hotel."

"Sure." I watched Bradley scanning for the nearest restrooms. "I think they're down this way."

He motioned to our right and reached for my hand. "We'll be right back, Jensen. Would you mind staying here with our bags?"

"No problem," Jensen answered. "I'll make a quick call and let our Atlanta office know we've arrived here on time."

We arrived back to find Jensen turned away from us, engaged in a deep and heated conversation. My heart started to pound when I heard him say Joe's name laced with disgust. My stomach felt nauseous. I knew it was a bad idea coming here. I wanted to back away from them. Run. To where I'm not sure. Bradley sensed my fear and before I could even move, he wrapped his arms around my trembling body. I heard him whisper into my ear.

"Kelly, it'll be okay. Please don't worry. Trust me."

All I could do was nod my head. Slowly Jensen turned around, maybe seeing us in his periphery, I wasn't sure. But he froze when he saw me standing there. He quickly looked into my eyes and then turned away to continue his conversation.

"Listen, Greg. I need to let you go. Thanks for giving me the heads up. I'll discuss this with my client." Jensen paused. Listening intently. The seconds ticked away and as they did I was dying inside.

"I agree. He doesn't have a leg to stand on really. I wish we could throw more at him too. But it will just delay things, so let's stick to the plan we agreed on." Jensen went silent.

What were they talking about? Was Joe's attorney's pulling out something fancy to use against me? My head started to swim and as I became faint, Bradley's two strong arms circled tighter around me, holding me up.

Jensen ended the call, then swearing and muttering under his breath, turned back to face us. I couldn't quite make out his words but I knew they meant trouble for me.

Trying not to imagine defeat was pretty much impossible, though.

"Let's head to our car. It's waiting for us outside." Jensen grabbed the handle of his luggage and pivoted toward the exit's sliding glass doors. Bradley and I did the same and followed dutifully behind.

The walk to the outside pick-up area seemed to take forever. I couldn't wait to know what Jensen had learned. I glanced at Bradley who was dragging both of our suitcases and he appeared as tense as I was. It was the unknown that was eating at us.

Jensen flagged a car holding up his name. The driver pulled the car up in front of us and jumped out of the driver's seat to handle our bags. Silently we climbed into the car. Jensen took the front seat while Bradley and I hurried into the backseat. Nothing was said until all the doors were shut.

"Here's the deal," Jensen finally started to explain. "Joe has decided to play hardball. We figured he would but his attorney's claiming he has an old prenuptial agreement that you signed, Kelly. Do you remember signing one?"

"What?" I felt like someone had slapped me in the face. A pre-nup? He had to be lying. "I don't remember signing anything like that."

"Do you remember signing anything before the wedding?" Jensen asked.

"I signed some papers related to his family's company. He told me they would protect me if anything happened to him. I'd be fine financially is what he told me."

My mind raced. I tried desperately to envision those papers again in my mind. It'd been a crazy time and I'd been right in the middle of last minute wedding plans. I think he'd even brought them to me at the country club when I was going over the guest headcount and seating.

"I'm worried that you signed something he can use against us. Our office here is emailing me a copy. They're just waiting for Joe's attorney to fax it over."

"Jensen, what in layman's terms does this mean?" Bradley questioned. "Will this affect what you're planning on presenting today?"

"I'm not sure yet. I'll know more when I get my hands on a copy of that fax. I still think we have the upper hand. Joe and his team have no idea that Kelly is coming today. They believe I'm here representing her in absentia.

"It's best that we stick to the plan no matter what happens with this crazy paper his council produces. When you walk in seven months pregnant, the game totally changes."

"Thanks, Jensen. It's hard to believe Joe has kept his lawyers in the dark about the baby. It's a game changer for sure." Bradley was pleased with what he heard.

I was still struggling, on the other hand. Maybe it was all those years living with a tyrant. Those kinds of memories fade slowly if at all. I knew what this man was capable of. I hadn't followed his orders to get rid of the baby. And when I'd left him... Well, no one leaves a man like Joe. He would be out for revenge and it was likely to get ugly.

Finally, the car pulled up to the hotel in the downtown area. I scooted out of the backseat and Jensen's hand reached to help me out of the car. Once on my feet, I knew Bradley was right behind me, felt his hand placed on the small of my back and then he found my hand. Our fingers once again intertwined. His touch gave me support. Reassured me.

"I'll have the bellhop take the bags to our rooms. We need to discuss what's going to happen again over a quick lunch. You all go ahead. Get Kelly out of the sun." Jensen seemed concerned about me. "They have a nice restaurant and it's usually quiet. I stay here when I'm visiting our Atlanta firm."

"Sounds good, but make sure they place Kelly's bags in my room. She'll be staying with me. That's protected information under the attorney client privilege, okay?" Bradley smirked.

"Got it." Jensen winked back at us.

Oh, great. Nothing like broadcasting that we're going to be sleeping together later. But I really couldn't think about that now. I needed to focus on the matter at hand. Getting out from under Joe's control once and for all, not about having sex with Bradley. God, could my day be anymore mixed up?

Bradley led me into the hotel. It had a beautiful lobby with shining marble and sparkling crystal light fixtures everywhere. There was a restaurant off to the side and we made our way toward it, walking together side by side. It felt like we were one and the same. A united front. I looked up at his face to find him gazing at me lovingly. His love was really all I needed today when it came down to it.

There was definitely something about this moment. It shook me. Woke me up and made me realize what was important. Bradley. My future and the baby. Until now, I'd lived my life on "what if's." Afraid to leave Joe. Paralyzed by fear. I was sick of being weak, so it was time to change, starting now. Somewhere I had the strength to fight this cruel man and I wasn't alone this time. I had the love of a beautiful man standing beside. As beautiful inside as out.

"You know what, Bradley?" I had his attention now. "I can do this, *we* can. No matter what happens, at the end of the day I have you. I can't ask for anything more."

Suddenly, I found myself pulled to the side in a corner next to some big tropical plant. With Bradley in front of me, I was likely hidden from view, which was good because the next thing I knew his lips were all over me.

Kissing my face, behind my ear, and up and down my neck. Oh good God, his lips on my neck. I hadn't felt them there in years. It was so intense. He had just a touch of scruff that tickled my skin. I was getting so worked up and felt hot all over. My knees wobbled as he made his way back up to my mouth. His arms were the only things supporting me. I can't believe how just a few kisses made me go mad. I'd probably combust later tonight.

His lips left mine and I moaned in protest. He cupped my face with his hands, holding me tenderly, preciously. Our eyes gazed into one another's. Words of love didn't need to be spoken because they were felt somewhere deep down inside. God, how I loved this man.

"I'm tempted to tell Jensen we're skipping lunch. Dammit, having you in my arms, kissing you, it's maddening." Bradley's hands left my face and moved to my waist, what little waist I had at seven months pregnant.

"I know, but we have so much riding on today. We need to keep our heads on straight and not get swept away. It's like we're teenagers again." I giggled and leaned into him, laying my head on his chest.

"You're right but it's tempting knowing we have a bed somewhere upstairs just waiting for us to ruffle it up."

Bradley hugged me quickly then led me into the restaurant. We entered just as Jensen arrived too. His eyebrows rose when he saw us. My face felt flushed and I'm sure I looked a bit dazed too. He was a smart man so I'm sure he figured out what we'd just been doing.

"You two need to get a room." Jensen joked. Who knew he had such a sense of humor? He'd been Mr. Play Hardball for weeks.

"Got one for later thanks," Bradley quipped back.

All I could do was roll my eyes as we followed the hostess to our table. Jensen had asked for something private, which seemed silly, as there were about ten people there. The place was practically empty. Jensen went over the plan again detail by detail. Nothing had changed really. His office said the prenuptial contained a clause about what I'd receive in a divorce if I committed adultery. I choked on those words. So did Bradley, especially knowing that Joe was the one that admitted to being a cheater.

Either way, Jensen said the settlement he'd put together would blow away anything Joe's attorneys would offer. Jensen had played this game before and I had to have faith in him. He'd done Bradley right and I had to believe he would do the same for me.

Chapter 7: Bradley's Turn

It was just before two and our scheduled showdown with Kelly's hopefully soon-to-be ex-husband. He was a royal ass for playing the pre-nup card at the last minute, which I guessed wasn't all that surprising considering whom we were dealing with. I'm sure he'd tricked her into signing all kinds of crazy things before they were married. Fucking jerk. I didn't use that word often as my father taught me it was best used when doing two things, moving furniture and the actual act. But Joe would be the exception to that rule and I'm sure my father would agree if he were still alive.

Jensen, Kelly and I rode up the elevator to Joe's attorney's office. We were quiet as we mentally prepared for what was ahead. Kelly had my hand in a death grip, but I loved her getting strength from me. However, I was more worried about her poor bottom lip as her teeth were constantly chewing on it.

"Hey, sweetie. Your lip," I whispered leaning toward her. "It needs a break." Her eyes went wide and she just smiled. I bent over and kissed her freed captive. Her lips were soft like silk. I pulled away quickly and eyed Jensen. He just rolled his eyes. I thought we were paying him to keep his thoughts to himself...

Once off the elevator, Jensen directed us to the attorney's office and opened the door. The place felt like a library with its dark wood-paneled walls. It reeked of wealth and made it rather obvious that Joe had invested in the best. Even though he was a paid public servant as a deputy district attorney, his family had deep pockets. Deep Old South money from what Jensen said.

We checked in at the reception desk where a young woman was seated. She informed us we were joining the other parties in a conference room and rose from her seat. We followed her down a long hallway with wooden floors. The clicks of our collective heels echoed off the surrounding walls. The sound was eerie as it broke the silence among us. I exchanged a glance with Kelly, trying to encourage her, as she appeared rattled. Holding her hand now was out of the question, Jensen warned us. No public displays of affection. Not even a simple touch. That one might prove to be hard especially if Kelly was floundering and needed my support.

After stopping in front of an expansive set of wood doors, the receptionist tapped on them. From inside the room, a man's voice spoke the words, "Please, come in." She opened both doors for us, and I watched them swing open wide practically hitting the wall behind them as our way was cleared.

A grand presentation appeared before us as we stood there staring into the conference room, one meant to intimidate and give them the upper hand, I'm sure.

The long side of the rectangle table was facing us and on the other side of it was Joe, sitting tall, sporting a dominating air and surrounded by his legal team. They looked us over impassively with papers placed purposefully in front of them their hands on the desk folded just waiting to make a move. They put up a good front, appearing ready and prepared, but then again so were we.

Kelly was protected from their full view as she stood behind Jensen and me, but when she walked around to a chair, I heard a couple gasps from the boys across the aisle. Yes, they saw Kelly and the time bomb she was carrying. I raised my head just in time to see them whispering angrily at Joe.

Just as we thought, he'd not said a word about the baby. What a bastard. Jensen was smart to keep the baby's existence a secret. But I still didn't get it. How could Joe deny his own child? It was unfathomable to me. Evil, actually.

I pulled a chair out for Kelly then Jensen sat between us, likely a good idea. I already wanted to give her a hug, hold her for a second, and let her know that I was here for her and that everything would be okay. I had to say it silently instead. She glanced over at me after we were all seated. I mouthed the words, "I love you" and she smiled weakly but seemed resolved. I think seeing all the feathers getting ruffled when she walked in signaled to her that we did indeed have Joe by the balls today.

"Good afternoon, gentlemen," Jensen started. "I'm Vince Jensen with Thomas and Martin law offices, the representative council for Kelly Parker Jefferies who is seated beside me. Also joining us is Bradley Dawson, a lifelong friend of Kelly's. Lastly, I'd like to mention another person here on our side of the table today, Joe Jeffries' and Kelly's unborn child."

I closely watched Joe as Jensen spoke each word. When my name came up, Joe fumed and moved in his seat. His lawyers had to hold him back as he tried to get up. I heard them tell Joe to calm down, pull himself together. He was creating quite a scene and then when the baby was mentioned, the baby he failed to tell his legal team about, his attorney once again spoke quietly to him. I could tell they were pissed. Likely felt deceived, as they should. Their well-laid plans now tumbled on the ground all around them. I quickly glanced at Kelly and winked. I felt victory in the air.

"What the hell is he doing here, Kelly?" Joe screamed as soon as Jensen finished his introduction. "Are you sleeping with him? I knew it. Leave me and run back to Dallas and him. Does he know what a whore you are?"

I was out of my chair instantly ready to fly across the table and pounce on Joe. Who did he think he was to call Kelly that? I wanted to pummel his face in, make him take back and regret every damn word he said. Jensen restrained me and told me to sit down or leave the room. I knew he was right but it took all my strength to control my anger. How dare he speak of Kelly like that? This time when I turned to her she was the one doing the encouraging.

"Bradley, please. Do what Jensen says." Her voice was shaky. I knew she was upset no matter what she was trying to tell me. "Please, it's all right."

"It's not all right," I answered back a little too loud. "But I'll keep my shit together for now. If there's anymore name calling though, all bets are off."

One of Joe's attorneys stood up and cleared his throat. "Would you mind if we had a few minutes with our client? A quick five. We have a comfortable lounge I can have Mindy escort you to."

"Certainly," Jensen replied.

The attorney who spoke came around to our side and shook Jensen's hand. "Matt Byers. I believe we spoke on the phone yesterday. As you can imagine we didn't know about the child. I'd like to speak to my client if you don't mind."

"No problems," Jensen again agreed. I was surprised to see such a change in the attorney's demeanor. He appeared so assured and ready for battle at first glance, but now he seemed ready to retreat.

Byers leaned over the table, and pushed a couple buttons on the phone in front of him. He spoke to Mindy, who I assume was the receptionist who'd escorted us to the conference room. I guessed correctly when the room's doors opened and Mindy appeared. Once again we followed her to a swanky lounge with a couple of couches and a desk. After she left, Jensen was the first to speak.

"We need to keep our voices down in here. No strategy talk at all. I don't trust them. Who knows if the room has hidden mics?" Jensen scanned around the room. His eyes stopped on a large contraption sitting on the wet bar's counter.

"I'm going to make some coffee. You behave," Jensen said to us before heading toward the coffee machine.

"How are you doing?" I searched Kelly's face, looking for any signs to tell me how she was holding up. Under the circumstances she appeared all right.

"It's funny. You'd think I'd be frazzled and upset after Joe called me a whore. For Pete's sake, I never was anything but faithful. His outburst showed me how awful a human being he is. Convinced me that I'm, or we're, doing the right thing. I hope this is the last time I see him or have to deal with him ever again."

"I pray so too, Kelly." I stuffed my hands in my pockets because they didn't want to behave at all. They itched to touch her but I had to play it cool.

As Jensen walked toward us, Mindy entered the lounge area and announced that we were wanted back in the conference room. The break was super quick and I wondered if they were able to calm Joe down and get him to be halfway reasonable. I'm sure his attorneys were shocked as hell when Kelly walked in. It was our trump card and I think we played it well. Now off for round two.

When we arrived back at the conference room the mood was different and somber. Joe looked like his legal team had taken him to the woodshed. The proud peacock that'd confronted us with his feathers puffed out was nowhere to be found. Instead, he held his head low avoiding eye contact as we sat down, once again, across from him.

"Thanks for allowing the break. We understand that both of the parties were aware of the child before their separation so there isn't a failure of disclosure on your client's part." Byers, Joe's main attorney went right to the point. His client hadn't told him about the baby and it wasn't Kelly's responsibility to disclose it. The blame lay right at Joe's feet. Actually, the whole damn mess did.

"That is correct," Jensen replied. "We came prepared today to offer a settlement. We have laid out the terms and conditions. I'll pass around the papers."

Jensen stood up, took out a folder from his briefcase and shuffled through some papers. He passed out the settlement agreement he hoped Joe would agree on. My hands started to perspire as my eyes found Kelly's. She gave me a halfhearted smile and I returned it as best I could. So much was at stake here, her future, the baby's, and ours together.

Once everyone had the papers in front of them, the seconds turned into minutes as Joe's legal team absorbed the offer in front them. It was straightforward and to the point. A set dollar amount. No maintenance or alimony for Kelly. No long term pay-offs from Joe.

All he had to do was sign the documents and write a check, but I knew nothing would ever be that simple when dealing with this man and his ego. I'd known plenty of jerks like him in my life. They liked to make people pay when they felt wronged. Then add all the zeros behind the number one... I was certain Joe would make Kelly sweat before he signed

"Before we discuss the financial part of this settlement, I'd like clarification on Mr. Jeffries giving up any parental rights to his unborn child. In the State of Georgia, the juvenile court will not allow this type of separation if the mother is planning on raising the child by herself." Byers' eyes shifted to me. "Another man would have to be seeking to adopt the child with the mother. The State doesn't want to be burdened down the road for the child in the event the mother can't provide financially for the child."

"An understandable concern," Jensen replied. "We have legal documents prepared by my offices here in Atlanta that petition the court for Bradley Dawson's adoption of the unborn child. He intends to raise the child as his own in partnership with Kelly Parker Jeffries."

The room went quiet again. Joe's hands clenched into fists. His knuckles were white and jaunting out toward the ceiling. He looked ready to come undone and I prepared myself for the announcement of another break being needed to calm him down. And I was right.

"We will need some time to with our client to discuss this. Perhaps we can meet again in a few days?"

"Unfortunately, this offer is for today only. The financial settlement outlined in the offer will double if there isn't an agreement today." Smartly, Jensen foresaw the potential delay and had a document ready to prove his point if needed.

"Fair enough. It says the juvenile proceedings for Mr. Jeffries' revocation of parental rights will be sealed. Is this correct?"

"That is correct. All the proceedings and documents supporting our legal actions will be sealed where the child is involved. We will also petition the court to seal the records of the divorce settlement since they make reference of the unborn child."

"If you all wouldn't mind waiting in the lounge again?" Byers asked. "You might want to make yourself comfortable as this discussion may take some time."

"No problem," Jensen replied.

And off we went to the lounge again. Kelly and I followed behind Jensen and this time my hands reached for her as we walked down the hall. At this point, the cat was out of the bag. They all knew my intentions. I wanted the baby as my own, and even though it wasn't discussed, they had to know that I felt the same way about Kelly.

"What do you think Bradley?" Kelly asked me, her eyes looking up into mine. "Joe seemed fit to be tied?"

"He doesn't want the baby. We know that for a fact. But he probably doesn't like the thought of another man, especially me, taking his place. It's crazy and doesn't make any sense. But his pride and reputation as a man has been called on the carpet."

"True," Kelly agreed. "His attorneys are getting to see the real Joe. And it's a pretty damn ugly show. Thanks for being here for me and the baby."

"I'm just a man hopelessly in love with you." I placed my hands on her stomach. "And this little one too. You can count on me, darling."

We sat next to each other on the couch, pretty much ignoring the fact that Jensen was in the room with us. Kelly's head rested on my shoulder. I felt her exhale a deep breath, and her body relaxed against mine as she did. I leaned my head against the top of hers.

Chapter 8: Kelly's Turn

A little over an hour after we made the trip into the lounge, Mindy appeared and said we were wanted back in the conference room. Finally. I wanted to get this whole thing over with. *Now.*

I'd drifted off a couple of times as I wedged myself into Bradley's side as we cuddled on the couch. His warmth and protection made me feel safe enough to succumb to a quick snooze. My body was exhausted from the travel and emotions of the day, but I felt refreshed, ready to see what Joe's attorneys thought of our offer.

This time Bradley and I walked into the conference room together, hand in hand. There was no need to hide what we felt for each other. He was willing to adopt my baby. Only someone in love with me would be willing to do that, right? I knew when he agreed to be the father if Joe gave up his rights that it meant love on his part. He lifted and buoyed me above my fears when he declared his love for me on the plane ride here. And the love I felt for this man was overwhelming. Mere words couldn't express what I felt. I guess I'd have to show him later. *There goes my horny brain again.* I needed to make it heel as my energies needed to be dedicated to the task at hand—Joe's signature on the damn divorce offer.

We settled into our seats again. It was clear that our opponents had something on their mind to share. It was as if they couldn't wait for us to sit down. Byers began before I had thoroughly scooted my chair to the table.

"After reading over your offer and discussing it thoroughly with our client, we have a few points to discuss and clarify." Byers waited for our response.

"I'd be surprised if you didn't," Jensen answered.

"Firstly, my client will agree to the financial figure as long as he will have nothing pending in the future to pay Mrs. Jeffries. Correct?"

"That is correct. If he agrees to the settlement, pending the court's approval of course, he will have no further monies due to my client. There will be no recourse available for changes either." Jensen summed up what I knew to be correct.

"We have advised our client to agree to the financial settlement offer. However, there is a concern about the unborn child." Byers paused and glanced sideways at Joe perhaps needing an okay to continue on. "Mr. Jeffries will give up his rights to the unborn child on one account. Mrs. Jeffries needs to make a public statement concerning the reason she left Joe."

"A public statement?" Jensen asked interrupting Byers.

"Yes, Mr. Jeffries is concerned about the political fallout of his divorce and the speculation some might have about the unborn child Mrs. Jeffries is carrying." Byers stopped and swallowed. It looked as if whatever he was about to say required effort on his part. Likewise, I prepared myself for what was coming from him too. "He has requested Mrs. Jeffries release a public statement, a press release would suffice, in which she admits to leaving him for Bradley Dawson and that Mr. Dawson is the child's father."

"What?" Jensen practically yelled. "You're asking my client to publicly humiliate herself and admit to adultery. Which, by the way, is one thing your client just might be guilty of himself."

"Yes, we have advised our client against this course of action, but Mr. Jeffries remains steadfast in his request, or should I say demand." Byers couldn't hide the disgust he felt for Joe.

Jensen had reared back in his chair and Bradley was standing up ready to take on Joe, but I had a secret weapon that neither of them knew about, one that would turn Joe's world upside down if I chose to use it. The time to lay down my cards had arrived.

I stood next to Bradley and placed my hand on his shoulder. He looked surprised that I was standing next to him. But it was my turn to play hardball now.

"Bradley and Jensen," I spoke to them. My voice was steady. "I have something to say to Joe that will likely clear this whole mess up. Please sit down and let me talk."

"Kelly, are you sure?" Bradley asked with a confused look on his face.

"Yes, I'm sure. Trust me," I replied.

Both Bradley and Jensen hesitantly took their seats for me. They both sat on the edge of their chairs ready to take my defense on a moment's notice. I smiled reassuringly at them. I didn't relish in what I was about to do, but Joe, being the pig that he was, had left me no other choice.

"What I'm about to say to you Joe is difficult for me to utter. It's hard to admit the man I married would behave the way you did toward your own child knowing I wanted to keep it." I took a deep breath. Joe was now sitting on the edge of his chair too. I had his undivided attention now.

"I have already prepared a press release related to the child." I swear I heard a couple of gasps, but I kept on speaking, not deterred. "A dear friend in Dallas owns a PR firm and has a press release prepared for me. All I have to do is text her, 'GO,' and she will release it to all strategic media in Georgia and around the country for that matter."

Boy, did I have their attention now. No one, especially Joe, moved a muscle. It was like my words put them in a trance and kept them spellbound.

"I'd like to read you the statement that will be released if you don't agree to what my attorney has stipulated in my divorce offer."

I cleared my throat and pulled a paper out of my purse. It was folded over a couple of times, so perhaps it didn't appear too scary and definitely not professional. But the punch from what I was about to read would flatten Joe to the floor. I'm pretty sure he didn't think I had it in me. Well, he was about to learn otherwise.

"Kelly Parker Jeffries, wife of Joseph Jeffries, the current Deputy District Attorney for Cook County in Atlanta, has chosen to end her fourteen-year marriage to Mr. Jeffries. Mrs. Jeffries left her husband after he found out she was carrying their child and insisted that she terminate the pregnancy. The previous statement can be substantiated by an email conversation from Joe Jeffries to Kelly Jeffries."

I let the paper drop from my fingers as I finished reading it. The paper landed softly but the words hit like a bomb. My head rose from watching the white paper fall to see Joe's white face. He was a ghost or looked as if he'd seen one. Spooked.

One of his attorney's lips quirked into almost a smile. He nodded his head at me as if he was my ally and with Joe as a client he likely was one.

"Well, this makes things a little different now, doesn't it Joe?" I heard the sarcasm in Bradley's voice. His distain for Joe sounded out strong.

"Unfortunately for my client, I'll have to agree." Byers spoke and leaned into Joe, whispering in his ear. Joe remained pale, and I almost became worried about him… almost.

"Kelly, I wish you would have disclosed this little PR move to me," Jensen said but his smile gave away his true feelings. I think he might have been a little impressed. It definitely wasn't what he had seen in me prior to today. Thank God Tina owned a PR firm. She'd helped me concoct this whole plan. She was the genius behind it all really. I just had to have the gumption to use it if needed.

"Sorry, but I thought I'd keep it secret. I really hoped I wouldn't need to bring it out into the open. It's hard to admit I was married to such a man," I half-whispered to Jensen not wanting the other side of the table to hear me.

"Either way, you've got him by the balls, Kelly." Bradley held my hand tight. "Look at them all over there. Joe's getting a come to Jesus talk from his attorneys right now. Guy looks like he's about to puke too."

"He does, doesn't he?" I said and turned back to look at my beautiful man. "I think it's over, Bradley. He'll do anything he can to cover himself publicly. He has an image to uphold after all."

My side of the table sat silently, watching Joe implode in front of us. It didn't take long for him to come around, though. They knew I was in my perfect right to disclose the truth behind Joe's reaction to my pregnancy. And since he was a pro-life, family values political figure, his days were over in politics if the press release was circulated.

"All right, Jensen. My client will sign the settlement today. As soon as it's filed with the courts and approved, we will transfer funds into Mrs. Jeffries', I should say Ms. Parker's account as the agreement also restores her maiden name."

I watched Joe sign a paper and then his attorneys signed too. It was over. The feeling of being free was almost euphoric, heady. Bradley pulled me to my feet and wrapped his big arms around me and for some strange reason I began to cry, sob really. I think it was relief. All the feelings and fears over what I'd been through came together and were released like a break in a dam. Tears of sweet relief.

"Oh, babe. It's all right and it's over." Bradley's words soothed my soul and helped me quit crying. My life was set on a different course now. Love and commitment. It was ours.

"You're right." I was smiling up at him and my tears blurred his face a bit. He wiped them from my cheek gently. We were in our own little bubble. It was as if no one else was around us. No attorneys a few feet away. No crazy ex-husband either. Until we heard Joe from across the room.

"Well, you got what you wanted all along didn't you, Bradley?" The venom in Joe's voice was undeniable. Ugliness laced his words and I had a feeling he wasn't finished yet.

"What are you talking about?" Bradley asked.

Bradley had turned to face Joe and appeared to be ready to walk around the table. I was afraid of what he might do to Joe, as he was beyond upset.

"You know what I'm talking about," Joe hissed. "You have my sloppy seconds and a whore's son to raise."

The next few seconds seemed to be in slow motion as Bradley moved around the table and drew back his fist. I knew what was going to happen as he made his way to Joe. The next thing I heard was a simultaneous sound of a smack, a thud and what might have been bones being crushed.

Holy shit. All hell had broken loose. Joe had fallen to the floor and his attorneys gathered around him, shielding him from Bradley. I ran to Bradley's side, trying to pull him away from the commotion that he'd caused.

"You're going to pay for this, Bradley," Joe spit out. Blood poured from his nose, a nose that appeared distorted and broken. "You deserve that whore and her bastard child. Who knows? It's probably yours anyway."

"You'd better shut up, Joe," I warned as I watched Byers calling for Mindy on the desk interoffice phone. He told her to bring paper towels from the lounge and stressed the word "lots."

"I'm not raising a bastard child and you know it!" Bradley yelled. "You're the only bastard in this room. What a sorry fuck up you are too."

I clung to Bradley and wrapped my arm through his punching arm as I felt we'd had enough violence for one day. He'd stood up for our child and me. I couldn't believe I could say that now but it was true. Bradley would be my baby's father.

"Don't even think of pressing charges either." Bradley voice was steely. Not an ounce of emotion in them. "Press releases have a funny way of popping up when one least expects them. Really funny how that works."

A silent Joe lay on the ground in front of us, defeated and cowering. It was a picture in my mind that would never be forgotten.

"Let's go, Ms. Parker." Bradley pulled me away from Joe and his attorneys. Jensen was watching from afar talking animatedly into his phone while giving us a thumbs-up signal as we walked to the door of the room.

"I think we have a bit of unfinished business back at the hotel," Bradley whispered into my ear and a shiver of anticipation ran through me. His seductive words worked as an aphrodisiac and I was thankful the hotel was just a block or two away. If I wasn't pregnant, I would have run the distance.

"Lead the way." The thought of what awaited us back at the hotel made my blood race through my veins. I wasn't sure how long this body of mine would hold out. I think I was operating on adrenaline at this point. If I could just keep it together and not give in to the exhaustion, I was pretty sure Bradley would make it worth my while. Those kisses he'd given me earlier still lingered on my lips, neck, and behind my ear. They were truly wicked and lethal to me.

"Jensen, I think we're finally finished here, don't you?" Bradley crossed over to Jensen and extended his hand. "I have to say this one more time. I hope I never need your services again."

"Me too, Bradley," Jensen agreed. "But this time I'm pretty sure they brought you the best thing in your life."

"Indeed." Bradley and Jensen shook hands. I thanked him too. But before I could extend my hand, Bradley had me out the door and clambering down the hallway to the office's reception area. He was a man on a mission and I was fairly certain that mission was me. Lucky, lucky me.

Chapter 9: Bradley's Turn

Giggling and holding hands like a couple of silly lovesick teens; we walked back to the hotel. We didn't say much to one another. I think the promise of what was going to happen once we got there kept us quiet with goofy smiles on our faces.

We'd won today and it was time to celebrate. Once we arrived at the hotel, Bradley nearly had us sliding across the marble floors of the lobby. My man was ready to come unleashed. I felt the tension rising as we rode the elevator up with another couple. When we got off at our floor, he scooped me up into his arms, carrying me like a small child. Instinctively, my hands went around his neck and then his lips found mine. He kissed me with his eyes open to avoid running into the hallways' walls.

"Reach into my suit coat pocket. The one on my left side, darling. I think you'll find our room key."

My hands searched the inside of his jacket and I felt the keycard resting there and pulled it out. My fingers ran across its outline. It was in my grasp at the ready when we arrived at our door. I turned in his arms and pushed the key into the slot. The green light appeared and somehow Bradley pushed down the door handle.

But oddly enough, he only put his foot into the room, using it to hold the door open and keeping it from shutting before us. I couldn't figure out why he didn't want to enter the room. We had both been hell-bent on getting in there to mess up those sheets. His actions didn't make sense.

"What's the matter?" I asked. My eyes gazing into his, as our faces and lips practically touched.

"I need to ask you something before I carry you across this threshold." He appeared a little nervous, maybe even timid. Not the typical Bradley that I knew.

"What is it, Bradley?" Surely he wasn't having second thoughts? I couldn't bear that today. "You're starting to worry me."

"Oh, please don't worry, beautiful." He kissed all over my face while pulling me a little tighter to his chest. I enjoyed his kisses but I worried that I was beginning to get too heavy for him.

"I want to ask you something that I wish I could have asked you years ago." He gazed into my eyes. They were so intense, full of fire, and mixed with a love that I couldn't deny.

"Will you marry me, Kelly? I want to make us, you, me and the baby, an official family."

"Of course, I'll marry you." I giggled a little. What a sweet and beautiful man. "But right now I'm dying to get into our room. I don't think I can wait another second. These pregnancy hormones. They're brutal and making me as horny as hell."

"Say no more, darling. I'm at your service tonight."

Bradley used his foot to push the door fully open. I heard it slam shut as he carried me to the bed. The room was semi-dark. The blinds half closed. It gave the room a sexy ambiance and also I wasn't sure how much daylight I wanted streaming in on me. I doubted that Bradley had ever seen a seven-month pregnant woman without clothes on. I didn't want to scar him for life.

He laid me across the bed, not letting my feet touch the floor. Propping myself up on my elbows, I looked up at him. His eyes were on fire and hooded. Their heat seemed to scorch me as he slowly browsed over my body.

"Lay back, Kelly. This is all about you. It's my gift to you for letting me back into your life."

I wasn't going to argue with that. So I lay back and closed my eyes letting the moment sink in. I was finally going to be with him. Was he ready to see me? Would my pregnant belly be a turnoff? I tried to squelch all the insecurities, but it didn't work. They floated around in my silly brain.

He removed my low-heeled pumps. Sensible pregnant shoes, but still rather ugly. Then I felt his fingers on my feet. Massaging them, pressing into the arches. This simple touch ignited me, set me on fire. I couldn't close my eyes any longer. I needed to see him and let him see what he was doing to me.

"Bradley," I moaned. "What are you doing to me? I can barely hold myself together and you're only touching my feet."

"Hush," he whispered. "Concentrate on the pleasure, babe. Let it work through you."

His fingers moved up to my calves stroking lightly, but even his light touch made me squirm. I was not too proud to beg for more.

"I need you. Please, Bradley."

"Relax, babe." He moved his hands to my thighs and slipped them under my dress. My breathing stopped as I felt his finger grazing across my sex, touching me intimately, pressing into me and making me arch my back in almost a pleasurable pain.

"You're killing me."

"No, I'm going to make you come. It's all right with the baby and all?" Sweet Bradley. We'd never really had this discussion and right now, it was the last thing I wanted to think about.

"No holds barred sex is what the doctor ordered." I panted as his fingers slipped inside my panties. "Please don't stop."

His thumb found my clit and pressed against me, then began moving in a torturous circle. I was so close to coming and we'd only just begun to make love.

"Too many clothes." He stretched out beside me on the bed and kissed me on the lips as his hand reached behind me and gently pulled the zipper of my dress down. Once it was unzipped, he rose on his knees next to me and slipped the dress down my arms. My black, lace bra was exposed, rising and falling with my rapid breaths.

"Beautiful."

His hands possessed me as they covered my breasts. My nipples became hard and ached for his touch. His fingers began to pinch and pull them like he did on the plane earlier. I could hardly control myself.

"God, Bradley. I feel like I could come with just this."

"Not yet." His voice was raspy with need too. "I've just started to have fun with you."

Holy crap. Just started? I couldn't remember the last time I'd had a real non-battery operated orgasm. It might have been years. Joe had never given a shit about my needs once we were married.

"It's been so long since I've been touched like this. I don't think I can hold out long."

But something told me that he was going to take me to the edge and pull back, over and over again. Sweet torture was on the menu today.

His hands slid behind me and unhooked my bra. My arms were quickly freed and he threw my bra onto the floor.

"Love black lace, but I love these even more." His lips were kissing around my nipples. I felt his tongue licking. Teasing me. Driving me wild. I took his head in my hands, weaved my fingers through his hair and pushed him into my breast demanding more.

"Greedy little thing aren't you?"

My body cried out as he answered my want with his teeth rubbing across a nipple. The feeling sent heat through me down to my sex. I wanted him. I wanted more. I was an aching mess of want.

He continued to suck on my nipples as I felt him removing my dress. Bradley was a good multitasker as my dress found its place beside my bra on the floor. Now the only barrier between us was my panties. But I cringed when I thought of how large my belly was right now.

"Bradley, I hope my big, fat tummy isn't a turn off. I would…"

"Hush, right now. Not another word or thought. You're sexy and beautiful. Lay back and let me show you."

My panties joined their fellow brethren on the floor. And my eyes meet Bradley's. I wanted to see if he was being truthful when he saw me fully nude. His eyes were dark and full of desire. So I had to believe that he wanted me as much as I wanted him. His head dipped lower as I watched him.

His lips landed on the top of my thighs and his hands pulled my rear to the edge of the bed. I couldn't really see what he was doing, but I had a pretty good idea what was next and he didn't disappoint either.

Fingers ran up my inner thighs as his hands pressed my legs open as far as they could possibly go. Then I felt his tongue. Oh, God, his glorious tongue was inside me.

Flicking over me. I was so close and had to ball the sheets up in my hands to keep from screaming like a banshee.

When he placed his fingers inside of me and twisted them around toward the front, I felt my orgasm getting even closer. He'd brought me to the edge and my legs began to shake. Oh damn, it was going to be an epic one. I hoped I didn't pass out, as I was feeling so lightheaded.

His tongue left my clit and I heard him speaking to me. Telling me to let go and come. His tongue returned to find me again, but this time it was joined with his lips. Those sweet lips began to suck on me and sent me falling. The pleasure was almost too much to handle. My screams were likely loud enough to get security called. I'd never had an orgasm like this. It went on forever as he twisted his fingers around inside of me and flicked my clit with his tongue.

Finally, my orgasm subsided, and truthfully, I was spent. I felt limp, lifeless. It was like every tense muscle in my body became shaky Jell-O.

"Jeez," I found myself giggling. "I've never felt anything like that in my life."

"That's just a start." I felt Bradley's fingers playing with me once again. Teasing. I was so sensitive where he lightly touched me and knew it wouldn't take much to get me worked up again. I'm not sure where he learned to make love like this, but he definitely had learned a few things in the fourteen years we'd been apart.

But I didn't want it to be all about me. He needed this as much as I did. He confessed that he'd not been with anyone in a year. Well, that drought was ending tonight dammit.

"It's your turn now." A quizzical look came from his eyes, wondering what I meant most likely. "Lie down."

He hesitated and I had to get stern and bossy. "*Now*, mister. I have plans for you too."

Gone was any self-consciousness on my part. I moved over his body completely nude. After all he'd just had me in his mouth, there was no need for modestly at this point.

I started with his dress shirt. Button by button I worked away, licking my lips and stopping a few times to kiss his newly exposed chest and abs. Hard and toned, I felt his muscles flexing under my lip's touch. He seemed to really like that, but I had other ideas for my lips. I had a feeling he'd like that plan too.

Once unbuttoned, I pushed the shirt off of him. Then I removed his socks and pants as he helped.

Now he was down to his boxer briefs. My beautiful man. He appeared fully ready for me too, filled out in all the right places, not a love handle in sight either. Carved well and defined.

I'd seen him before, made love to him countless times as a teen even. Granted it was years ago and he was a man now, but tonight there was something totally different between us. All the past memories didn't seem to count. They'd faded and felt like a lifetime ago. We were truly having a new beginning.

My fingers found the waistline of his briefs and I heard him gasp as I felt under the elastic, stretching them and pulling them down and over his erection. My tongue licked the length him, making him twitch. He was perfect. Tall, muscles, and all man. I could hardly stop staring at his perfection.

His hands laced through my hair and subtly guided me back to his erection. I licked and sucked. Listened to his moans. They were telling me that he liked what I was doing.

"Damn. I'm too close." He pulled my head away from him. I looked up at him confused. I didn't really know what he wanted me to do next. I was willing to do just about anything. Well, anything my body would let me.

"Is it okay if you ride me?" His request was so sweet and sexy.

"Yes. Would you like that?" His eyes were glazed and heavy with desire.

"I want to be inside you so damn bad. I want you riding on top of me if it's okay."

I gingerly straddled my legs on each side of his body as he helped to line himself up to me. One of his hands prepared me for him as his other brought his erection to me. When I felt him at my opening, I gently sank down, feeling him stretch me.

We were completely one and it felt so empowering. I threw my head back and moaned. The feeling of him inside of me was too much and I couldn't keep quiet if I tried. Then he started moaning too. We took a moment to adjust as my body took him in fully. Exquisite. Nothing better described the feeling of him inside of me. I began moving in a grinding motion against him.

His fingers found my sensitive clit as I continued to work against him. Grinding away. His fingers were unrelenting. His touch was pure heaven and soon another orgasm came flying through my body leaving me spent. I wanted to collapse into Bradley's chest, but he wasn't there yet. My arms started to shake from fatigue as they tried to hold me up.

"Oh, Kelly. I've got you." He rose up and placed his hands under my backside. My head pressed into his chest. I felt him gently lifting, raising me up then bringing me back down. His rhythm became erratic as he drew close. Seconds later, his orgasm pulsed its release into me.

Afterward, we sagged against one another trying to catch our breaths. He continued to rub my back with soft, tender caresses. But my arms were too lifeless to return the favor.

We fell back on our pillows and eventually spooned together. He was to my back with his arm wrapped around my belly.

"Kelly, that was unreal." His words were barely a whisper but in the silent room I didn't miss a single one.

"I love you, Bradley." I was practically asleep as I said his name. It was time to sleep for a bit and rest up for another round... We had some catching up to do.

Epilogue: Her Arrival

The nurse had just left my room. She'd stopped by to check up on me, take my blood pressure and see how we were faring as first-time parents. With one look around her, she knew all was well. Bradley was lightly snoring as he slept in the reclining chair. Little Sydney was lying across his chest sound asleep as she snuggled into him. Looking at them made my heart swell and I couldn't help tearing up. Bradley had been there for me since the first night at the Love Handles' get together. It was his strength that got me through some dark days. I knew that he would be there for me and little Sydney no matter what we faced. We were a family now. The Dawson's of Dallas, Texas. I couldn't ask for anything more. I felt like the most blessed woman in the entire world.

DRUNK and DISORDERLY

by Liv Morris

Chapter 1

People often ask me how I met "The Infamous Andrew Cooper." He's rather a big deal here in Atlanta. You see, Andrew is a former NFL star and tight end for the Atlanta Falcons. The best way to describe Andrew? Chiseled, sculpted from head to toe, drop dead (or your panties) handsome and he sports a rather luscious tight end himself. Basically, he's a rival to Michelangelo's *David*. Can you hear me sighing at the comparison? Oh, another important thing I almost forgot. He's also the man I fell desperately in *hate* with. Yes, hate. I'll explain that part later.

Who am I? Well, I'm, Amelia Montgomery. My friends call me Millie. I'm just an average girl who was raised in the Deep South. Nothing spectacular or unique about me except perhaps my freakish love for art. I'm just your normal, everyday girl next door. This little fact makes the story of how Andrew and I met even harder to believe. And to think it all began with a simple phone call one August morning...

Somewhere in my purse, I hear my cell phone's ring tone going off. When I finally get my hands on it and view the screen, I see a number I don't recognize. My heart starts to race when I realize it's an Atlanta area code. I've been hoping and praying for a call from there. Maybe the man upstairs isn't too upset with me after all.

"Hello?" I answer quickly.

"Is this Amelia Montgomery?" an older man asks.

"Yes, sir. This is she." Gotta love those good old-fashioned Southern manners.

"Good morning, Ms. Montgomery. This is Stuart Reynolds, the principal of Peachtree High School in Atlanta. I hope I'm calling at a good time."

Be still my thumping heart. It *was* the call. "Oh, this is a perfect time. I'm not doing a thing right now."

Hell, could I sound any more pathetic? Truth is I'm beyond desperate. Panic mode is more like it. I haven't heard back from a single high school that I've applied to for a position as an art teacher. Wait, sorry, that's not totally true. I've heard back from them, but they've all given me a big fat, *NO! No, we aren't hiring. No, we don't want you.* And last but not least, *Please, no more phone calls or inquiries; we'll call you if and when we have an opening.*

Four years of undergraduate studies and a master's degree in education and I haven't had even a tiny nibble. Until now.

"Glad this is a good time." I swear I hear a little laugh in his voice. I cringe and try to take a few deep breaths away from the phone. I didn't want to sound like a perverted heavy breather through the receiver. "I'm calling to discuss a position that has just opened up at our high school. Our current art teacher is retiring. A very sudden thing. I guess winning the lottery will do that to you."

He's really chuckling now. I like this guy, Mr. Reynolds. He's made me relax, put me at ease, and I'm actually breathing normally again.

"I can imagine," I pipe in.

"That gets me to the purpose of my call today. I would like to have you come to Atlanta for an interview as the art teacher's replacement. Your friend, Priscilla Caldwell, has recommended you to us and it looks like we have your resume and information here too."

I know, I know. That name! Priscilla. Her mother is a big Elvis fan. Did I mention her middle name is Presley? Crazy, right? She's my lifelong friend and also a biology teacher at Peachtree. And right now, she's my favorite person on God's green earth. Oh, by the way, no offense if your name is Priscilla.

"I'd love to come interview for the position." I want to start jumping around like a monkey but I manage to keep myself still. Not an easy feat for me. "And yes, you should have all my information and the most up-to-date resume too. I sent it a few weeks ago just in case an opening came up."

"I see you have references from your student teaching days as well as photos of your own art portfolio. You're very talented, Ms. Montgomery."

"Thank you." I feel like he can see me blushing through the phone's connection. "Art's my passion so that really means a lot to me."

"Well, your work is definitely impressive." I can't hold the excitement in any longer and start pumping my fist into the air. I hope I'm not celebrating too early, but I can't imagine this conversation going any better, other than Mr. Reynolds telling me I'm starting next week. "I'd like to have you come in this Wednesday at 10 a.m. Does that time work out well with your schedule?"

I almost said, *"What schedule?"* but thankfully, I held my tongue.

"Let me check—." I pause for a moment. I'm lying as you know, but I hate to appear too anxious. "That works out well for me. I'm really looking forward to meeting you, Mr. Reynolds."

"I'm looking forward to meeting you too." Again, I swear there's a quiet laugh behind his words. Maybe he's just a jolly guy, but his demeanor is so different from the jaded principals I've met over the last few years while working as a student teacher. "Come to the front office, and my assistant, Mrs. Peterson, will give you some forms to fill out. General employment documents. Boring bureaucratic paperwork."

"Thanks again for calling and considering me for this position."

"You're welcome, Ms. Montgomery. Have a good day and see you on Wednesday."

As soon as our connection ends, I pull up Priscilla's number and call her.

"Hey, Millie."

"Oh, my God! Guess who just called me?" I am officially jumping up and down now.

"That's an easy one, Mr. Reynolds, right?" She's laughing at me.

"I guess I don't have to wonder how you knew. But, Priscilla, I can't thank you enough."

"It was nothing, really. I think you have a good chance at getting this job. They're only interviewing two people. You and another teacher from the area." I stop dead in my tracks. Her words hit me like a punch to the gut.

"Another teacher? Someone with experience?" I'm hoping she says no.

"Yes, but don't worry. I think you're a shoe-in. Honestly, I do." I flop myself back onto the sofa as the air is being released out of my happy balloon.

"Well, I hate to get too excited about it, but I hope that you're right. I really need this job. All those student loans I have freak me out."

"Don't I know. When's your interview?"

"In two days, on Wednesday. Ten in the morning. Which is perfect. Not too early." I can do mornings, but I should wear a sign around my neck stating, "Proceed with caution."

"I'm assuming you'll drive to Atlanta tomorrow?"

"I just got off the phone with Mr. Reynolds, but that makes sense. Do you mind if I stay at your place? I don't think I can spring for a hotel right now." I can't borrow another cent from my folks, as I've been a leach long enough.

"Mi casa's your casa. You know that. I'm leaving Wednesday morning to visit my mother in Florida. She wants me to see her new place."

"Oh yeah, I forgot that your mother moved away from Augusta." Priscilla and I grew up in Augusta, Georgia. Great place, but I want to live in Atlanta so badly. It's always been my dream.

"I'm not staying there long. I'll be back in Atlanta on Friday. Why don't you stay at my place until I get back? We can hang out over the weekend together. Hopefully celebrate your new job."

"Sounds great and thanks. Thanks for everything. I wouldn't have this job interview if it wasn't for you."

"It was no biggie. You'll do great. I have a good feeling about this. You know the teacher who's job your applying for won the lottery? The mother effing lottery. Seems like fate to me that this came up for you."

"Yeah, Mr. Reynolds told me that. I hope you're right as I could use a big dose of fate right about now."

"I hear you on that one. What time were you thinking about coming in tomorrow?"

"I'll shoot for around noon. That will give us the whole afternoon and evening to catch up. Does that sound okay?"

"Works for me. Can't wait to see you."

"Same here. See you tomorrow."

Chapter 2

So I'm skipping ahead to Wednesday morning at about 9:30 a.m., a few minutes shy of my interview time. Priscilla and I had a great time together on Tuesday. We ordered pizza from her favorite place and drank a couple beers while watching the movie, *Romy and Michele's High School Reunion*, one of my personal favorites.

It was a great girl's night in but we ended it early. I wanted to get some sleep and look rested, not hung over for the job interview the next day, so lights were out just before eleven. The pizza put me into a carb coma, which let me turn my mind off and get a full night's sleep.

Anyway, I'm just now entering the main office Mr. Reynolds told me about. It appears orderly and quiet, most likely due to the fact that school isn't in session right now. I tiptoe into the room so my heels don't click on the hard tiles announcing that I'm here.

Toward the back office area, I see a woman typing away on her laptop. She doesn't hear me come in. Now I'm worried that I'll scare the shit out of her when I do speak so I let my heels fall onto the tile before I make it to the carpeted area.

We now have eye contact and the woman, who I'm assuming is Mrs. Peterson, smiles at me. A very welcoming sight indeed. I see she's dressed very casually and I feel a little overdressed in my interview attire. I'm wearing a navy dress, with a respectable hem length and little cap sleeves. I opted against pantyhose. You may not know this but a woman showing up to a job interview in the South without stockings on is almost a cardinal sin. However, it's ninety-one degrees outside and as humid as the rainforest so I left the hose at home. After seeing how casual this woman is, I'm thankful that I did.

"Mrs. Peterson?" I ask.

"Yes, you must be Ms. Montgomery."

"That's me." I smile big back at her.

"Well, welcome to Peachtree High. You're early." I like arriving early to important things like this. I bet that surprises you. Most people would likely peg me as being late to everything, but in this one area of my life I've risen above my chaotic, scattered self.

"Just a little bit. Mr. Reynolds said there was some paperwork that I needed to fill out, so I thought I'd get here a little early. Get a head start on it if possible."

"You're right. There *is* a lot of paperwork for you. Forms galore." She reaches for a clipboard and hands it to me. "Here's everything you need to fill out. If you'd like, you can sit at the empty desk up front. The receptionist is on vacation until the week before school starts up again. I'm pretty much Mr. Reynolds' gatekeeper for now." She laughs but I have a feeling she keeps good guard for him. I see something in her eyes. They have a keen, observing look to them like she misses nothing.

"Thanks." I take the clipboard and proceed to the desk Mrs. Peterson suggested. As I'm finishing the forms a door opens up and I hear two people speaking behind me. Their voices fill the silent room. Looking in the direction of the sounds, I see a portly man standing at the door behind Mrs. Peterson's desk.

I think it's safe to assume the man in the doorway is Mr. Reynolds. Funny thing though, he resembles Boss Hogg on the old TV show *Dukes of Hazzard*, minus the white suit. As a southern girl, I suffered through watching reruns of that show with my dear father. A few years ago, Jessica Simpson starred in the movie remake of the TV sitcom. Truthfully, it isn't even close to the real thing. Most remakes never are.

"It was a pleasure to meet you, Mr. Reynolds." I hear a sex-laced, sultry female's voice. You know the kind that makes men fall to their knees. With my eye trained on the office door, I watch a woman walk through the threshold and stand a couple feet from Boss Hogg's twin brother.

As I get a closer look at this woman, I believe a better term for her is drop-dead gorgeous. Jeez. She's tall, statuesque-like, and her silky, long hair would make any Crystal Gayle fan hot under the collar. Who's Crystal Gayle you're likely wondering? She's an old-school country singer whose brown eyes turned blue with hair so long it was likely a safety hazard.

The interaction between Mr. Reynolds and "The Hair" is blatantly flirtatious. She's coyly batting her eyelashes and he appears to be blushing a bit too. She reaches out and shakes his hand. The way he's looking between her and their joined hands makes me wonder if he might dip his head and plant a kiss on her knuckles.

"We'll let you know one way or another about the teaching position, Ms. Lannon. You should be hearing from us by the middle of next week. We need to get the art teacher position filled as soon as possible."

Wait. *What? This* is my competition?

Holy crap. Did you hear my hopes and dreams hit the floor just now? Hold it. That sound was just my pen crashing against the tile when I dropped it in shock. But the scuffle of my reaching down and retrieving the damn thing has everyone's eyes on me now.

Looking up from my half-bent position to pick-up the pen, I give my audience a weak smile. It says, "I'm sorry to have bothered you. Please look away." And thankfully they do.

"I look forward to hearing from you, Mr. Reynolds. If you have any more questions, give me a call. You have my number." The Hair continues on unaffected by my interruption. She's as smooth as silk.

She turns away from him to exit the office and it feels like her parade across the room's in slow motion. Each step she takes with her long legs, every flip of her glossy hair, and each twist of her hip, all in slow motion. She floats by the desk I'm cowering at without even a glance in my direction.

All I can think of is how totally and utterly screwed I am. Maybe I should just gather up my purse and leave. Avoid the humiliation. But I really need this job desperately, so I sit up straight as a board in my chair and pray that my confidence returns. I plaster on a fake smile that says the glamazon's beauty pageant presence means nothing to me. But you know that I'm a big, fat liar. That woman totally outshines me. She's a hot bonfire and I'm just a flickering flame compared to her.

After she's left the office area, I pick up the clipboard on the table and start walking back toward Mrs. Peterson. All the paperwork is filled out, as if it even matters at this point.

"Here's the paperwork. I believe it's all completed." As I'm standing at her desk, I swear I smell the lingering scent of some expensive perfume. I bet The Hair left it behind. Dammit. I have to admit it smells divine.

"Thanks, Ms. Montgomery. Let me introduce you to Principal Reynolds." Mrs. Peterson rises out of her chair and motions for me to join her on the other side of her desk and I politely comply.

"Mr. Reynolds, this is Amelia Montgomery." Sweet Mrs. Peterson. She winks at me as she finishes the introduction. I wonder if she can sense my disappointment after seeing the last candidate breeze through here.

"Ms. Montgomery. Pleasure to meet you. Thanks for coming in all the way from Augusta on such short notice." We shake hands quickly as he welcomes me.

"Nice to meet you too and it was no problem. Two days was plenty of time to get to Atlanta."

"Why don't we step into my office?" Mr. Reynolds speaks to me as he turns and walks back through the open door of his office.

I smile back at Mrs. Peterson and follow behind Mr. Reynolds. Once in the office, I see a wall of windows taking up the entire back wall giving the room a nice view. The office isn't too large but there's enough space for a couple of chairs.

"Please have a seat." He points to one of the chairs in front of his desk.

I sit down gracefully and then the questions begin...

"So tell me a little about yourself, Ms. Montgomery."

That's also when the lies begin to pour out of me like a gusher. I sure as heck can't tell him the sad truth. That I'm an unemployed, overeducated slacker living back at my parents' house. A place I swore I'd only visit on special occasions and government holidays. But reality bites, so I basically lie my ass off. Literally, there was nothing left of said ass when the interview was finished. It's a good thing I didn't wear pantyhose after all or they'd have fallen down around my knees. There isn't anything there now to hold them up.

By the last question, I feel like I'm hanging on by a thread, like my fingers are holding on precariously to the side of a cliff as the world of unemployment waits below to catch me.

"I have one more question for you today. We're a tight-knit community here at Peachtree. What could you contribute to our school as an art teacher?"

I think I can answer this one honestly. No padding the response this time.

"People hang artwork on their walls. It beautifies their homes, makes them more welcoming. I'd like to bring that same feeling to Peachtree. Have the students here realize how much more beautiful our world is because of art and all its different forms."

"Interesting. Can you be more specific? What exactly do you have in mind?"

"Well, football season begins the first week of school right?"

"That's right. The guys have been doing morning practices since July."

"Imagine the banners the art students can make for the games. Colorful, eye-catching. Artist meets Athlete. A good way to bring groups together."

"I'd have to run that by the football coaches and the cheerleaders. They usually do all the banners for the football players. But who knows? They may welcome the chance to share."

"Sure. It's just one idea. There are so many other ways to bring art into the students' everyday lives." Here goes the close. The pitch. "I'd love the opportunity to do that at Peachtree."

"You definitely have enthusiasm for your subject. It's a good counterbalance for the lack of teaching experience you have."

Ouch! And with those words, my heart sinks into a sea of disappointment. *Ker plunk.*

"Again, thank you for the opportunity to interview with you today, Mr. Reynolds." He stands as I'm speaking. I expect him to move forward and escort me to the door like he did The Hair, but he remains planted, not moving a muscle toward me. Crap, this is bad.

I shake his hand while he says a quick goodbye and tells me, "We'll call you later with our decision."

Completely discouraged, I head out of the office and see Mrs. Peterson's empty desk and I'm glad. I just don't have it in me to force another smile on my face. Right now I'm trying to hold ugly crying at bay.

You may be wondering why someone like me, a qualified teacher with a master's degree, is having such a hard time landing a job? The facts are hard to face. Across the country, art-teaching positions are almost impossible to come by because of budget cuts. Cost-saving measures by school boards all add up to few openings. Unfortunately, art departments are the first to land on the cutting floor when schools need to trim costs.

So it has come down to an art teacher actually winning the lottery for me to even secure an interview. Pathetic. There are times that I wish I were a science teacher like Priscilla. They're actually in demand. A scarcity.

Once I make it out to my car, I crank up the A/C and drive back to Priscilla's apartment. It totally sucks that she's not here right now because I could really use a friend. A shoulder to cry on and a drinking buddy would be great.

As I'm pulling into her apartment complex, I see a small bar across the street from the entrance. That's when inspiration hits me. I need some liquid encouragement. Pronto!

Chapter 3

Once inside her apartment, I quickly shed my interview attire. I decide on clothes more appropriate for this sweltering heat and hanging out at a dive bar. Now I'm wearing white, short shorts, a breezy aqua-colored sleeveless top, and a pair of sexy, gladiator-looking sandals, the ones with all the leather strings that wrap around the ankles. They also look great with togas. Think *Animal House*.

At this point in my story, it's important to clarify that drinking before noon isn't my normal behavior or routine. But you know how my morning has gone. Straight down the crapper. So, hopefully, you can understand my need to get a little buzz going.

If my mother knew what I was up to she'd kill me. Heading off to a neighborhood bar by myself no matter the time of day, isn't what a young woman raised in Augusta, Georgia, does. Oh well, I'm not in Augusta anymore. Thank God.

After locking up the apartment and donning my favorite sunglasses, I head back out into the bright midday sun. One good thing about Joe's Gather'n Place, the bar across the street, I can crawl home if need be. No driving necessary.

Heading toward the bar's entrance, I cross the street and feel the pavement heat radiating up around me. It's going to be a scorcher today. Gravel dust stirs as I walk through the small parking lot. I finally arrive at the door, grab the tarnished brass handle, and tug on it. The hinges let out a protest as I walk into the darkened bar. The door shuts behind me. All sunlight disappears. It's like walking into a cave. I remove my sunglasses, but my eyes still have a hard time adjusting to the darkness.

Finally, I see the beer signs illuminated above the long, wooden bar to my left. The neon lights beckon me to belly up and partake. I select the stool the farthest from the door, not sure why, but I guess I'm not really in the mood to socialize. Which isn't a problem as there's no one here but the old bartender. He has to be pushing seventy. Maybe he's Joe, the bar's namesake.

"Welcome, Miss," the old-timer greets me. His smile shows he's missing one of his front teeth. Poor guy.

"Hello," I answer back.

"What can I get ya?" he asks. "Something to drink?"

"Definitely something to drink." I'm just not sure what my poison should be. It's about high-up noon, so I can move past the morning standards of Bloody Mary's or Mimosas. "I'd like a vodka tonic. In a tall glass with lots of ice, please."

"One vodka tonic coming up for the pretty lady." He ends with a little wink. What a flirt and I have to laugh.

"Are you always this busy around here?" I joke.

"This place is usually pretty crowded at lunch. Must be the heat." I watch him pour a scary amount of vodka into my glass. I need to eat something if I plan to drink this much or I'll be sliding off the stool onto the floor after two drinks.

"Lunch? So you serve food too?" I ask.

"Been told that our hamburgers and fries are the best in the area." He puffs out his chest and boasts. "Have folks coming from all around here for them."

"Sounds good to me." My neglected stomach starts to rumble. I was too nervous to even think about food before the interview. "I'll have a burger with cheese and can you—"

As I'm getting ready to ask the man to hold the onion, the door squeaks and light floods in from the outside. It's blinding as I turn my head to see it flood through the door. But what catches my eye is the shape of the man standing there. The sunshine streams around the darkness of his form, almost looking like it's jetting out of his body's edge. He appears to be glowing. It reminds of a scene you might see in a western movie. The outlaws are at the local saloon, hiding away at the bar, and in walks the sheriff. A dramatic moment.

When the door closes behind him, all I can make out is his height. He's a giant but, damn, my eyes are not working right. The shock of light from outside blinds me again and they need to readjust.

The silhouette of the man begins moving toward the bar where I'm sitting. He walks toward me taking long strides. Before I know it he's actually standing one place away from me at the bar. I find this interesting, as there are about ten empty stools to my left. But when my eyes start focusing clearly again, I'm damn glad he's close by because he's as hot as the dashboard of my car on a sunny summer day. Burn your fingers when you touch him hot. Sizzling. Lucky me.

I'm guessing he's at least 6'3." Towering tall. He's more a presence then a mere man, the kind that turns your head and makes your eyes follow. Muscled arms press against the sleeves of his gray t-shirt, the material also stretches tightly across his large chest and shoulders.

He sports a pair of cargo shorts. I'm not normally a shorts fan for guys, but I get a little peak of his thighs along with his toned calves. I gulp down a bit more of my drink. Damn, his body has more definitions than a dictionary.

"Afternoon, Coop." The old man greets the guy who decides to perch himself one empty stool away from me. Seems safe to guess his name is Coop too.

"Afternoon, Joe. What's up?" Whoa, the way this Coop guy speaks gets my attention. His deep voice is commanding. Confident.

"I was just taking this lovely lady's order for a burger." The old man tilts his head my way. "Tell her about them, Coop. I think she's a first timer."

And just like that, Coop and I begin engaging with one another. Thoughts of food or the old man standing in front of me fade away when this guy named Coop turns toward me.

I bite my lip waiting for the full view of him as he slowly turns his head. Anticipation builds. I notice his eyes first. He looks directly into mine. Consuming. I feel this strange flutter in my stomach and my breathing stops. It's an unusual and intense connection and he doesn't break it by looking away. His gaze is keeping me paralyzed, pinned to my stool. Add his high cheekbones, the light stubble outlining a razor sharp jawline and he looks like a model in GQ. He's a total panty-soaking machine.

The bar is too dark for me to make out the exact color of his eyes, but they appear almost black, piercing. Like they know unspoken things about me. It's unnerving, really. Then he takes his sweet time while giving me the once, then twice over. When he's finally finished perusing me, my skin feels sunburned, overheated.

"Hi there." His words float on a cloud of lust to my ears. Sexy just isn't a big enough word to describe him. I find myself shivering like a cold blast just ran over my skin. It's so bizarre. I've gone from hot flashes to chills in seconds. No other guy has gotten this reaction out of me. Never... Who is this dude?

"Hi there." I'm doing a great job as his echo.

"So you're new here?"

"I'm not even new. More of an interloper," I finish with a little chuckle.

"An interloper?" He appears amused as his smile appears a bit crooked, like he's trying to figure me out.

"Yes. I'm up here from Augusta. Had a job interview this morning." I turn to my vodka. I need some liquid courage and my mouth is parched, dry, unlike my panties. I take a healthy swig and continue. When I turn back to him, he still has that amused smirk on his face. It's cute. Don't get me wrong. He's still as sexy as sin but, hell, there's something endearing about his smirk... It's like he's transformed into this adorable, young boy mixed with a little orneriness. The pull your sister's pigtails kind.

"So, a job interview? I'm thinking it didn't go so well. Right?" Spot on, Sherlock.

"You must read minds." My sarcasm answers his question.

"Sorry about that." I examine his face to see if he seems sincere. His dark eyes have softened and to my surprise, *I think* he's truly sympathetic. Honestly sorry. Rather refreshing.

"Thanks. It was beyond bad." I hold up my vodka toward him. "I wouldn't be sitting here drinking by myself this early in the day if I'd hit a slam dunk."

He scoots over my way. Now he's sitting on the stool next to me. We're side-by-side now. He swivels his body toward me, and I feel his knee touch mine, knee-to-knee, skin-to-skin and I shiver.

"Well, I think we should do what we can to turn this day around for you...?" He ends with his brow raised in question. I'm deducting that he wants my name.

This is tricky for me. Do I tell him Amelia or Millie? I only have seconds to ponder this. I'm thinking Millie. It's casual. We're in a dive bar. The nickname is used mostly by my friends. I want to be his friend or get friendly with him. Easy guess on which one I use.

"I'm Millie." I shamelessly bat my eyelashes at Coop. Remember, I'm drinking on an empty stomach and my first vodka tonic is now all ice. My normal restraints are falling down. "And thanks. It's been a rough day."

"Well, the day is young. I bet we can turn it around." The word "we" makes me want to scoot closer to him. Have more than just our knees touching. And guess what? I do...

"I like that idea." I want to add "and you," but refrain. I need to ease into flirting even if I'm totally okay with him easing into my panties. My naughty thoughts make me snicker as I'm not usually this much of a bad girl.

"All right then. We have a plan," Coop commands and I melt. "Make Millie another one of what ever she's having, Joe. I'll have my standard."

"Coming up." Joe takes my glass and tosses the melting ice into a sink. "You still want that burger, young lady?"

"If I'm going to have another drink, yes, I better." I'm really feeling buzzed at this point. The carbfest from last night's pizza seems to be long gone.

"Have the cook throw one on the grill for me too," Coop adds.

"So where were we?" Coop says winking at me. I feel my face flushing turning red. "Helping Millie forget about her shitty morning. That's my game plan now. Are you okay with that?"

All I can do is nod my head and wonder what he means by game plan. But regardless, I'm totally on his team and shaking my pom poms while cheering, "Go Coop!" I'd be okay if he wanted to round a few bases with me too. A home run might be pushing it though.

"Sure, I'm game." And with that comment, my life forever changes.

Chapter 4

One thing leads to another. One drink becomes too many to count. And before I know it, I'm in big trouble with a capital T. R. O. U. B. L. E.

I'll spare you the mundane details and go straight to the sordid ones. They're what you want to know about, right? Do I hear an, "Amen, sister?" Yes, I think I do.

It's now pushing three in the afternoon, and I've sufficiently soaked myself with enough vodka to prune a pickle. Joe's bar has had a few more folks drop by for the day, but Coop and I are in our own little bubble at the bar, chatting, flirting, and drinking. Finally, he makes his move, steps up to bat, goes for a home run.

"Whatta ya say we go back to my place?" He speaks with a voice that makes me melt like butter over hot toast. He's so smooth. And I fear this means he's had some major practice with that line. Like there's a bevy of babes strung across Atlanta who have heard this same question and most likely have succumbed.

In my drunken haze, I try but can't look away from his eyes as they blaze with lust at me. Millie. The girl next door who's now being asked by a hot piece of ass to go home with him. It's decision time and I decide right then that I need to go visit the ladies' room, needing to regroup or possibly throw up if my head doesn't stop spinning.

"Hold that question, Coop. I'll be right back." My words sound slurred even to my own ears. Placing my hand on his hard as a rock forearm, I start to rise off the barstool. "Could you point me in the direction of the ladies' room?"

"Back through the hallway on the right." He seems disappointed. Undoubtedly, it's not the answer he usually hears.

"Thanks. I'll be right back."

"And I'll be waiting for that answer, baby."

Holy shit... That little endearment and my vodka'd blood make me almost fall to my knees where I stand. But I pause, smile at him and head to the restroom. As I make my way to it, I can feel his eyes perusing my backside. I'd be lying if I said I didn't add a little more sway to my hips.

Once inside, I handle my business quickly and do what every girl should do when faced with a decision like this: call a girlfriend.

"Hey, Millie. How'd the inter—"

"Oh, my God!" I completely interrupt. "Priscilla, you're never going to believe where I am."

"In Atlanta still, I hope."

"Yes, but I'm across the street from your apartment building at that dive bar, Joe's Place"

"Wait. What are you doing there? Are you by yourself?" She sounds worried but I continue on.

"Well, yes and no. The interview went horrible. Terrible." I have difficulty pronouncing those last two words. Too many "B's."

"Oh no. What happened?"

"'The Hair' totally has the job, not me."

"Millie, you're not making a lick of sense right now. And who's 'The Hair'? Have you been drinking? For Christ's sake it's only a little after three!"

"I've been drinking, maybe even a tad tipsy, but I've run into the hunk of all hunks here. Coop the Divine."

"Now you're really worrying me. So you've just met this guy. There at Joe's?"

"Yes. He's a regular here. Tall and gorgeous. Built. I think he likes me too."

"Of course he likes you. You're the hottest friend I have. Uber sexy. That was said in a non-lesbian way, okay?"

"You're so funny. I'm not even a little sexy." I lean against the sink to steady myself. No more drinks for me. "I just wanted to let you know who I was with in case things heat up and I'm never heard from again. He's asked me to go back to his place."

"Oh, Millie. I don't think that's a good idea. You really don't know who this guy is, you're drunk, and it's only three in the afternoon." She pauses and I hear her sigh. "And if he's as hot as you say, I think your 'never sleep together on the first date' streak will be over."

"He seems like a nice guy, though. Joe, the old bar guy, knew him by name. Anyway, he's been trying to cheer me up after the interview from hell."

"I don't like this at all, Millie. Please be careful. If I don't hear from you in a couple hours I'm calling this Joe guy."

"I promise to call. And what can happen to me in broad daylight?"

"A lot, believe me." There seems to be a bit of "been there, done that" in Priscilla's words.

"I'll be careful." Deep down inside I'm not sure that's the truth. "Okay?"

"Okay." She appears to throw in the towel on talking me out of going home with him. "Remember, call me or else."

"Bye, Priscilla."

"Love you crazy."

"You too."

After getting off the call with Priscilla, I look into the small hazy mirror over the bathroom sink, assessing my reflection. I'm a little bright-eyed, and excited. It's Coop making me appear this way. I know it has everything to do with him. A hot guy flirting with me, finding me attractive, and wanting to be with me. It's as intoxicating as the vodka I've been drinking. And to be quite honest with you, I've not felt a thrill like this in a long, long time.

Drinking early, alone, and having an encounter with an unbelievably hot guy who's interested in me, well, let's just say this isn't my normal day. The thought of stopping whatever direction it's going in makes me feel sad. I'm not ready to let anything kill the buzz I feel from being around Coop.

It's been awhile since a guy has shown any interest in me. Since graduating with my master's degree in May, I've been cloistered in my hometown where the guys are either married or my distant relative. Recently, my life has been as boring as a fifth grade band concert. Maybe it's time to spice things up? Throw caution to the wind?

If I go home with him, that doesn't mean I'm going to sleep with him, right? But realistically I know I'm fooling myself. Will I be able to say no if things heat up with him? Would I even want to? It's been so damn long since I've been with someone and I've never felt this instant connection with any man like this before. There's some weird, jazzed-up energy between us. One that really seems a shame not to be explored. But just how much exploring do I want him doing with me?

Pushing away from the sink, I make my way out of the restroom and walk out to the open bar area and see that Coop's gaze is trained on the hallway leading to the restroom. Our eyes instantly meet. Just knowing he's waiting for me, watching attentively makes me happy, very damn happy.

I walk slowly to him, enjoying the head to toe appraisal he gives me. He has a sexy smile that gets wider across his face with each and every step I take.

"Well, hi there," I whisper now standing in front of him where he's sitting on the barstool looking deliciously handsome. Eat him alive delicious, in fact. And his blatant perusal of my body has left me feeling almost breathless.

"Hi there," he quietly answers back. But his voice doesn't sound weak like mine. It's seductive as if some kind of naughty promise is behind it. My knees suddenly become a little weak at the thought.

"Well, I've been thinking about your question." I pause and as I do he reaches for me, grabbing my hands in his then pulling me forward. He widens his legs as he sits atop the stool and brings me to rest between them. His hands rub softly up and down my forearms. I feel him pressing his legs against my hips keeping me in place. I can't move from his hold. Constrained. Hunter to prey.

"And do you have an answer for me? I'm hoping it's yes."

All I can do at this point is nod and agree with him. He's touching my skin, his legs pushing against my body. I'm experiencing complete sensory overload and I'm so lost I can't even answer back.

He's grinning back at me and looks as happy as a man whose horse just won the Derby and I'm his prized blue ribbon.

"I've settled up with Joe here." I notice that our drinks and dishes have been cleared away from the bar. Coop anticipated my response. I'm not sure if that's good or bad.

"So I was a sure thing?" I ask raising my brow.

"A man can hope, Millie." Just hearing him mutter my name, makes me lean against him even more. Our faces are now close together. Lips not too far apart. I smell his woodsy scent and my eyes close for just a second as I breathe it in, so masculine and heady.

"You okay, Millie?" he asks, his voice laced with concern. "Have you had too much to drink?"

I open my eyes and see *his* eyes looking intense and a little worried. I swear they can see right through me down to my soul. I'd find this a little creepy if the intensity between us didn't turn me on so much.

"I'm doing real good." Truthfully I am. Who wouldn't be in my shoes?

I look straight into his eyes and bite my lip, flirting with him. Being coy. From the hungry look in his eyes, it works.

"Let's go, you!" And in a flash he's standing up by my side with his arm wrapped my shoulders. At his height, that's where his hands naturally land on me. I'm now melting into him walking stride for stride to the door. But not before he says good-bye to sweet old Joe.

"See you later, Joe."

"See you around, Coop. Make sure that nice young lady gets home safely." I swear I hear an admonishment in Joe's voice, like a father, telling us to be home by curfew.

"Will do. You know me, Joe." Coop's response is followed with a chuckle. I'm hoping that's not a laugh because he's not one to get girls home safely. At least two people, Priscilla and Joe, know that I'm leaving with this man.

I dig my sunglasses out of my purse before we hit the door. I know the sun's going to blind me if I don't as I've been inside of this cavern-like place for over three hours.

Coop opens the door for me. I exit outside and wait a couple feet ahead of him. There are only three cars in the gravel parking lot, a rather beat-up truck, with rust just about everywhere, and a red compact car. But neither one of them say *Coop* to me.

I'm thinking the last one of the three—a hot looking sports car. I have no clue what the make is but everything about it screams *expensive.* It's dark navy blue, shiny, and brilliantly sparkles in the sun like Edward Cullen, that brooding, hot vampire in *Twilight.*

Glancing back at Coop, I see him pulling a set of keys out of his pocket. He points a receiver toward the sports car and I hear a beeping sound. I'm assuming this signals the doors of *his* car are unlocked now.

I guessed right, but what the heck does this guy do? I can't even imagine how much a set of wheels like this costs. Likely more than the entire year's salary of the art teaching position I interviewed for this morning.

"Wow, Coop," I say walking toward his car and standing by the passenger door. "This is magnificent."

"Thanks, I've had it a couple of years. She's my baby." *His baby?* Spoken like a true guy. Boys and their toys. It's so true.

But this is more than a toy, it's a statement that says, *Hey I'm rich. Look at me.* Now more than ever, I really think this guy's totally out of my league.

"I bet it's a chick magnet too." I speak before I can catch myself. Those words would've been better thought than actually said. But I can't take them back now.

"Well, it's not a deterrent," he retorts sarcastically. I feel him at my side, his body lightly touching mine as his hand rests momentarily on my back. Even this slight connection between us makes me want to check my back and see if it's smoking where we're touching, the feeling between us is so hot and sizzling.

Coop opens the door for me. He's definitely scoring points for being a gentleman. But once I slide into the seat and feel the hot leather against my legs, I immediately scream.

"Holy shit. My legs!" I shout and push myself back out of the car. Coop's arms grab my shoulders and hold me in place.

"Millie, I'm so sorry. I should've warned you. Are you okay?"

"I'm fine. I think." I turn around with the back of my legs facing him. "Do they look red?"

I'm looking at Coop over my shoulder and watch as he squats down behind me. His face is parallel to my ass. This close of an inspection is a little unnerving. I fear those little bitches called cellulite bumps might be right at his eye level. You know the ones I'm talking about. Cottage cheese on the legs.

"Not red, but definitely hot babe. Real hot." He gently grazes his hand over the backs of my thighs. Just a whisper of a touch and I'm feeling like my legs are on fire again. The sensations he gives me, well, I've never experienced anything like it before.

He raises up beside me. I'm motionless. Still tingling.

"I have a clean t-shirt in the back of the car. I'll put it on the seat. Those legs are going to stay protected. I might have plans for them later." He winks at me while reaching in the back seat and grabbing a duffle bag.

Later? Plans? I watch him carefully prepare the hot seat for me. It's sweet how concerned he is but going home with him is crazy, nuts. However, I don't think I can or want to stop what's already in full motion.

"Okay, my lady. Your seat awaits." He's such a charmer and I'm thinking he's likely going to charm the shorts right off me.

"Thanks." I ease into the car once again, holding the shirt in place. This time everything's fine and the heat doesn't reach my legs.

He walks around to the other side and I notice the expensive wood on the console. Gadgets and displays everywhere. He said he was looking for a new job too. It was something we both had in common, but what the heck did he used to do? He didn't tell me much just that he had a job-related injury that made him leave his last position.

He opens his door and climbs in next to me. I watch as his legs fold and the rest of his tall body eases into the seat next to me. Even though we were closer sitting leg to leg in the bar, it feels more intimate in the car as he closes the door. We're cocooned in this small space, like there's no escape.

"I need to get the air blowing." Coop pushes on a remote that's located on a key chain and the car starts. I feel a cool blast of air hitting me right after the engine turns.

"I love your car. It's so cool, literally. My car takes forever to cool down."

"Well, I'm glad you left yours at your friend's apartment." I'd shared with him earlier that I was in Atlanta applying for a teaching job and was staying at Priscilla's apartment across the street.

Ending up at Joe's? Best damn thing I did today, maybe this week. Heck, likely my whole life, but I didn't have a clue about this yet.

"Me, too." A worry hits me. "Are you okay to drive? We've been drinking all afternoon. I'm not sure how I'm walking or talking, really."

"I'm good. I had my usual at Joe's. Lemonade. Straight up." Oh, he's not been drinking but making sure my drink was never empty.

"You're kidding me. No alcohol?"

"None. I knew I'd be driving home." He gives me a quick side-glance and I swear he looks apologetic. "But I promise to catch up when we get to my house."

"You better. I'm light years ahead of you now." I lightly punch his shoulder half in fun, half in anger for not joining in earlier with me.

Chapter 5

The ride in his car is quiet. I can't even hear the hum of the engine. There's complete silence until he turns on his radio and the bass reverbs all around me. In my semi-drunken state, it's a bit overpowering. Like the band is playing live from the space behind us with the drummer hammering away on the back of my seat.

As we listen to Pit Bull tell us to not stop the party, good advice by the way, I watch Coop pull the car up to a gated community, one of those exclusive places where rich and powerful people hide, I mean live. I've never been behind a private gate until now.

"Is this where you live, Coop?" Still can't figure this guy out.

"A lot of my friends live here and I like the privacy." What kind of friends does he have? Gazillionaires? He makes it seem like living here is no big deal. It isn't if you can afford a million dollar plus home. The houses are enormous, beautiful with immaculate lawns, the kind that are tended by professional gardeners. Professional everything, really.

"It may be private, but I'm thinking a better word is impressive."

"Thanks. It's home to me." Coop turns the car into a driveway where a palatial looking home sits back from the street. There has to be three acres surrounding this house.

"Is this yours?" I can't hide the surprise in my voice as the car approaches the now open garage.

"This is it. My home."

"Your compound is more like it."

He laughs, but seriously this place is unreal. I can't even fathom what it must have cost him. I want to ask him what he does, or did before he was injured, but I can't seem to get up the nerve. Maybe I'm afraid he'll say he robs banks or is a drug runner.

After entering the garage, he shuts off the car and turns to me. "Well, we're here."

"Yes we are," I respond nervously looking anywhere but at him.

This is it. What I want and also what I'm worried about. I was all bravado and sass on my phone call with Priscilla. Those feelings are fading now that I'm facing reality. I hope to God I made the right choice.

"Sit here. I'll come around and get your door." Still as charming as ever.

Coop opens the door and escorts me out of the garage. He guides me with his hand placed against my back. The garage is detached from the house but a tall portico connects it to the house. It's more for show than a protection from the elements and definitely grander than a porch. At least the porches in Augusta.

As we approach the main door, he pulls the key ring out of his pocket, inserts a key into a large brass lock, and opens the door. With a sweep of his hand, he invites me in.

I take a step over the threshold. No turning back now. I'm here and officially have crossed over the line into his lair. Looking around the open foyer, my eyes see the living room ahead of me. There's a massive stone fireplace directly in front of me against a far wall. It's more of a statement. I mean who really needs fireplaces in Atlanta?

There's something unusual hanging above it though. The item appears to be in a shadow box. My legs move me toward it and I can't believe what I'm seeing. An Atlanta Falcons jersey is encased in the large wooden frame with a glass covering. But what I make out on the black and red shirt stops me dead in my tracks. Across the back shoulder is the name, *Cooper*.

"Wait a second. *Cooper*?" And it all starts making sense to me. His car, this house I'm standing in, and his "job-related injury." He's a football player or was one.

Holy shit. If I were a fan of football, I most likely would've figured this out. But here's a little tidbit for you. I hate football. Despise it actually. Love the sports player, hate the sport?

While trying to process what I'm seeing, I don't hear Coop walk up beside me so I'm startled when I feel his touch on my arm.

"Sorry, Millie. Didn't mean to make you jump." I look up into his eyes and can tell he needs to know what I think about his being Mr. Football.

"Yes, I confess. I'm the Cooper on that jersey. Played here in Atlanta for nine years. Since I was a rookie."

"Why didn't you tell me?" I can't believe this. Neither one of us got specific about our jobs when we were talking earlier, but this is a big oversight. Like a multi-million dollar one.

"I don't know. I thought about saying something. But honestly, when you had no idea who I was. Well, that was a change for me." His eyes have a serious look about them like he's trying to drive home a point. "I wanted you to like me for me. Coop. Not some big NFL player."

"I guess it's hard when you meet people, wondering if they're interested in you as a person or you the athlete. I get it. But truthfully, I'm not a big football fan. So I wouldn't have been impressed if you'd told me."

"So you're not impressed?" he questions me with a smirk on his face. "Not even a little bit?"

"Jeez, I thought you wanted me to like you for you." He's confusing me now. "Make up your mind already."

"Oh believe me, Millie. I've made up my mind." He gazes at me. Something in his eyes unnerves me. Makes my stomach flutter, my breath hitch. "And it's set on you."

He closes the gap between us and stands so close that we're almost touching. Looking up at him, I can see want in his eyes. And I'm fairly certain I'm returning the same look back at him.

Here's where things take a *really* sordid turn. I bet you're saying, *"Finally. It took her long enough to get the good stuff."* Sorry about the delay, but I needed a little more build-up. I hate looking like a wanton hussy too soon. Hopefully, my decision to get hot and heavy with Coop is more palatable now. At least I know he's not a serial killer.

Coop wraps his strong arms around me. All of me presses against all of him. He's a wall of steel. I feel his strength all around me. It has possessiveness to it. Like I'm his and not moving from his arms. Which is fine by me. His upper body lowers, bringing his head next to mine. I feel his lips on my neck kissing me in a small nibble-like fashion. But the effect his lips have on me isn't small. It's more like a gust of wind catching me off guard, making me unstable.

I let my body collapse into his arms, calming as his lovely assault continues on my partially exposed shoulder. The scruff on his jaw prickles my tender flesh driving me wild. But somehow I find my voice amid all the pheromones circulating between us.

"Coop, whatever's going on here, it's not my usual thing." As I speak, his lips inch their way up behind my ear. The sensation makes it hard to concentrate. "Hook-ups aren't me."

But who am I kidding? He's a pro-football player. Women likely drop to their knees on command for him. Trouble is I've never been one of *those* women before.

"I know." His breathy words hit my ear. He's almost panting. And that turns me on even more. "Just relax, baby. Gonna make you feel so good."

And on command, I throw in the towel. Admit defeat. Give into the fire I'm feeling inside. But this is one battle where the surrendering party wins too. At least that's my hope.

His mouth finally makes it to mine. Our lips unite and his hands push me farther into him. Like he's hungry for me. Needy. My softness hits his hardness. Yes, that hardness! Impressive too. Everything about him is larger than life so I shouldn't be surprised.

I push my hips forward against him in a grinding motion. And he responds by kissing me harder. One hand clasps behind my head while the other makes its way under the back of my shirt. I feel his fingers lightly stroking my skin. His touch. Skin to skin. It's almost too much.

"God, you're so soft," Coop mumbles his words against my lips not wanting to break our connection. "I want you in my bed. Okay?"

"Okay," I whisper.

And that one tiny word, sets Coop off on a series of motions. He bends and places one arm behind my knee. The next thing I know I'm airborne and being cradled in his arms baby style, pulled to his chest.

"Oh..." I let out a small cry when he's lifting me from the ground, a reaction to his actions as they've caught me totally off guard.

He answers me by returning his lips back to my neck while drawing me up even higher in his arms. I fling my head back to give him better access, completely submitting to him.

I can't believe what's happening to me. It's a scene from a movie. A page out of a romance book. That's what this feels like, being totally swept off my feet and carried away. He's my Rhett and I feel like Scarlett. We are in Atlanta after all. Now he's moving and heading to his room, I think.

Let's be honest, ladies. We've all dreamt about this kind of a swoony experience. A hot man finds you so desirable he can't wait another second to have you. He's not even willing to wait for you to walk to his bedroom. He wants you there *now*, so he takes matters into his own hands, literally.

His bedroom. After walking down a long, arched hallway, that's where we are now. Even though it's a bright afternoon, the sun hides behind dark stained plantation shutters that are closed snugly against the windows. Rays of light peak through tiny cracks in the slats, flickering across us as he transports me toward his bed.

The setting is perfect, dreamlike. It's intimate, enticing, and so dangerous for someone like me. But I close my eyes and just feel, lost in the sensations as he lowers me to his waiting bed below.

The comforter he lays me on is soft, plush. I sink into it and he climbs on to the bed next to me. Gently, he rests part of his body on top of me and his perfect lips find mine again, continuing to build the passion between us. His weight shifts a little and I feel his erection pressing against my hip. I move against him and he groans.

Me, Millie, just made Mr. Football moan out loud. I can't believe the effect I'm having on him. God knows he's had me under his spell since he walked into Joe's bar.

His hands make their way under my shirt, unclasping my bra with practiced skill. But I remove that thought from my mind as his fingers find my breasts then nipples. I arch my back into his touch, wanting and needing more. He raises my shirt, exposing me to him for the first time. While he gazes at my breasts, I remove my top and bra. His eyes look into mine and I swear he's thanking me just by his look. And then he descends. He finds a nipple with his mouth. His fingers discover the other one.

It's pleasure and ecstasy as he twists, sucks and pulls at me. His attention to my sensitive nipples makes me squirm and shift under him. During my movement my legs part and he positions himself between them, spreading me wider. I do nothing to stop him.

"I've wanted to touch you since I first saw you."

His words are shocking. Me?

"Yes, *you*. So fucking sexy." Oh damn. I must've said that question out loud.

I want to tell him I feel the same about him, but the words don't come. Instead, I try to show him my feelings by pulling his shirt up and running my hands down his back, grazing my nails across him until he shivers at my touch.

Muscles, tensing and relaxing are what my fingers meet as they wander aimlessly, learning his body. He's solid. Not an ounce of fat. He radiates strength.

He starts to descend lower on my stomach. Kissing and licking a trail to the top of my shorts. I look down at him. Our eyes meet and his are trained on mine. Hot with desire, I'm panting with anticipation. He's totally in charge right now. He's calling all the shots, but I'm not sure where he's headed.

Quickly Coop rises to his knees and places his hands around my left leg. He raises it up almost to his shoulder. I watch him reach for the tied strings of leather on my sandals. He tugs on a strap releasing it from its knot. The ends are free now and he torturously unwinds them around my ankle. Deliberately slow. It's like he's making a meal out of this act. Three courses including an after dinner drink!

When the last of the straps is freed, he pulls my sandal away from my foot and tosses it to the side. Before it lands on the floor, he's already working on the other one. It too succumbs to his slow and methodical removal. I'm practically ready to scream, *"Just take the damn thing off and screw me already."* His slowness is killing me.

From the smirky grin on his face, I'm rather certain he knows what he's doing to me. It's on purpose like he wants me begging for mercy. And I decide that I'm not too proud to beg.

"Oh god, Coop. Please..." I hardly recognize my voice. I've never felt this kind of passion before. Maybe it's the naughtiness. Who knows?

"Please, what, baby?" God he's gonna make me say it.

"I want *you*. In... Me... *Now*..." Maybe it's still my tipsy head, but I've jumped off the cliff.

After my declaration, Coop growls like a tiger. It's more of a roar and he rolls over me stopping somewhere between my thighs. I want him in a desperate way. Like he's my next breath. So I yield to his hands as they paw at my shorts and my panties. I think only my shorts survive his claws as my panties disintegrate into several pieces. Nothing appears to be safe and I hope that includes me.

Swiftly his fingers find me, part me, and caress.

"Oh, God. You're so wet," Coop practically moans.

Normally, I would die at words like this. I mean I don't know him at all. We're strangers, but just the opposite happens as I push myself against his fingers. Wanton. Eager for more. And he doesn't disappoint. His head lowers and you know what's next. Yes, his tongue. And now it's my turn to cry out.

"God! Yes!" I'm literally screaming now. My first not self-induced orgasm in a year feels so close. He licks and pushes his tongue against me. I run my fingers through his hair and push him down even harder, needing a little more as I feel myself starting to explode.

I shatter, fall apart. My body splinters like a million pieces of me are scattered around the room. Crying out, I hold his head tightly in place. Damn if I'll let him move.

Slowly, I release him from the death grip of my hands. He sits up again and I'm greeted with a salacious smile. He's rather proud of himself it appears and so am I. As a teacher, I think he deserves an A+ for all his efforts. And a towel for his face, if you know what I mean. Nothing says a job well done like a dripping chin!

"Enjoy that, baby?" he says while standing up from the bed. I nod, as I'm not sure if my voice is functioning yet, my entire body still humming from my orgasm.

Watching mesmerized, I see him remove his shirt and cargo shorts. He's beautiful. Chiseled. I feel like I'm back in art class studying works carved in marble. I can't wait to feel him, touch him.

I hold my breath as his hands come back up to his boxer briefs. His erection is hardly contained and with one swift move, it's freed. My breath hitches at the sight. There sure is a lot of him to fit in little old me, but I'm all for trying. God, Coop may ruin me for other men.

"Ready or not, here I come?" He smiles all sexy, teasing.

I nod again, silent as he crawls up between my legs and lies some of his weight against me. I instinctively bend my knees and place my feet flat on the bed. They dip into the softness, gripping for a foothold.

I feel him run his length against my sex. Up and down. Pressing. I'm still sensitive from my orgasm. All my feelings are heightened. I've heard of multiple orgasms but have never gotten even close before. But those times were Pre-Coop. I think my sex life will now have a dividing line called BC/AC: before Coop, after Coop.

Slowly he moves up my body and reaches for his nightstand. I thought he wanted me to return the oral favor at first, but when I see him pull out a shiny foil packet, I'm relieved. Even though I'm on the Pill, I'd be the lucky girl who got some horrible STD the first time she had casual sex.

The foil packet's dangling in front of my face as he holds it between his fingers. "Suit me up, baby." I have to chuckle, because even with my limited football knowledge, I know players use this term. What a typical guy. Chocked full of romance and all.

Coop places the packet in my waiting hand. I've never done this before. All my boyfriends and I were monogamous so there was no need. But I attended a public high school, sat through health class as we sheathed bananas so this should be easy. I hope.

I tear the foil at the little cut indent and pull the condom out. I pause and look up at his face. His eyes are definitely giving me the go-ahead signal. I scoot down beneath him just a little as he's on knees with his legs resting on both sides of me.

I come face to face with the part of him that needs to be suited up. My hands rise up to touch him. He's velvet and stone. Hot and strong. Daringly, I pump my hand up and down the length of him. He moans and I squirm at the sound. There's something powerful about making him come undone.

His reaction spurs me on even more and I bravely open my mouth, letting my lips enclose around him. Ridges of him meeting my tongue while my hand still holds him, moving. Now I swear he's starting to shake. The arms that are holding him up are trembling as a result of what I'm doing to him.

"Oh, God." He moans with words slurred together. "I want you now."

He moves away from me in a flash. I eye him in question, but his intentions are made clear quickly when he grabs the condom out of my hand and rolls it down himself in one quick motion. He settles between my legs one more time, lining himself up with me, then bucks his hips.

In that one solid motion, he's in me and I cry out, not from pain, more from the unexpected onslaught. He stills as my cry subsides then looks me in the eye, searching my face to see if I'm okay.

I push my hips forward while he's motionless, wanting more, he gets the message I'm sending and unleashes. Lifting my ass in his hands, he sits up more on his knees and starts relentlessly thrusting into me. He's in total control of my body. It's his alone right now.

I close my eyes as my back arches off the bed; greedily receiving everything he's giving me. I've never had sex like this before. Bordering rough. It's a forceful, intense passion. I know I'm totally ruined for anyone else now as I feel another orgasm approaching. All I can do now is submit to it and chant *Oh my God* over and over. A litany to his rhythmic thrusts.

"Oh... My... *God*..." My final chorus is a long, drawn-out shout as I explode again.

He falls forward, leaning on an elbow, but his pounding continues as his fingers touch me where I'm detonating. They're gentle but potent, prolonging my high. Coop sure knows what the hell he's doing. Fortunate for me.

As I'm descending from some place on the ceiling, he follows me calling my name out as he comes. It's the sexiest damn thing I've ever heard.

Coop collapses on top of me. We're trying to catch our breaths, as he looks down into my eyes. Honestly, I'm a little nervous at this moment. What does one say in the afterglow of hook-up sex? *Thanks?* I'm clueless.

"Hi there." Thankfully, Coop breaks the silence with the first words he spoke to me at Joe's Bar.

"Hi there," I reply back but giggle as I do. I find it funny, but oddly comforting. He's definitely not brushing me off which is a plus in this situation.

Rolling over to his side, Coop breaks our connection. But he wraps an arm around me and draws me to him. His fingers brush the hair away from my face and neck. I gaze up at him and find him smiling at me. He has a content look on his face, one that I helped to place there.

"Millie, that was unreal. God, I don't want to let you go."

Wow, I wasn't expecting that at all. It's completely unexpected and maybe a little over the top. Does he say that to all the girls that warm his bed? Keep them from regretting their decision to sleep with him? I wish I knew.

"Unreal is an understatement." That's the best I can do right now. I'd like to say, "Thanks," but that seems a bit strange. It's not like he just passed me the potatoes.

I snuggle closer into him, closing my eyes as his fingers skate over my back. Sweet, light circles...

Chapter 6

I am hot, overheated. My eyes are closed but I know exactly where I am. Coop's bed, where a plaque should hang saying, "The site of Millie's first illicit rendezvous."

I slowly open my eyes and realize why I feel like a furnace is blowing on me. I'm right up against Coop's body. He's asleep on his back and I'm tucked into his side, my face plastered to his chest.

We must've fallen asleep like this. Both of us. An exhausting round of sex can do that to a person. I'm speaking like an expert here, which is the furthest thing from the truth. But I believe we were both spent.

How do I move without waking him up? I have to get up and go to the bathroom, but don't want to face him awake yet. The alcohol's effect on numbing my brain in the decision-making department has left me. I'm facing reality now as well as a naked man. Jeez, what the hell was I thinking? Oh right, I wasn't. Silly me.

Slowly, I wiggle away from him, stopping every few inches, hopefully making less of a disturbance. He doesn't move a muscle as I reach the edge of the bed and gingerly scoot off it, my feet now on the floor.

There's a set of double doors on the wall opposite the bed. I pray it's his master bath and proceed toward them. When I quietly open them, I see a room straight out of a magazine. A shower for ten, encased in glass with a mosaic tiles on the wall. It's breathtaking. I've decided it's good to be an athlete.

I tiptoe across the cold tile floor to the toilet, which has its own special little room. Nice and private. After finishing, I stop in front of the mirror over the double sinks. I am completely naked and my hair's a hornet's nest. Medusa has nothing on me other than being clothed.

I collapse onto the counter with my head in my hands. It's decision time for me and like the chicken shit that I am I decide to flee. Get the hell out of his house before he wakes up. I know what you're likely saying. "He told you he didn't want to let you go." Wonderful comment in the moments after our shared bliss, but I didn't want to face the fact that it was likely just a line, a comeback.

Gathering up all my clothes, I put them back on in record time. I stuff my shredded panties into my pocket. Not the kind of DNA evidence I want to leave on the scene.

Coop is still asleep. He hasn't stirred at all since I left his bed and looks dead to the world. Seeing him quiet and peaceful is such a contrast to when he was screwing my brains out. I sigh and quietly say goodbye to him.

I find my purse back in the main room of his house, a little brown spot sitting on the white carpet in front of his fireplace. It was dropped when I realized Coop was Mr. Football.

I look up at his jersey one more time. If he was a normal guy, more in my league, I would likely stay around and see what happens. But he's light years and a few million dollars away from unemployed me.

Checking my phone, I scroll through the alerts on my screen and see scores of missed texts and calls from Priscilla. She's likely phoned Joe by now. Sent out the National Guard. I text her quickly saying I'm okay which is a big, fat lie. I'm *not* okay; I'm a mess all around.

I make my way outside his front door safely then sit on his entrance steps and lace back up my sandals. I start my way down his driveway and break into a slight run. Trying to remember which direction we came from in his car does me no good. Between the alcohol and being awed by his subdivision, I have no clue.

Gambling, I turn left when I reach the street in front of his house. I start running again and glance down a side street as I approach it. The entrance gate appears down at its end. Bingo! I head straight toward it praying that someone drives up to the gate soon and it swings open. When I'm only a few feet away, a car pulls up behind me and the gates move. I slip out of them and I'm free.

However, I also have no idea where I am. An unenviable predicament to be in for sure. Who uses GPS to find their way home after a one-afternoon stand? Me, that's who. Pathetic.

But I need to get the hell out of here. The booze has worn off and I'm not feeling too proud of myself. Out of sight (even though he was such a pretty one) hopefully means out of mind.

As I'm walking down the sidewalk I input Priscilla's address and a map appears which will hopefully direct me back to her apartment building. The screen shows that I'm really not too far away. It's an easy walk, so I hoof it to her house, the map and its little blue GPS dot leading my way.

Once I'm back at Priscilla's, I take a long, hot shower, almost to the point of scalding. I don't believe I want to wash away my experience with Coop, at least not totally, but I do.

Would I have slept with him if I were completely sober? Probably not. But I wasn't rip-roaring, forget my morals drunk either. I think I was more intoxicated with *him*. He was beautiful. Found me attractive, hot even. And there was some crazy chemistry floating between us. A girl can only take so much. It's the resisting part that I failed at and I'm likely just another woman who's fallen under his same spell. Bewitched.

I made it through the rest of the week and weekend thanks to Priscilla. She arrived back in Atlanta earlier than planned. I think she worried I was in a "hide the knives mood." I wasn't *that* bad, but I was definitely down.

Likely unemployed still and trying to process my liaison with Coop had left me in a tizzy. So Priscilla smothered me in chocolate—ice cream, brownies, and candies. You name it, we ate it. Add a lot of, "You'll find the right guy," and "He's not good enough to shine your shoes," talk and I headed back to Augusta feeling a bit better.

That's where I find myself now, driving down the highway on the outskirts of my hometown, remnants of me left behind in a posh gated community in Atlanta.

It's time for me to put Coop and our time together out of my mind. Erase it from my memory. Instead, I'll focus on what's next—facing my parents with their twenty million questions about how my interview went. I avoided conversations with them about it over the last few days, telling them via text that it went all right and I'd give them the run down when I got home.

Well, now's the time as I see my mother's car sitting in the driveway. I collect my bags, head inside, and try to prepare myself for her grilling. She means well, but I think she's ready for me to truly leave the nest, get out on my own. You know how much I want that too. It's my constant hope.

Chapter 7

Another Wednesday rolls around. It's been a week since my disastrous interview and I haven't heard squat, not even a peep after writing a thank you note and emailing Mr. Reynolds. Not a good sign at all.

I'm scouring the Internet for new teaching postings when my phone rings. It's an Atlanta number and I'm thinking Mr. Reynolds or his assistant, Mrs. Peterson, is calling to tell me the bad news.

"Hello," I answer with absolutely no enthusiasm in my voice.

"Is this Ms. Montgomery?" Yep, it's Mr. Reynolds. Here we go...

"Yes, this is she." Southern manners die hard.

"Ms. Montgomery, This is Mr. Reynolds. I'm sorry that it has taken me a week to get back in touch with you. But we have finally come to a decision." I hold my breath, preparing for the worst. "And I'd like to offer you the position of art teacher at Peachtree High School."

After hearing those words, I'm transported somewhere else. Another planet? Jupiter or Mars perhaps? His offer is totally unexpected.

"Wait," I bring myself back down to planet Earth. "You're offering the position to me?"

"Absolutely. We are very excited to have you here with us a Peachtree. As a matter of fact, I need you to come back to Atlanta as soon as possible. If you decide to take the position that is."

Decide to take the position? You've got to be kidding me; of course I'll take it. Sweet Mr. Reynolds doesn't have a clue how my last shred of hope was long gone, likely sailing on a boat to the Bahamas.

"I'd love to teach at Peachtree. And getting back quickly to Atlanta isn't a problem at all. When do you need me?"

"I'm so pleased that you can join our faculty here. And I hate to ask this of you on such short notice, but something you said in the interview has me thinking."

He pauses and I wonder what the hell he's leading into. I made up a *lot* of things in the interview and the thought is making my palms start to sweat. You know that old saying, "Chickens coming home to roost."

"I remember you talking about bringing athletes and artists together." At least this part in the interview was true. "Well, one of our parents was chairing a fundraiser for the football team. However, her mother has taken ill. Sudden thing. And we need your help." He stops, waiting for my response. And being eager and excited, I jump right on it.

"Of course! I'd be glad to help in any way that I can."

"Thank you. I was hoping you'd say that. It's a Casino Night. Off-site too. No students. We have a new football coach here who's also going to be helping. Just got off the phone with him."

I'd like you both to be the master of ceremonies at the event then divide the proceeds amongst the art department and the football boosters. Everyone's on board with the idea here. You two will be the face of the event."

"Wow, I think this is a great idea. When do you need me there?" The wheels in my brain are already starting to churn with ideas of what I can have art students do with a little extra money.

"The event is this Saturday. Short notice I know, but if you could possibly drive to Atlanta tonight and meet with me in the morning. The football coach is coming in at nine."

"I can definitely be there. No problem at all." Thank God, Priscilla is in Atlanta right now.

"Great. I think you and this new coach will get a long fine. He's rather a big star around here. Maybe you've heard of him, Andrew Cooper?"

That's right, the one and only Andrew Cooper. Better known as Coop. I don't really remember the rest of my conversation with Mr. Reynolds. I have the important things down, though. I got the teaching job. I need to be at Peachtree tomorrow morning. And lastly, Coop is the new football coach.

Kill me now!

When I'm a little more coherent and stop shaking, I give Priscilla a call. She needs to talk me down off the ledge here. I'm perched atop a thirty-story building fearing that I'm going to be pushed to my death.

"Hey, Millie. I've been waiting for your call."

"You have?"

"Yes, I have some inside sources remember. I teach at Peachtree." She's laughing, but I'm still dying.

"Right, well I got the job." My voice is flat.

"I know. I found out the other woman they interviewed was leaving her position due to personal misconduct. Or more commonly know as having an affair with a married teacher."

"I knew there had to be a reason I got the job over her."

"What's wrong with you, Millie?" She seems concerned. "I thought you'd be going crazy."

"Oh, I don't know. Maybe it's the new football coach that was hired today at Peachtree. Andrew Cooper. Ring any bells?"

"No shit." She seems shocked too. "How did you find that out before me?"

"Mr. Reynolds informed me that Coop and I are needed to work together on a fundraiser this weekend for the football booster program. A casino night. We're headlining the event."

"This is bad on so many levels. What are you going to do?"

"I don't know. But I feel sick at the thought of seeing Coop again let alone working with him on something. It's turned my dream of getting this job into a nightmare."

"It's unbelievable. What are the odds?" Priscilla knows me better than to ask that question.

"Me and Murphy have been friends all my life." That's Murphy's Law in case there was a question.

"Funny, Millie," she retorts.

"If it's okay, I'm heading to Atlanta tonight. Mr. Reynolds wants me in his office at nine tomorrow morning."

"Wow, that's quick. But I don't have any big plans tonight, so come on in. I think I'll run by the liquor store too. We may need a few drinks to help us strategize for tomorrow."

"Thanks so much. I need to go tell my parents what's up. And pack for a few days. Is it okay if I stay with you until Sunday?"

"Sure. No problem."

"I'll text you when I'm leaving for Atlanta."

"Okay. And keep your chin up. Somehow you'll get through this."

"I hope you're right. Talk to you later."

I end the conversation and prepare for telling my parents. I have to muster up some excitement or they may not believe that I was offered the job. Time for a Meryl Streep worthy Academy Award performance.

Chapter 8

My stomach is tied in knots. My nerves are completely shot. I hardly slept a wink last night just tossed and turned, worried and fretted about seeing Coop again today. I pull into the parking lot of Peachtree High School at 8:45 a.m. The lot's practically empty since school's not in session. But I see a familiar car. An expensive sports car. Damn, it's Coop's sweet ride, which means he's here already.

You know what really stinks? I should be thrilled about this job. Bouncing off the ceiling and walls with excitement. Instead, my palms are clammy and I feel like I'm going to throw up.

I walk the long sidewalk that leads to the doors of the building. Each step brings me closer to a fate I never dreamed of—facing my first and only sexual regret; even if it is only a partial one.

Sheryl Crow's song, "My Favorite Mistake" keeps playing in my brain, a tribute to my misery. But I have to admit it's true. Deep down inside I know I'd probably succumb to Coop again. He was just so damn perfect in his lovemaking. I've tried to forget what his hands, mouth and everything else felt like that day. But it's no use. The more I try, the more I remember. Ruined, I'm completely ruined.

Once inside the building, I smooth down the cotton material of my sensible dress. Priscilla dressed me this morning, styled my hair and applied my makeup. My mind was too scattered to make decisions or concentrate. She chose a respectable appearance for me, not quite schoolmarm but close.

I reach for the doorknob to the main office. My fingers freeze over the shiny metal. I dread the moment when I will face Coop, when our eyes meet. The thought petrifies me. What will his reaction be of seeing me again? At least I have the advantage of knowing what lies ahead of me. He's completely clueless.

Mr. Reynolds probably used the name, Amelia Montgomery when he spoke of me and Coop only knows me as Millie.

I clasp my hands together as I enter the office, worried that their shaking might be visible.

I spot Mrs. Peterson in the distance. Her head down as she shuffles through some papers. I start walking toward her. My movement must have been detected as she looks up and smiles at me. God, how I needed to see her warm smiling face right now. It's comforting.

"Hello, Ms. Montgomery," she sweetly greets me. "Congratulations on your new position here. We're super happy to have you."

"Thank you. I am so happy too." I try to muster up some enthusiasm, but it's just not there.

"Mr. Reynolds is in his office with Andrew Cooper. He's a real looker. Single, I've heard too." She winks at me and I want to sink into the floor. I'm tempted to turn and run out the door. "Let me open the door to his office for you."

I follow her a few steps to the principal's office and the space where Coop awaits. My knees are weak, hardly holding me up.

As she pushes the door open, and I peek in around her. Mr. Reynolds reacts to her at the door and rises from his chair behind his desk. Coop sits in front of him in the exact seat I sat in during my interview. I gingerly take a couple steps toward the desk as Coop turns his head and pivots his body my direction. Our eyes meet across the space. There's only a few feet between us.

It takes him a second to register who I am, like he's trying to place me. His brows are pinched in concentration. But the second he figures out that it's me, Millie, the girl he screwed last Wednesday, I know it. His jaw drops. His eyes widen in shock. His hair might even be standing on end. It's like a bolt of electricity ran through him and he jolts straight up to his feet.

Now Coop's whole body is turned to me. We're staring at each other. Deadlocked. Each of us standing as still as soldiers guarding Big Ben. I forget that there are others in the room until I hear Mr. Reynolds coughing slightly to get our attention.

"Hello, Ms. Montgomery," Mr. Reynolds says breaking the spell between Coop and me. He walks to me and shakes my hand. "Great to have you here with us and on such short notice. I'd like to introduce you to our new assistant football coach, Coach Andrew Cooper. He goes by Coop."

I take Coop's outstretched hand into mine. He does more than shake it. He presses his fingers a little too firmly around mine. Then he holds my hand in his tight grip a little longer than is proper. We each mumble a, "Hello, nice to meet you."

He releases my hand and his fingers slowly trail the length of mine as he pulls away. All I can think about is what those fingers did to me in his bed. How they pleasured me. A rush of heat floods over me at the memory. I'm betting my face has turned a fire engine red too, betraying my thoughts.

"Please have a seat, you two, and welcome again. I'm very glad to have you both here. Our newest additions to Peachtree."

"Thank you," we both say at the same time. I give Coop a nervous glance.

Somewhere from deep down inside, I force my legs to move. They bring me just inches away from Coop as I sit down. Mr. Reynolds and Coop follow my lead and sit down too. Pure southern gentlemen waiting to take a seat until the lady sits down first.

My eyes are turned toward Mr. Reynolds but I can feel Coop's hot gaze on me. I move my head slightly to catch his face and see his expression. It's more of a glare. An unhappy one. He's pissed, angry. His nostrils are even a little flared.

My uneasiness makes me fidget and shift in my seat. I nervously wring my hands in my lap, looking anywhere but Coop's direction. But I can feel his anger directed toward me. It burns my skin. But I can't figure out why he's so pissed off at me. I swing my hair to cover the side of my face that's facing him. It serves as a wall of protection. However, body armor might be better right now.

"Cecilia Barnes, the parent who was going to be the master of ceremonies at Saturday's event, wants me to thank you for helping her out. She's also the event chair but has delegated her organizing work to other parents. So, simply put, we need you two to show up a little early and run the event from a microphone. Encourage people to open their wallets if you know what I mean."

"I've done this for charities many times. Mostly for the Children's Hospital here in Atlanta. It's all about trust.

Having people believe what you tell them," Coop says passionately.

I know his last words are directed at me. Literally. He looked right at me as he spoke them. Shit. I just need to make it through this meeting and Saturday night's event. I'll be fine after that. How often will I see him once school starts? Art teachers and coaches don't usually cross paths. Thank God.

Mr. Reynolds instructs us on the whereabouts of Saturday's fundraiser. Since it's held off campus at a hotel and not a school-sanctioned function per se, alcohol will be served, a fact that leaves me feeling pretty damn happy. I'll need a few drinks to get through an event where Coop and I are working together.

Though too much drinking likely landed me in Coop's bed in the first place. I'll just have to pace myself Saturday night and institute a two-drink, two-foot rule. I can't get too buzzed or too close to him. He's rather lethal to me. I glance over and scan his profile. Yep, he's very deadly. Damn, his sexiness. I swear it streams off of his body and creates a puddle in my panties. I lean as far away from him as I can, my body practically half over the arm of my seat and anymore leaning will have the chair tipping over.

"I know you're an old hat at this, Coop. You'll have to show Ms. Montgomery the ropes. Teach her how to get everyone excited about a cause and willing to donate to it." Sadly, Mr. Reynolds doesn't realize that Coop has already shown me his "rope."

"Getting people excited and willing to donate is something I'm good at. " Coop's tone is sarcastic. And yes, he says these comments right to my face. Looking down at me with anger in his eyes. I shiver, but not from fear. Damn, my traitorous body.

Mr. Reynolds finally starts bringing this meeting from hell to an end. I'm close to bolting from the room, claiming

I feel sick. It really isn't a lie. Priscilla made me eat a bagel and cream cheese this morning and it isn't sitting well on my stomach.

"You two have all the information you need, I believe." Mr. Reynolds hands us each a sheet of paper. "I've taken the liberty of putting your contact information on here. Phone numbers, emails, etcetera. The street address of the hotel, along with the details of the people helping run the event. I think you two are all set."

"Thank you, sir," I respond. I've been mute throughout the meeting afraid to utter a word just letting the men do all the talking. A sweet little southern wallflower who was soundly plucked by the man sitting next to her. I didn't know what to say, preferring to just recoil in my chair.

"You have a passion for the arts, Ms. Montgomery. Coop has one for football. I'd like to see you two combine your passions. Bring them together." I lower my head, beyond mortified by these words, while Coop coughs or chokes. I'm not really sure. But I'm not daring enough to look his way. "I'll let you two get acquainted. I have a meeting with the math department in a few minutes. Thanks for helping us out in a pinch."

Did Mr. Reynolds just say that? Combine our passions? Shit, I hate to break the news to him but we're long past that point. Passions shared, spent and still being replayed over and over in my mind.

We all rise out of our seats. I quickly shake Mr. Reynolds' hand and thank him for the opportunity to teach at Peachtree. Then I turn to leave his office in double time completely ignoring Coop, stepping past Mrs. Peterson without a glance in her direction. I just want the hell out of there. I don't feel like I can breathe. As I break free and make it past the front doors, I hit the warm, summer Atlanta air then break into a run and head to my car.

Over my heartbeat pounding in my head, I hear someone calling my name behind me. Shouting it. It doesn't take a rocket scientist to know who it is. But as I said before, I'm a major chicken shit. I don't do confrontations. Not my kind of thing. Southern breeding perhaps? Grin and bear it. Suck it up and take it. Not the best philosophies but it's who I am at heart.

I'm digging around in my purse for my keys as I continue to run away from the voice that's calling my name. Getting closer to my car, I now can hear his feet hitting against the pavement behind me.

My keys are out and ready as I try with shaky hands to unlock the car, but a hand grabs my arm and spins me around. And I'm met with the one and only Coop. He's mad, fuming, and hot as hell. His blazing eyes are leaving me breathless. I lean against the door of my car. I need help standing up. Being this close to him has a horrible effect on my knees. They've become Jell-O.

"Well, if it isn't Millie?" There's no way to miss the disdain in his voice. "Ms. Love 'Em and Leave 'Em, herself."

Crap. I want a quick comeback, but what can I say? His words are completely true. There's no way around them, so I decide to barrel right through them instead.

"That's right. You know me. Hook-up queen."

"It would appear so. So you got the teaching job after all."

"Yes, I did. And you found one too, it looks like. Slumming with the regular folks now." I match the tone of his voice. Passionate disgust. But I'm really dying inside and just want to leave before I pass out from being so close to him. His scent is driving me wild, making me want to kneel before him and do bad, bad things.

"I can't believe you. After spending all afternoon with me. Great sex with no complaints, right?" Oh shit, he had to bring it up. The sex part. "You leave me without a single word. Not even a note saying, 'Thanks for the fuck.'"

"I don't want to talk about this right now." I need distance or I'm going to be all over him, tearing his clothes off in the parking lot. It's one or the other. So I shake his hands off my arm and turn around toward my car. I opt for the choice that won't get me arrested or fired.

"Right. Run away, little girl. You're apparently great at that." I cringe at his comments, but finally get my door unlocked. Damn, I hate my car. It's so old and cheap that it doesn't even have automatic doors. "If I didn't care so much about the football team and the support of the booster club, I'd move hell or high water to get out of Saturday night."

"Well, I'll be praying for both. Hell *and* high water." I open my door and slam it behind me. After getting my old bucket of bolts started, I peel out of the parking lot not even peeking at the rearview mirror.

When I'm two blocks away from school, I pull into a store parking lot and stop. Leaning my head on the hard plastic of my steering wheel, the tears I'd been holding back start pouring out. Ugly crying again, like I just finished watching *The Way We Were* or *Old Yeller*. It's that bad. In my haze of tears, I reach for my phone and dial Priscilla.

"How did it go with Coop?"

"I—" is the only word that escapes through my tears. Priscilla knows that I'm a mess and does the talking, thank goodness.

"Come on back to the apartment. I'll have a batch of brownies in the oven when you get here. It's going to be okay, Millie. I promise."

I mutter an unintelligible word back to her and hang up. I find the monogrammed handkerchief I carry around in my purse. Southern women tend to have one floating around them at all times; a scarce artifact, but when you need a hankie, there is no substitute. I wipe off my face and blow my nose. Somehow, I make it back to Priscilla's apartment for round two of, "How to forget Coop" chocolate therapy.

Chapter 9

Over the last two days, Coop emails me a few times about the Casino Night. Every email has someone else co-copied in the exchange. Nothing out of the ordinary is said by him. Just logistics about the evening and our responsibilities. He completely ignores me. Never talks to me directly. More like he's talking over me or patting me on the head like a small errant child. Okay, I admit he's the celebrity, but we were supposed to be working on this together.

So since he's ignoring me, I decide to return the favor and say nothing in response. Mature, right? Since my sob fest on Thursday, my feelings for him have definitely evolved from timidity to something closer to rage.

Now he's just pissing me off. Treating me with no regard. I'm as mad as a New Jersey Real Housewife. Even felt like flipping a table today at Starbucks when I read his latest email to me.

Coop asked if someone on the fundraising committee would write up small note cards with the lines I needed to read in front of everyone. He thought I might crack under the pressure of having all the eyes on me. Okay, maybe he's totally right, I hate speaking to crowds, but he's being a royal jerk about it. It was like I wasn't even on the email chain. Shouldn't he have asked me first? I'm so mad right now I could punch him.

Sadly, if I didn't have to emcee this event with Coop, I'd be excited. It actually looks like a lot of fun. A makeshift casino is being put together, people will pay money for the poker chips and use them to play everything from roulette to blackjack, but no one wins cash prizes. Instead, winners take home items donated by local businesses. The biggest winner of the night gets a week stay at a lovely condo in Destin, Florida. Not bad for a high school fundraiser.

Priscilla prepares me for the evening. I borrow everything from her except underwear. She's assembled my wardrobe—black three-inch heels, a fitted black pencil skirt and a red blouse with short sleeves. My outfit screams career girl. She wanted me to have an air of authority, build up my confidence, perhaps.

Priscilla drives me to the hotel where the event is being held. I climb out of the car in front of the hotel and speak to her through the open door.

"Thanks, Priscilla. I'll see you back here in thirty minutes, right?"

"It might be closer to an hour. I'm picking up two other girls and one of them is notorious for being late. But an hour, tops."

"See you." I shut the car door and make my way inside to the hotel's lobby. There are official signs pointing the way to the event in Ballroom A. Stopping just outside the door to the ballroom, I pull out my compact and check my lipstick and hair. Everything appears to be okay so I walk right through the open door.

My feet stop and so does my heart when I see Coop. Damn him. He's wearing a charcoal gray suit with pinstripes. Quite the change from the casual attire I've always seen him in. He looks as sexy as hell. Polished and authoritative. Dare I even say dominating?

My mind starts to wander back to a bedroom in a gated community with beautiful streams of light peeking in through wood slats. Dangerous thoughts that have to be controlled. I see the bar to the side of the room and make a beeline toward it. A drink in hand is needed before I come face to face with Coop.

I order my standard vodka tonic, but not after being carded. Really? I'm a damn teacher here. Once I have my lifeline sitting in my hand, I start walking toward Coop. He sees me coming and I don't care one bit for that scowl on his face. I decide to finish my drink on my way to him. I give a fleeting thought to turning around for another cocktail, perhaps a shot, something quick acting. But I press on. No turning back now.

"Well, good evening, Ms. Montgomery. I see you found a familiar friend." He says this while pointing to my glass. What an asshole. Really? The nerve.

"At least this friend knows how to make a woman feel good." Boom and burn. Yeah, that left him a little shocked. What is the football term? Touchdown for Millie.

"Nice, nice. But I'm pretty sure those two orgasms I gave you felt better than whatever you're drinking," he continues, smirky smile and all. "Unless that drink makes you scream, 'Oh, my, God.'"

"How dare you!" I have a notion to throw the drink in his face but I need the alcohol too bad to waste it.

"Listen, we could play this 'hate' game all night, but we have work to do." I roll my eyes at him. I want to duke this out with more words. "I'm not anymore happy about this arrangement than you are."

"You don't know anything about my happiness," I answer defiantly.

"So you're happy to be here then?"

"You know that I'm not," I spit out at him. "I'd rather be at the zoo watching a baboon scratch its ass."

He looks at me confused and starts to laugh. Hard. A doubled-over and holding his side, kind of laugh.

That's the craziest thing I've ever said. How did I come up with that? Baboons? What the hell did that bartender put in my drink?

"Quit laughing at me." I'm getting really pissed now.

"Let's... quit... monkeying around... and get to work." He speaks each word through his laughter practically choking on them. It's completely annoying. People in the room are starting to notice us now. The workers who are setting up the event are probably thinking he's as mad as a hatter.

"Stop the stupid monkey comments. You're making a scene." He finally calms down and quits laughing.

"Here are your cue cards for the night." I snatch them out of his hand.

"You were such a jerk to me about them. You brought up the subject without even asking me first. Who do you think you are anyway?"

"I'll be a monkey's uncle if I wasn't the best sex you ever had." Now my drink is almost gone. Just a few drops left with some melted ice. And I bet you know what I'm about to do. That's right. The contents inside my highball glass land on Coop's face and bounce off onto the floor. He stares at me stunned. I'm stunned too.

"That's it. You're crazy. Completely nuts." His voice is raised, almost to the point of yelling. "I think it's better that we stay away from each other tonight. I'll see you when it's time to step in front of the microphone. Until then get the hell out of my sight."

"For your information you weren't the best sex I've ever had." I know. I'm lying through my teeth here but no way am I letting him get away with thinking that he was all *that*. Even though he was. Well, you get my drift.

I turn on my heels and head back to the bar and straight into the chest of Mr. Reynolds. He's standing with his hands across his chest looking between Coop and me. It would be safe to assume he heard some of what we said. Likely witnessed my ice toss. I'm tempted to crawl under one of the casino tables.

"I have no idea what is or has gone on between you two. But the success of tonight's event is too important to let some lover's spat affect it. I expect both of you to act like grown ups. Am I making myself clear?" Oh boy, Mr. Reynolds isn't his usual jolly self.

"Sir, we just came to an understanding, right, Ms. Montgomery?" Coop says.

I nod in agreement. "I can assure we won't let anything like this happen again."

"Okay." Mr. Reynolds eyes us speculatively. "I need to help with a display, but I'll be watching."

Mr. Reynolds heads to a table by the stage where Coop and I will be standing later. I swear I heard Mr. Reynolds muttering under his breath, but I couldn't make it out.

Now with an empty glass in my hand, I continue my trip across the room to the bar. I don't even glance back at Coop, but I feel his eyes on me. Burning my backside. Deliciously. *Damn* him.

People start arriving about thirty minutes after the "incident." I'm finishing up my second drink and contemplating a third. The room isn't spinning. I'm still able to stand, so I order one more. This next drink was my big mistake as the third one was what tipped the scales of sobriety.

I feel a hand gripping my arm hard, just above the elbow. Fingers dig into my flesh and I let out a little cry protesting the pain.

"Hey," I say, wincing from the discomfort. Following the arm attached to mine, I see it belongs to none other than Coop. "What the hell do you want?"

"For one, that this night was over. And second, for you to sober up. How many drinks have you had?"

"Sober up?" I ask. "I'm fine. Just dandy."

"Good God." He holds my hand while pulling me with him. He's likely twice my weight and a good eight inches taller than me, so all I can do is follow him. "I think you're going to be Vanna White tonight. Just stand up at the mic, look beautiful and smile."

"I'm fine. Seriouz…" The word won't come out of my mouth right.

"See what I mean. You can't even talk."

I decide to keep my mouth shut, afraid that anything I say will make his point valid. He practically drags me across the floor to the front of the ballroom. There's a little stage for us to stand on. Coop helps me up a step to the platform then guides me on to the raised floor. He steps up to the microphone, which is attached to a podium and raises the mic a few inches. He side eyes me. It's a quick glance but he conveys a lot with it. Mostly, *Keep your damn mouth shut.*

He taps the mic to gather the crowd's attention and so the evening begins. Tap… tap… tap.

"Good evening, ladies and gentleman. I'm Andrew Cooper, Peachtree's new assistant football coach." There's a roar of applause, shouts and hollering. I guess he truly is a big deal after all. Whatever. "Thanks for the warm welcome. I'm looking forward to giving back to the Atlanta community here at Peachtree. Joining me tonight is Ms. Montgomery. Our new art teacher."

I do a perfect Vanna White impression and wave at the crowd smiling like I'm Miss America. All the pageant practice came in handy after all. Wouldn't my mother be proud?

"The proceeds of tonight's Casino Night will be split between the football booster club and the art department. So please support Peachtree by throwing some dice or turning a few cards..."

Just as Coop is speaking mid-sentence, there's a loud commotion in the back of the room. I stand up on my tiptoes to see what's going on back there. Coop steadies my balance by placing his hand on the shoulder opposite of him. I *am* swaying a bit.

I see a woman escorting a police officer toward us, zigzagging through the tables with people standing motionless at them likely wondering what the hell is going on. The woman walking our way is clearly upset, but the officer shows no emotion. His face is totally impassive. Not an expression shows. I can't for the life of me figure out what the hell is going on but I have a feeling this angry woman is about to clear things up for me.

"Officer, these two are the leaders here tonight." I gasp as she points to Coop and me. *What the heck?* "This whole evening is a game of chance. Unauthorized gambling in the eyes of the law."

Now the two intruders to the event are standing in front us. "I think we can clear this whole thing up quickly," the officer says in a commanding way, full of authority. His voice is the only sound in the room and strangely echoes off the walls. "We just need to see your permit to operate a charitable evening of gambling. I'm sure the fundraising chairperson has it."

Holy shit! I don't know the first or last thing about a gambling permit. And the chairperson is out of town taking care of her sick parent. All this adds up to us being royally screwed.

"Sir," Coop begins. "I think I can clear this up quickly. You may know me as Andrew Cooper, former tight end for the Falcons."

"Son, I don't give a rat's ass if you're the Pope. I need to see that paper."

Now's when things get a little crazy. I decide to pipe in here and it's not very helpful at all. Shocking, I'm sure.

"See, Coop. Finally someone who's not impressed with you and your superstar status."

I push him with both hands, but he hardly moves. In frustration, I start beating on his chest. Not one of my finest moments. He grabs my hands, more in defense from my slight beatings, but still I protest with gusto, struggling and fighting with him.

"How dare you hold me like that? Let go of me." I try to free myself to no avail.

"I'm not letting go of you until you calm the hell down." I'm pretty sure the entire room hears him say that through the microphone. The gasp I hear somewhere in the room proves the point.

"How can I calm down when you're such an asshole?" I hear even more gasps after that one.

"Okay, you two." The officer comes up onto the platform with us, moves his face in front of mine and takes a deep breath. "Just as I thought. Drinking. Both of you."

"What?" Coop asks incredulously. "I've not had a single drink tonight."

"Well, I've heard that one before. How about this then? I'm taking her to jail for being drunk and you for being disorderly. She did ask you to remove your hands and you didn't comply."

I look to my wrist and see Coop's fingers still wrapped around them. Then in a split second, he releases them. Like they're hot coals, burning his skin.

"Officer, I apologize for their behavior tonight." Mr. Reynolds appears in front of the podium, hopefully coming to our rescue. "It appears that we do have a permit, though it's in the hands of our event's chairperson. She was called out of town on a family emergency."

Mr. Reynolds comes up on the platform, stops at the officer's side, and whispers something into his ear. I watch as the officer nods his head up and down agreeing with whatever Mr. Reynolds told him. Hope springs up that this is all getting cleared up and the Casino Night can resume.

Mr. Reynolds finishes his secret conversation and moves to the side leaving the officer alone in front of us.

"Right now, I'm more worried about the display I just saw between these two than the gambling permit." I watch the officer pull a lone pair of handcuffs out of his pocket. "I think it's best to take them in, Mr. Reynolds. Let them cool down for a bit. Don't you?"

Mr. Reynolds looks between Coop and me. There's the oddest half-smile on his face. It surprises me, as I would've thought he'd be furious with our outburst and my drunken behavior.

"Yes, I agree. Some time cooling off is a good idea," Mr. Reynolds agrees with the cop. Wait a second. I'm going to jail for this? A silly quarrel. What universe am I living in anyway?

"Give me your hand, Miss." I extend my arm, and feel the cold metal as it encompasses my wrist, hearing the simple click securing the cuff. Damn, I used to think handcuffs were sexy. Not anymore.

"And now yours." He points to Coop's arm and repeats the same process. One handcuff and both of us bound together. Would someone please wake me up now? Surely, I'm dreaming and this is an awful nightmare.

The officer takes my arm gently and leads me off the platform. Coop has no choice but to follow. I walk through the room with my head down in shame until I hear Priscilla speaking somewhere to my left side.

"Don't worry, Millie. I'll call my cousin. He's an attorney." I look up and see her, and realize I'm crying, tears streaming down my face. I nod at her and mouth the words, "Thanks."

But I'll need more than an attorney. There's a good chance that I'll need another art teacher winning the lottery. This job, my dream one, is probably over before it really began. More angry tears follow. I'm frustrated, mad at Coop and myself.

I want to kick him in the shins. Take out all my frustrations on something, anything. I'm afraid to even look his way. If he returns my gaze with anger in his eyes, it could get ugly fast. I don't remember the last time I've been this upset. Steam might even be coming out of my ears.

Keeping my eyes trained on the ground, I see that we're in the lobby as the flooring changes to marble tiles. Shit, next up is the patrol car. Then the police station. After that the unemployment line. What a clusterfuck of a night.

The warm evening air hits me as the officer leads us outside. My skin is overheated and I wish there was a cool breeze blowing. Between all the alcohol and getting cuffed, I'm feeling feverish. Flush, too.

Now that we're outside, I peek up just enough to see the officer's awaiting patrol car in the distance, lights off, thankfully. Any more drama and I'd be screaming. As we approach the car, Coop finally speaks. He's been oddly silent the entire time.

"Officer, there really isn't a need to take us to the station. Surely, we can work this out here."

"Forget the speeches, hotshot. I'm not listening. You can tell your story to the precinct captain. He loves to be entertained." For the first time the police officer shows some emotion and laughs. At us. In Coop's face. We are so going down for the count now. I can almost hear the jail cell's door slamming shut.

Coop sighs in frustration. I look up at him and I swear he looks a little scared, uneasy. His record as the perfect celebrity is about to be tarnished. The press will have a field day when they get ahold of this. I'm a nothing. I'll go back to Augusta where I belong and find a job cat sitting or something. No one will care.

But he's going to have to answer for this one. The reporters will likely grill him and sensationalize the whole ordeal. And as Coop looks into my eyes, registering some feeling that I'd never seen on his face, a little sympathy pushes past my anger, making me just a little bit sorry. Dare I say remorseful?

"Hey." Talking just above a whisper, I pull on the handcuff we're both connected to and get his attention. "I'm sorry about all of this. I egged you on."

"Yes, you did. But I wanted to get back at you." Now I see anger in his eyes. He wanted a pound of flesh from me. Well, he's already had a few pounds of my flesh, but not like this.

"Get me back?" I ask. "Well, you sure picked an asshole way to do that."

We're standing at the car before Coop can answer me back. But I'm sure he'll fill me in on how wrong I am. The officer unlocks the back door for us.

I've seen this exact scenario a million times on TV shows. The bad guys under arrest have to climb in the backseat. The officer guides them, placing a hand on their heads so they don't knock themselves out on the door's frame. This is one art form I don't care to imitate. But we have no choice and climb into the back. Sliding across the leather seat, I make room for Coop. I lean against the far door. Far, far away from him.

"You have no idea, do you?" Coop asks me through gritted teeth, anger seething from him in waves. "Answer me."

"Wow, you're quite the jerk." My response is spoken more like a hiss. "No, I don't have any idea why you're so mad, and honestly I could care less."

"Here's the whole damn truth." He pauses, waiting until I make eye contact with him and we're staring into each other eyes. All my attention is his right now. His anger makes him appear so intense, dangerous, and deliciously sexy. He's as beautiful as hell and I find myself shifting in my seat. It's the damn Coop effect. No woman is immune to it. "I've never, I mean never, had someone leave me after having sex like you did."

And boom it hits me. This has nothing to do with me, Millie, the person. It's his big, fragile ego. I bruised it. Hit him where it *really* counts. The simple act of my leaving him without a word was a bull's-eye aimed straight at his pride.

"I was right. It's all about you. I was just the first one who stepped on your ego. Welcome to the real world, Coop. It's called rejection."

I really didn't mean that, you know. There never was any rejection on my part. More like an escape before he rejected me. But I'll never tell him that.

"Here's the deal, Millie. I really liked you. Maybe that's why it's bothering me. I thought you felt the way same way about me too."

Another bomb was just dropped on me. I wasn't expecting that response from him at all. He liked me. Coop, Mr. Football, the man who ruined me for all others. Hell, what a dumbass I am. He's looking at me. Heart on his sleeves vulnerable. God, he's too adorable right now.

So I do what every smart, single woman in my shoes would do. I scoot across the seat and basically attack him. But this time with my lips not my fists.

Epilogue

I've heard it said that there's a thin line between love and hate. Sexual chemistry blurs that line. Erases it, in fact. Coop and I are a perfect example of these truths.

We stayed in that police car for a long time, kissing, groping, panting and steaming up the windows. Trying to make out in the backseat of a car, handcuffed to a 6'3" dude was a challenge but one I succeed at, thank you very much.

I bet you're wondering about the cop. Did he take us to the station? Book us? Throw us in a jail cell? Nah, nothing like that happened at all.

You see Mr. Reynolds overheard our *entire* little quarrel. He particularly loved it when I tossed my drink in Coop's face. And being a wise, sweet man married for close to forty years, he saw what Coop and I didn't. A basic, undeniable attraction. Oh, and two super stubborn knuckleheads.

When Mr. Reynolds spoke to the officer privately, he concocted the whole scheme. He asked the officer to cuff us, get us alone in the backseat of his patrol car, and leave us there. They both watched from afar just in case it turned violent, but left when they saw us getting jiggy with it.

Wondering how our story ends? We've been together now for two whole years and will be married next month with Mr. Reynolds officiating. Who knew he was an ordained Methodist minister? But most importantly, Coop and I are both hopelessly in love with one another.

I feel like Disney's Cinderella because our love story is my fairytale. And in this game called life, I feel like I'm the second art teacher at Peachtree to win the lottery. That's how lucky I feel having found Coop.

We had some obstacles to overcome and probably still do, but we're a team and ready to tackle them. Yes, even his football jargon has rubbed off on me. I'm not sure if we'll always live happily ever after but we're sure going to try.

The End

Dear reader,

Thank you for taking a chance on an independent author. I truly appreciate you choosing to buy and read my book.

I'd love to hear from you too. Perhaps leave a review on Amazon, or a comment on my web site or Facebook page.
www.livmorris.com or
https://www.facebook.com/livingwrite

You can also connect with me on twitter. It's a favorite of mine.
http://twitter.com/Living_Write

All the best,
Liv

Read a preview of *ADAM'S APPLE*, my EROTIC BEST SELLER.... Uniquely told in Adam's point of view.

Adam Kingsley reigns as the young prince of Manhattan. Everything he touches turns to gold, making him the envy of Wall Street. Women swoon at his feet, money is no object, and his killer good looks are as wicked as sin. A dangerous trifecta that allows him to possess anything or anyone he desires.

What more could a thirty-two-year-old man wish for? Maybe that his life never changes and his murky past stays far away...Sounds reasonable, yet life seldom is.

Kathryn Delcour is an alluring socialite with unique erotic tastes who helps others find true sexual fulfillment. When she suddenly appears on the New York City social scene, Adam finds this complex woman too tempting to resist. He will stop at nothing to have her, yet she is warned to stay away from him and his player ways. Kathryn tries to keep him at arm's length, but her arms may not be strong enough to hold the charismatic Adam Kingsley at bay.

The passionate lure of ancient sexual practices, a past that isn't content to remain buried and a present filled with intrigue, danger and revenge. An erotic story sweetened with secrets, seduction, and suspense.

Love in the City

Adam's Apple

(Touch of Tantra #1)

by Liv Morris

Prologue

April 23rd, 2005. Laurel Hill Cemetery, Philadelphia, PA.

The sky shines a crisp, azure blue, but my heart is a lifeless gray and quickly turning as black as the muddied dirt I'm holding in my hands. I squeeze my fingers so tightly into a fist that my hand begins to shake and bits of grit embed into my palms.

The task set before me is customary and very common among men. But the woman I mourn today was anything but common. She was brilliant, wise, and beautiful.

Now she's gone... Forever.

Sorrow will no longer consume her heart and soul. Instead it passes on to me.

I toss the black dirt into the dark and musty grave and fall to my knees. The eerie hollow sound of the clumps of dirt hitting the wood below is more than I can bear.

The tears I've been suppressing for days now fall freely down my face like a dam's flood after a breach. An unrestrained sorrow pours out of me, and the whirl of emotions I've hidden within myself is no longer concealed. My grief is freed as I realize all I love is now six feet below me, but it might as well be a million miles away. The distance will never be broached this side of heaven as she is God's angel now.

Returning to the hearse, I see a man's face in the distance. We make eye contact before he raises the tinted window of his black limo. His vehicle pulls away, disappearing into the morning's mist. Anger rises above my grief because he has no right to be anywhere near this solemn ceremony.

He's the bastard who slowly and silently destroyed the woman I'm leaving behind today in this cold and wet cemetery. She was my mother . . . My selfless life-giver, and I owe her everything.

Chapter 1

My legs feel as heavy as lead pipes, but somehow they carry me through the marbled lobby to the sidewalk outside of my office high rise. I find myself standing on grimy concrete with the New York City rain pelting me, staining my yellow silk tie. I am numb to nature's onslaught, as my thoughts remain at the conference table forty stories above—where the last meeting of the day still haunts me.

My head of corporate security had informed me that my trusted partner and friend, Simon Edwards, betrayed me by stabbing me in the back. My stomach almost retches as I think about his deceit. I've known him since our freshman year at MIT fourteen years ago. Through random selection, we'd shared a dorm room together. We weren't extremely close because we were polar opposites and different personality types. Especially when it came to dealing with people. Basically, I tolerated them and he didn't. But we formed a common respect for one another during our college years and beyond. Maybe it was our desire to make our mark in the business world, as we both had something to prove to the fathers we hated. It was likely the only thing we had in common.

After graduating college, four of us from MIT, including Simon, headed to New York City and formed Kings Capital, largely using the inheritance I received after my mother's death. It served as the company's seed money and positioned me as the company's head. Although Simon seldom made his way to the boardroom, his presence there was felt by us all. We'd relied on his genius mind to design a way around any obstacle or shortcoming we found in our software ventures. We capitalized on so many deals thanks to Simon. We had a saying among the board, "If Simon says so, we buy."

Never in a million years would I have thought he'd try to sell me out. When others said my dreams were impossible or if a wall was placed in my way, he was my go-to man. Now he was the wall. Simon was caught trying to sell me out by giving away corporate secrets to another company. My corporate secrets. Secrets stained with my own blood, sweat, and fears. Although I was assured our company secrets never touched any outsiders' hand, his act of betrayal has set my world's axis askew.

I wipe the rain off my face and see Eddie, my driver, standing beside my black Escalade, New York City's newest version of a limo. He holds an umbrella in one hand and the opened back door in another. I observe his rigid stance; not a muscle moves in his face as he remains at attention like a soldier awaiting his commander's arrival. I hurry toward him, anxious to get out of the rain and away from my building. Kings Capital has been the center of my life since it was started, but now I want to run from everything I've built.

As I'm nearing the car, I hear someone calling my name. A quick glance over my shoulder brings my assistant, Mrs. Carter, into view. I notice she's waving a piece of white paper as she runs toward me. I compare the two extremes of the people who work for me: one is stoically robotic, the other is embarrassingly chaotic.

"Mr. Kingsley, sir, I neglected to give you your ticket to the Swanson event!" Mrs. Carter rests her hand on her heaving chest, breathless. "Security is at a high level tonight since the Ethiopian ambassador is attending. No one will be allowed inside without this." I stare at the ticket in her hand; the black ink is starting to blur from the rain.

Mrs. Carter places the ticket in my outstretched hand. I watch beads of water from the rain roll down her plump cheeks. The rain washes away parts of her makeup, revealing bare reddish skin underneath.

"Thank you, Mrs. Carter." A crack of thunder rumbles around us, echoing off the towering buildings, causing us both to jump. "You'd better get back inside."

"I just want to say how sorry I am, Mr. Kingsley, about Mr. Edwards. I—" Pity is written all over her face, and I detest pity.

"Thank you, Mrs. Carter. I know your intentions are good, but do not bring this matter up again in my presence. If it needs to be discussed, I will let you know."

My harsh rebuke might as well have been a slap across her face. Mrs. Carter appears wounded, and her skin has now turned more the color of fire.

"Certainly, sir." She hangs her head briefly and then looks up at me with the same pity in her eyes. Perhaps even more than before. Dammit to hell. "Have a lovely evening at the benefit."

"My apologies for being short, Mrs. Carter. It's just been a hell of a day." My conscience tugs at me. Fuck, I've overreacted, given into my easily roused temper, and penalized her for a crime she didn't commit.

"I'll see you tomorrow morning," I speak more calmly, the angry tone in my voice now gone.

"Yes, sir. And I understand." I watch a timid smile stretch across her face. The rain has now fully removed any trace of makeup from her skin, and her pulled-back hair is soaking wet and plastered to her scalp. I should feel guilty for making her stand outside with me getting drenched, but the feeling doesn't come to me.

"Just remember, Mr. Kingsley. Karma is a wonderful thing." And with that quick statement she pivots on her sensible heels and runs back inside the building.

Karma. I have to laugh. I, of all people, know too well about karma and it's legend. However, I've chosen to operate under the old proverb of an eye for an eye. Karma requires no action and the hope of a chance. I rely on one thing in this world: my actions. I will leave nothing to chance and prefer playing the game of life with the strongest hand possible.

I turn toward my car and approach the open door.

"Good evening, Eddie." I greet my driver with a nod as I escape the pelting rain and ease into the backseat.

"Good evening, Sir." Eddie shuts the door behind me.

I immediately put on some rap music and turn the volume almost inhumanly high, hoping the noise will help drown out the stress of my day. Leaning back against the soft leather seat, I let the bass thump against me.

Eddie gets behind the wheel and mutes the volume of the music. I look at him annoyed. "Home, Mr. Kingsley, or do you have an engagement to attend?"

Normally, I confer with him on my agenda, but this afternoon's event with Simon has me off-kilter and I simply forgot. "I have a benefit at the Lincoln Center tonight. But take the long way so I can change into my tux."

"Yes, sir." Eddie pushes the mute button again, and the music blares from the speakers. I see him slyly smirk in the rearview mirror.

Eddie has been my driver since my company landed on the Fortune 500 list two years ago. It was shortly before I turned thirty. A magical year indeed. Heady and intoxicating. My first taste of obscene wealth and its rewards.

Since then I've fucked my way around this city, and poor Eddie has witnessed it all. I've burned through women like a wildfire roaring across a dry forest. Nothing has stood in my way. My passions have been all-consuming as I've indulged myself in all kinds of debauchery. I might think about settling down in a few years, maybe. But, for now, I'm content to sample the choice delights surrounding me. What single man in my shoes wouldn't say the same? Temptation is just too fucking tempting for me.

As Eddie prepares to pull away from the front of my building, I spot Simon being escorted out of the glass doors. A team of two security officers, one on each side of Simon, has their hands placed tightly above his elbows. I watch as they roughly release him once they have him fully outside. Simon stumbles but remains standing.

"Hold up, Eddie," I shout above the music before the SUV moves into the traffic. "Stop right here."

The SUV lurches to a stop and I brace myself against the back of the front seat. I shift slowly on the leather, wet from my rain-soaked clothes, until I'm totally facing Simon through my window. To my surprise he is approaching my vehicle and the look on his face is murderous. Never have I seen him show this much emotion. Never. Even when his fiancée left him a few weeks ago. It's unnerving.

Simon slowly approaches the Escalade and stares into the tinted glass of my windows. His eyes are wide and crazed, the veins in his forehead protruding. He appears ready to fight. Part of me wants to fling open the door and pummel his ass into the sidewalk. Pulverize him. Make him pay. I have about five inches on him and maybe forty pounds of muscle. He's no match for me. But something about his face, his eyes make me reconsider. I grip harder into the seatback, grounding myself into place.

Simon leans in closer, his nose almost touches the

glass as he shouts something at me, but I can't hear him. His words are silent to me as I sit behind the car's dark wall of glass and listen to the loud music piped through the speakers and vibrating around me.

As I am getting ready to tell Eddie to pull away, Simon makes a move that conveys what his words could not. He places his finger beside his neck and drags it across from one side to the other. The universal symbol for you're dead. An eerie feeling runs through me, and I consider calling security to remove him from the sidewalk, but Simon turns away practically running from me.

Throughout Simon's angry display, Eddie is silently observing his behavior through the window. He's known Simon for as long as he's worked for me, so this stunt has to come as a shock. Glancing at Eddie in the front seat, I see a look of confusion mixed with concern on his face.

"It's been a hell of a day, Eddie." I take a deep breath and release my white-knuckled fingers from the seatback. An indent in the leather remains, a ghost outlining where my tension lay. "Get me the fuck out of here."

I'm tempted to tell Eddie to take me home and skip tonight's benefit, but I have committed to be there and make a major donation. I will likely be called by name and asked to stand and be acknowledged for my charity. An empty chair in my absence would be an affront to the organization. One that I'm actually quite fond of, which in this town is rare.

Resolved to keep pressing on, I remove the bag that's hanging from the hook behind my seat. Inside there is a black tux, brilliant white shirt, and shiny black shoes. I start to undress and as I do, Eddie, on cue, raises the divider between the seats. I laugh as he does. He's seen and heard just about everything in this backseat. Surely a flash of my briefs won't offend him. But he remains a gentleman as usual, even when I've given him no cause to believe that I am one.

As soon as I'm fully dressed, Eddie pulls up in front of the Lincoln Center, the location for tonight's benefit. I comb my fingers through my hair, trying to settle it back in place. It has a mind of it's own. Sex hair, I've been told.

Other than my white shirt, I'm adorned in black from the top of my head to the soles of my shoes. It's the color of success in New York City, and likely the color of most people's hearts attending tonight, too.

I'm scheduled to appear at two similar events this weekend, each one as stimulating as a prostate exam. Since my company made the Fortune 500 list, the invitations and requests from charities in this city have poured into my office. Poor Mrs. Carter practically needs an assistant to weed through them all. I think it's time to cut back on my attendance. I've frankly had my fill.

During the last two years, I've found the conversation at these affairs to be mundane and as boring as hell. The attendees address me speculatively, shocked by my success and youth. At thirty-two how I've succeeded is not the norm unless one's empire is built on family wealth and prestige. In a sick way my empire was built on family money—the hush money given to my mother when she fled this city thirty-two years ago. Funny thing about hush money, though, it's rarely kept quiet.

But tonight I'll have to endure all the disgusting verbal fawning. I can hear the people now, those shocked by my accomplishments.

"Hello, Mr. Kingsley. I've heard so much about you."

"Good evening, Mr. Kingsley. It's amazing how you've taken Wall Street by storm."

"Oh, Mr. Kingsley, what a striking man you are...blah...blah...blah."

The eyes on the nameless faces of my commentators have one thing in common: fear. Fear that I will dislike them, fear that I will crush them, and fear they will never obtain the wealth and power I have. It's pathetic how each dinner, gala, or benefit turns into a sycophant ball. A wicked dance where I'm placed in the center to be admired and envied. Displayed on some invisible pedestal until the sands shift beneath me and another up-and-coming man replaces me. Someone with more money, more power. The next bright and shining star. No one remains on top forever, and I have no illusions about my tenuous position among New York's power players.

Eddie opens the door and I exit with a quick nod to him. "Plan on company tonight. I need something fun to look forward to."

He nods back in a silent reply because he knows my routine and sexual appetites very well. It's a waiting game for him. He will receive my pick-up text and appear in five minutes at the curb. I'll let him know in my message if I'll have a friend at the end of the night. He will then prepare my arrival accordingly. Tonight, since I've alerted him early, he'll have some champagne ready when we enter the car, the backseat divider up, and seductive music playing in the background. Later, after I'm finished with the night's delight, he'll drop her off at her Upper East Side condo lovingly bought by her rich father who I've probably done business with.

Making my way to Lincoln Center's entrance, I pull the ticket Mrs. Carter gave me from my jacket's pocket. I see a line has formed in front of the building, and I dread having to stand with everyone outside. When I decide to bypass the line and proceed inside through the doublewide doors, a young woman with an official-looking badge pinned across her flat chest approaches me. Her blond hair falls haphazardly against her shoulders and she appears overwhelmed. I notice a little perspiration glisten on her forehead as she forces a smile at me. Sweating is so weak,

I think to myself. I plant a smile on my face and prepare for her compliments, the inevitable suck-up that asks me to open my wallet and hand over its contents.

"Good evening." I decide to speak first.

"Good evening, Mr. Kingsley." She offers her hand to me in a formal greeting, and on reflex I respond in kind. "My name is Natalie Vincent. I'm the assistant to Ava Swanson, the executive director of The Swanson Foundation. It's an honor to have you attending our benefit tonight. We have special seating for you in the ballroom." She doesn't spew the usual false platitudes. How refreshing.

"This way." She tilts her head toward the direction she wants me to follow. She appears to be on a mission, and her high heels begin clicking with speed against the marble floors. Pulling my eyes away from her long, slender legs, I stop briefly to acknowledge some pompous men from whom I've legally stolen money. It's the Wall Street way, and the only place on Earth where stealing is applauded and rewarded.

I shake a few clammy hands and endure a couple slaps on my back, then hurriedly make my way back to Ms. Vincent. She's halted her march toward the ballroom and stands waiting for me a few feet away. Her patience may be running thin as I watch her feet tap away until I'm back by her side. I have to smile to myself as I've never had a charity executive show such disregard to me. Me, the person who will likely be the biggest donor of the night.

"Excuse me," I say and add the best devilish grin I can produce. "I hate to leave a woman waiting." But I see her discreetly roll her eyes and huff as she turns in the direction she was headed. And I have to say I'm enjoying the view of her backside as she walks a few steps ahead of me.

Ms. Vincent and I enter the main dining area for

tonight's event. I watch her stop at the head table and I start to tense. I despise sitting at the head table as it ensures that I am front and center. I prefer to blend in and watch others, not have all eyes fixed on me. Turning toward me, Ms. Vincent points out my seat and the identifying place card with Adam Kingsley written boldly across it.

"You will be sitting by the speaker, Sir Lawrence Scott. He's the organizer of The Hope House in Ethiopia. A wonderful outreach and a wonderful man."

"It should provide some stimulating conversation for the evening, I'm sure." I attempt to sound sincere but become distracted when I notice the elaborate diamond necklace lying on her pale chest. The clasp is moved to the front and ruins the piece's declaration of importance. After pulling my gaze away from her chest, she eyes me speculatively and continues.

"Stimulating might be a stretch, even for Sir Scott." She gestures toward a wall of open doors. "If you'll follow me, I'll show you the patron's reception area."

Once again, I'm trailing behind Ms. Vincent and wondering what's underneath the tight black dress she's wearing. My imagination conjures up lace encasing soft silk. If I found her more attractive, I might try to see if I'm right.

After entering the reception area off the main ballroom, Ms. Vincent departs, assuring me I will be speaking with her later. I head straight toward one of the several bars scattered throughout the large room and order my standard scotch, Glenlivet. If they have my favorite brand, I'm likely to contribute more money. Otherwise, my donation goes down considerably. After I successfully place my order, it appears The Swanson Foundation is in luck tonight.

Scanning the crowd as I wait for my drink, I see the

usual suspects: balding men with pooching bellies holding on to their latest trophy wives or girlfriends. Some of the women meet my gaze with a knowing look as I've already been improperly introduced to certain parts of them when they were less attached.

I spot a former friend, Sarah Edmonds, I believe it is now. She has wonderful auburn hair that cascades against her alabaster skin, but her hideous laugh sounds like a hyena. I need to turn my gaze away from her quickly or she'll interpret my perusal as interest. I don't touch the merchandise once it's bought. And she most surely is bought. Poor fucker, Mr. Edmonds.

I take a couple more swigs of my scotch and let some of the better memories with the women I've known in the room come to mind. Between the scotch and brief sexual fantasies, I feel my body start to relax for the first time since this afternoon. I signal the bartender for a refill. I need a few more before subjecting myself to an evening next to Sir Lawrence. Fuck, this night needs to speed by.

In the far corner there's a stunning raven-haired beauty, and I shift my body slightly so I can watch her more closely. I've noticed her at a couple events the last month, and both times she has appeared alone. No one seems attached to her, which I find extremely odd as raw beauty like hers is uncommon in Manhattan. I wonder who she is and where she came from. No one suddenly appears on the New York social scene without some fanfare, especially at her age and her likelihood of being single. I bet she's family money, or a trust fund baby beautifully grown up.

I would guess she's older than I am, but I have never been close enough to see the details of her face and determine what her true age might be. Early thirties possibly. Her luminous skin gives her the glow of youth, so it's hard to tell. I enjoy watching the men around her as they hang onto every word she speaks out of her ruby lips.

Her congregation reminds me of a scene from Gone with the Wind when Scarlett O'Hara had all the naïve southern boys circled around her and eating out of the palm of her hand. I can almost hear this stunner mocking the men with a little fiddle dee dee thrown at them.

She ceremoniously extricates herself from the crowd of fawning suitors and moves toward the bar where I'm located. My heartbeat quickens at the thought of seeing her up close, maybe even sharing a word or two.

As she approaches me, I watch the sway of her hips and damn how they sway. Her tight dress accentuates her every move and I'm mesmerized, completely in her thrall. Her stature is petite, but curves grace her body seductively. Everything I see makes me thankful I'm a man. The sexy stilettos she's wearing belong in one of two places, over my shoulders or on the floor next to my bed.

Finally she looks my way and our eyes immediately connect, and at this moment I'm perfectly still. I can't break the intensity I feel in this first interaction between us. Her blue eyes are surrounded by creamy skin and framed with her long, black hair. She is a fucking masterpiece. An artist's beauty.

The next thing I see on her lovely face is a knowing smile. She doesn't appear to be mocking me, at least that's my hope. And I decide right then that I need to know who this mystery woman is and where she came from.

I have an unspoken rule of never introducing myself at these shitty functions, but this woman I've got to meet. Now. I walk toward her, blocking her path to the bar and making it impossible for her to ignore me. She places her hands on her hips and looks up at me expectantly.

Feeling a bit on edge, I revert back to full-on business mode. What is it about this woman's beauty and expressions that make me feel uneasy? I stretch out my

Love in the City

hand to her, but her hands remain solidly on her hips.

Well damn, this is interesting. There isn't a single wrinkle or line on her face, but the way she looks at me is intriguing, a confidence only acquired with time and experience. Everything about her fascinates me, and her sudden appearance on the social scene bewilders me. But most importantly right now, her body has totally aroused mine. This combination almost never happens with the women I meet at these things, so I start to speak.

"I'd like to introduce myself, I'm Adam Kings—"

She laughs before I can finish my name.

"Oh, I know who you are, pretty billionaire boy. Everyone in the room knows your name. Likely even the bartender I was on my way to visit knows you." She holds up an empty wine glass. "Do you know who I am, though?"

"I'm afraid you have me at a loss." Smirking, I draw my hand to my chest to feign feeling hurt and rejected. "And calling me 'pretty' and 'boy.' That stings."

"Please don't be offended. They're really meant as a terms of endearment."

She moves closer to me, so close I see the full swell of her breasts as they disappear beneath the silk of her dark green dress. My cock responds to my perfect vantage point as I watch her mostly exposed chest move slowly and evenly. This intriguing yet nameless woman is an enticing tease, and I have to say I'm thoroughly enjoying myself for the first time tonight.

"Let me introduce myself. In polite company I go by Kathryn." I watch as she winks and runs her little tongue across her bottom lip. I swallow, hard.

"We have a name. That's a start." I find myself smiling at her. A full-blown grin, which contradicts my usual behavior. "And what do you do, Kathryn?"

"You want to know what I do?" She keeps her eyes trained on mine, and I swear I see a mischievous twinkle in them. "In my case that's a loaded question."

"Loaded question or not, I would still like to know," I say, hoping she'll reveal more of herself to me. "I've seen you before at other functions. It's like you just appeared out of thin air."

"Not quite thin air, but close. And it's funny; I've noticed you, as well." She moves even closer, and now we are nearly touching one another. "I wondered if we'd ever meet. You know I've been warned about you."

"Warned?" My question sounds hollow, unconvincing: I know what she's likely been told. Adam Kingsley is a player. A skirt-chaser. And I can't deny it, either.

"Yes, warned to keep my distance." I see a touch of amusement in her eyes, and now I'm sure she's mocking me. "I know we've just meet, but I'm curious about something. Can I ask you a really personal question, Mr. Kingsley?"

"Sure, but you have to call me Adam." Honestly, I just want to hear her say my name. Watch her full lips mouth the sound.

"Let's stick to formalities, Mr. Kingsley. My question is actually a semi-professional one."

"A professional one?" I'm still left in the dark about her occupation, even her last name, yet she wants to ask me personal questions. Who is this ballsy woman?

"Yes, professional. I have a doctorate in psychology and coach couples in the intimacy department." The intimacy department? What the fuck does that mean?

"Well, Dr. Kathryn, I'm not sure how I can help with that subject. But okay, shoot away." I have a feeling I'm going to regret this.

"When I look around this room, I see women watching you and our exchange. Some looking sad, others looking envious. I'm curious to know how many of them you've slept with?" She stares at me with a serious look on her face. She doesn't blink or look away. It's then I realize she really wants me to answer her. Throw out a number. Fuck. I'm not sure how to respond or even count up the tally, so I decide to try a little humor.

"Somewhere between one and all of them?" She rolls her eyes to the side, not satisfied with my answer, but I'm not finished yet either.

"Honestly, I'd like to say you, just you." My voice is barely above a whisper. "That you're the only one I've fucked in this room." Kathryn appears a little surprised by my answer but then laughs, and I join her. I think she realizes I'm teasing her. But what I said might be partially true because no other woman in this room appeals to me like she does.

"They were right to warn me." Her mood shifts. Gone are her smiles. "Men like you will never understand what a woman really needs."

"Is that right? So you're an expert on me now. My judge and jury." I cross my arms over my chest as my temper starts to rise.

"Oh dear. I think I've touched a nerve," she says while throwing her head back and laughing at me. Quite frankly, I'm not amused. "Yes, Mr. Kingsley, I'm an expert of sorts."

"Care to explain?" My tone's short with her as I'm still a bit pissed.

"It would be my pleasure." She winks at me and I'm feeling conflicted. Do I really want to know what she's an expert at? Who am I kidding? Of course I do.

"I'm a specialist at taking boys like yourself and turning them into real men. I've never failed. Not once. At least that's what their wives and girlfriends say."

"So, what have you never failed at, in more specific terms?" I'm hoping she takes the bait and gives me the details of her exploits, as this woman confounds and frustrates me.

She brings her free hand up to my chest and runs her delicate fingers under the lapel of my Armani tux. My arms fall to my side as I feel her grasping my jacket and gently pulling my upper body down toward her, bringing our faces cheek to cheek. Her soft lips brush lightly against my ear.

"I take cocky, rich boys like you and teach them how to make love to women until they're barely able to mutter a word. Completely and utterly blissed. That's really what separates the men from the boys, Mr. Kingsley. Sex as an art form versus fucking for a release."

I find myself unable to respond, completely tongue-tied. Something I'm not used to experiencing. I always have a slick comeback. Always. I see fire in her eyes and notice her lips starting to move again, and good God, I realize she's not done with me yet.

"You see, Mr. Kingsley, when I said you were a pretty billionaire boy I meant every damn word. You're very pretty indeed, striking really, but still just a boy."

ADAM'S APPLE is available on Amazon and Barnes & Noble in both ebook and paperback. Also available on iTunes/iBook and Smashwords.

Made in the USA
Charleston, SC
08 March 2014